COWBOYS AND UNTAMED HEARTS

Natalie Acres

MENAGE AMOUR

Siren Publishing, Inc.

www.SirenPublishing.com

A SIREN PUBLISHING BOOK

IMPRINT: Ménage Amour

COWBOY BOOTS AND UNTAMED HEARTS

Copyright © 2009 by Natalie Acres

ISBN-10: 1-60601-435-8

ISBN-13: 978-1-60601-435-6

First Printing: June 2009

Cover design by Jinger Heaston

All cover art and logo copyright © 2009 by Siren Publishing, Inc.

Printed in the U.S.A.

PUBLISHER

Siren Publishing, Inc.

www.SirenPublishing.com

DEDICATION

For my friends 'back home' who are just discovering my books and don't quite know what to make of them. Keep reading. One day soon, you'll recognize yourself in some of my characters. Then you'll discover how much you're treasured, how much you're loved.

COWBOY BOOTS AND UNTAMED HEARTS

NATALIE ACRES

Prologue

Home in Virginia

Sydney Kane stood fifty yards or so away from her father and bent her ear. Several men, dressed in their thousand-dollar suits, gathered around him. They were from one of the federal agencies, or so she believed, and arrived with one purpose in mind—to describe a new danger looming. Sam Kane's involvement in a past operation resulted in these men showing up at Sydney's front door…again.

Something, or someone, threatened their lives once more. She wondered when, if ever, her father would tire of his business. He once told her in his line of work, men didn't walk away. She read between the lines. Some people never enjoyed a simple life and Sydney accepted her fate. She didn't have to like it.

At six foot five, Sam Kane towered over most men, even those standing in front of him appeared small in comparison and they looked intimidating enough. One in particular held her attention.

He was almost her father's equal in body type, with a solid build and long, thick arms. He was handsome, probably in his late twenties, as if age mattered when a man looked all rogue and prepared for anything. He stood out more than the others with his two-day old beard, set jaw and visible determination. After she spotted him, Sydney hardly noticed in any of the other men. Without a doubt, the operative in front of her was there to protect her.

He allowed his sunglasses to drift off the bridge of his nose while another agent gave specific orders and described upcoming plans. The simple act, while hardly extraordinary, gave the younger guy instant bad-boy appeal. He never changed his stance, and pretended not to notice anything around him.

Sydney wasn't fooled.

Sexy came easy for men like him, but his job came first. While he didn't necessarily look dangerous now, she understood more about him than most women might notice without a first introduction. The man standing next to her father delivered death when ordered.

He had a heart-shaped mouth and kissable moist lips, not that she cared. Her father's pawns rarely offered her companionship. It didn't matter. After a first look, Sydney was hooked.

He stared straight ahead through the most peculiar shade of green eyes she'd ever seen. She wouldn't define them as pretty, only strange, almost mesmerizing. Lime green with what looked like a splash of bright yellow in the center focused on her. If a man had the ability to see through someone, he possessed it.

The muscular bodyguard glared at her, but she didn't think he truly saw her. Most of her father's friends, or associates were always professional but this one existed in a class of his own.

She quickly realized the young gun undoubtedly earned her father's trust if he planned to hand her over to him, and he did. She never questioned it.

Once the sleek black cars arrived at her place, she typically packed and left within a few hours. In her estimation, they were keen on a fast departure this time. The familiar routine rarely changed but depending on the threat, the time it took to disappear often forced a speedy farewell.

Sam Kane turned and she heard the words she dreaded, but expected. "I'll have her ready in a few hours. Wait here."

Each of the four men took a military stance and looked on as her father quickly approached her. "Sydney," he began, "We need to go inside now."

"No, Daddy. Not again. Please, I really don't want to go."

She always hated this part most. She stood there staring at him, waiting for him to change his mind, but realizing he'd never consider it. She tried to buy time, silently bargain for a few more minutes of paradise, the place she called home.

"It's only for a little while," he told her.

"Yes, for a little while. I'm eighteen and can't start my life because I have to hide from yours. Why now when I'm ready to start college and my own career?"

"Because I made choices a long time ago and those decisions still follow us today."

And they would tomorrow and the day after.

"When do I start making some of my own decisions?" she asked, fury whirling in her veins.

Her gaze followed the fence line of the property. She watched a mare and her colt. They galloped across the fields moving closer and closer to a large pond. She wanted to run with them and never look back.

He grabbed her arm and led her inside. They argued while he packed her things.

"If you make me leave, I won't come home this time," she said sourly. Her threats were always the same and always empty.

"It doesn't matter, Sydney. My staff will follow you wherever you go. This is the last time. I promise. Go with my men and let them get you set up somewhere, anywhere you want to go, just name it."

"With a new identity and another new life?"

"Yes," he admitted reluctantly. "This is the last time I'll require it. I swear it."

He made the promise and it was a stupid oath she wanted to believe. She tugged her identification cards from the top drawer of her dresser and slapped her hand against the side of it, followed by a swift kick. "I'll leave, but I don't like it."

"You'll go and you'll stay alive. You're a good girl, Sydney. You mind me because you trust me to keep you safe, and I always will."

Four Months Later-Malibu, California

Sydney hated the way he made her feel and yet she loved the way he used her body. When she was with him, she trusted him completely. Whenever he left her, she felt abandoned, a longing so corrupt that she understood from the first time he touched her, he owned her.

She watched her Master run his hand over his long face and she questioned him, trying once more to challenge him, something she seldom attempted. Most of the time she failed and sometimes it resulted in her punishment.

"Master, please don't deny me," she pleaded, stretching her arms tight against the binds that held her. She flinched when his fingers slid across her inner thigh.

He pinched her damp skin trailing closer and closer to her pussy.

"Please, please make love to me."

"Sydney, you know I can't. I won't. I only want to touch you. Feel me, Sydney."

After a few twists and turns, she rolled her head to the side and tilted her nose upward. She smelled the salt in the air and heard the crashing waves in the distance. She longed to go outside with him and walk together hand in hand.

"You're mine, Sydney. It's enough. All I need."

Mine?

It wasn't enough, or was it? If she belonged to him, then maybe this was all she'd ever have and all she deserved anyway.

Sometimes, after long sessions of sexual pleasure stimulated by toys and contraptions, she felt lost, like she didn't belong to him or anyone else. Other times, when he used mental bondage practices, she felt more desirable as a woman, and more love than she'd ever known.

He played with her, pushed her to the limits but he never bothered to take her, to thrust his cock inside her and fill her with his size. Did he fear he'd hurt her? She knew she was small but wasn't a woman's body supposed to handle a man's penis regardless of size concerns? She wondered as she stared at it, watching the pre-cum slip from his slit. Instinctively, she smacked her lips.

Watching his excitement always made her mouth water. She felt like one of Pavlov's dogs, conditioned to respond favorably whenever she saw her Master's cock.

He sat on her bed and released the cuffs. He gently removed the nipple clamps and kissed her breasts after he discarded first one claw-like contraption and then the other.

The vibrator in her pussy hummed at a low speed. The butt plug, the one he often referred to as a bottom popper, continued to jerk in her rear impaling her with a continual beat, one uninterrupted thrust after another. His mouth soon trailed across her chest, and he lapped at her nipples.

Her juices gathered around her toy and she craved him. Sweet heaven, she understood lust. She came again and then once more. Her orgasms rolled over her like a slow moving tide that claimed her and still she needed more. She wanted him to thrust inside of her and make her scream.

Her body stayed covered in sweat beads. He scolded her time and time again when she climaxed without his consent. She didn't care. He threatened punishment but it was rarely harsh and they were running out of time. She sensed it in her gut and saw it in his cold stare. He received the order to send her home.

Realizing she faced time without him made her need him all the more. She hungered for him, ached for his cock to satisfy her completely before his body warmed her throughout the night.

The harrowing truth never deserted her. She knew better than to expect something for her efforts.

He planned to walk away and tomorrow he would kiss her goodbye. The men in her life always sent her away. It was for her own good, and she trusted her Master to make the right decisions. It was time to go home.

Prologue Two

Two Years Later
Fourth of July

Sydney and her girlfriends rushed through the county fair like they were afraid they'd miss something. Jett Donovan watched them from a distance and his eyes never left her even when his latest arm decoration pouted. Right then, he couldn't even remember the gal's name. The more she gripped his tight muscle, the more he wanted to lose her in the crowd. The only name he cared to remember belonged to the only woman who ever kept him guessing—his neighbor, Sydney Kane.

Sydney had a body he would sell out his daddy's farm just to see. His brothers felt the same and Luke, his youngest brother had carried a torch for her since they'd graduated from Virginia High.

Sydney used to chase them everywhere. When she was a kid, she looked for ways to win their favor, but something abruptly changed. Jett couldn't put his finger on it. Sydney Kane grew up overnight and when she did, she lost the twinkle in her eye but gained a mysterious sexuality he felt destined to explore.

Jett's brother Riley said something happened to her the last time her father sent her away. She came back into town and didn't make their farm her first stop. They rarely saw her after she returned.

Sometimes, Jett wondered if her father deliberately kept her under lock and key. He tested his theory of an ever-present threat. After using the resources he had at his fingertips, he couldn't find intelligence to lead him to believe Sydney faced new danger. For some reason, she kept to herself and there wasn't an explanation for it.

Hopping over the flimsy silver-coated rail, Jett waited until Sydney and her friends grouped together around five swings. He'd left his tag along over at the cotton candy stand when he saw a new opportunity and as luck unfolded in his favor, he jumped at the chance to get Sydney's attention.

Sydney took the swing behind her four friends who paired off and left her to fend for herself. Two of them giggled when he chose the outside seat next to her. So what if they arranged the chance meeting when they saw him headed her way.

"Jett Donovan, are you following me?" she asked, pushing the metal bar up and sliding under it.

He quickly strapped the safety belt across his lap. "I sure am," he said with a wink. "When did you get back in town, neighbor?"

"Recently."

Good for her, he thought. She didn't give away too much information. Her father would swell with pride.

"Glad to get back home, I guess."

"Sure," she said but she didn't sound too enthusiastic.

Jett understood the guarded answers. Her father certainly trained her well and if he failed in any capacity, Jett imagined she encountered a few good teachers in her father's men. The sudden thought made his skin crawl. *Her father's men.*

The ride operator lifted a lever and the chairs rose to their spinning position. Within a few seconds, they drifted high above the crowd. Jett watched her.

She tossed her head back and laughed as they moved faster and faster. At one point, he couldn't resist. He reached over and touched her chestnut hair. He quickly withdrew his hand when she froze with a painted smile instead of a sincere one.

Yep, he'd sell out the home place for a day with Sydney Kane because he knew women and the one next to him had about as much experience with men as a nun in a convent. It only drove his desires, and pushed his cock tighter against his dark denim jeans.

After a few minutes on the ride, the operator did them both a favor. The swings lowered to the ground and he grabbed her hand.

"Tell your friends I'm taking you home," he whispered in her ear.

"Jett, I can't ditch them," she stated flatly before her friends approached.

"You and I both know you want to. Watch how easy I can do it for you," he said, mischief lingering in his expression.

He squeezed her hand tightly in his palm after he shooed off the other ladies. He created the opportunity. Now, he planned to hold her in his arms and taste the lips of an innocent woman.

His brothers had ideas of their own for their little neighbor. He couldn't wait to see how she responded to them—every one of them—but there was no harm in taking his own course of action. There was no one around to stop him from stealing the first kiss if she'd allow it, and she did.

One Week Later

Sydney rarely made her Master angry, but this time she provoked him. Confessing a long time love for her neighbors somehow disturbed him but he made her tell him the truth and then he requested details.

He once explained how he knew when she was lying and she believed him. She couldn't look into his lime-green eyes and fib. She owed him complete honesty. He deserved her respect.

"Sydney, tell me exactly how you reacted to Jett Donovan," he growled. "Were you wet when his hands were on you? Did you feel a gush of excitement or a slow burn?"

"I...I don't remember," she whimpered.

"Were you drinking?" he asked. His guttural tone proved disgust lingered if she admitted to the consumption of alcohol.

"Yes, some…before I saw him."

"Do you blame your actions on substances?"

"No, it was my choice."

"And who gave you the right to choose?" he yelled, his solid fist landing next to her on the *Catherine Wheel.* The wood piece splintered with the blow.

"You weren't there," she said quietly.

"I shouldn't have to watch your every move, Sydney!"

"No Master, you're right. I should ask before I act. If you're not around, I know what to do and what not to do because I understand what pleases you."

"And you think I'm pleased when another man touches you?"

"No, Master. I'm sure it is upsetting."

His lips twitched. Upsetting, hell. It damn near destroyed him.

He studied her thoughtfully and with a smirk he tried to hide, he inquired more. "And how did the young Donovan react when you teased him and then denied him?"

She didn't answer right away.

"Sydney?"

"I don't think he liked it," she admitted.

"I imagine he didn't," he remarked, grabbing his black bag from under the wheel. He retrieved a paddle, a black leather crop, lubricant, a clit kisser, a short grey stone, and a vibrator. He situated the items on a metal table parallel to the wheel.

"Now, my little slave, how should I punish you?"

"Can I choose?"

"Of course not, but if you had the choice, what would you prefer?"

"I don't have the choice, Master, and I trust you to make the right one for me."

Chapter One

Three Years Later

Sydney stood in the middle of the field with a shiny red apple in hand. She'd chased Bitch around ten acres or so for most of the morning. Up and down the fence line, around the parameter of the corral, and straight into the largest pasture area of the ranch. Finally, she'd pulled out another sweet temptation.

The first two attempts failed miserably. She tried to wave a carrot Bitch's way and the horse only snorted. She ended up and ate it herself. A few minutes later, she pulled out sugar cubes. She held them flat in her palm and the blasted beast ignored her. She used them as weapons and threw them as hard as she could. All four missed the stupid mare and only fueled her anger.

Sydney soon realized a call over to the Donovan place was in order. If something happened to Bitch, her father would raise the roof. Mr. Donovan or one of his boys wouldn't mind helping her. She silently hoped for one, maybe even two, of *his boys.*

After she realized what she'd wished for, she let out a sigh of relief. She didn't experience guilt now. It had taken three years to get to this point but it felt good, damn good. She could think about the Donovans again and do it at her leisure.

Immediately, she looked around the property. Sometimes, she still felt her Master watching her. With her father out of town, she imagined him lurking in the shadows somewhere, waiting for the right time to reenter her life. If he was out there, he was probably laughing. She might laugh too if it wasn't so cold.

"Bitch," she talked to the horse like she expected a reply. "I'm calling the Donovans."

Bitch didn't respond. She took it as a sign.

She tossed an apple into the air again. The damn horse never noticed. Facing defeat, she took a bite of the fruit and headed for the barn.

She deserved some eye candy after what Bitch put her through and her neighbors provided plenty. She shook off the thought and the bitter chill while she stood next to the barn office heater and dialed the number on the wall.

It only took two rings. Riley Donovan answered with a husky, "Donovan's."

Sydney stared at the list of emergency numbers and thought of her nine-one-one. Grief, she thought. This was the kind of experience that earned her a good *Cowgirl of the Year* award, the special notoriety alerting cowboys that she belonged on her back, and not in boots.

"Is anyone there? Hello?"

She cleared her throat. "Is this Riley or Kevin?"

There were four Donovan hunks but only two of them sounded exactly alike and they possessed the most orgasmic voices around. Deep baritone and sexy as all hell, the men could've made a fortune selling phone sex to lonely women.

A short pause and then she heard, "Depends on who's callin'."

Flirt. "It's Sydney Kane."

"In that case, it's Riley. What can I do you for?"

Her heart stopped beating for a second, just like it always did when she heard one of the Donovan boys ask that sexy little question. It was a phrase all the cowboys used but it sounded so sincere, kind of like a true invitation, since the question fell from Donovan lips.

"What's the going rate?" she replied, sending two-thumbs up to heaven above that Riley wasn't around to see her blush.

"Don't tempt me, neighbor. I can make it over to your place in record time."

She almost choked upon hearing his loaded proposition and deliberately changed the subject back to her intended purpose for dialing his number. "Listen, I have a problem over here with a true bitch."

"Honey, believe me when I tell you, I am no help in that department. I seem to have a way with a few ladies but when it comes to bitches, I'll have to direct you to Kevin."

"I meant Daddy's filly."

"Ah, yeah, Dad told me Mr. Kane named her after her temperament. I've been meaning to drop by to take a look at her. Rumor has it she's a beauty."

"Yeah, she's something else. Let me tell ya."

Sydney paced a few steps. "Listen, I hate to bother you, but I'm in a pinch. Dad is out of town and he specifically told me to leave Bitch in her stall unless I let her run in the bull pen and well—"

"You didn't."

"Nope. I let her have the open fields today and after a few hours of trying to coax her back inside, I finally gave up."

"You know, the local weather reports are pretty bad, Syd. Abingdon residents expect blizzard-like conditions. I hope you're prepared for the worst over there."

"I hope so, too. I started foolin' around with this horse, and time got away from me. I've never seen anything like her. The prissy little filly is pure beauty in motion with her muscular legs pounding out at the cold, hard ground. She's also defiant, and stubborn as a mule." She stopped herself when she heard him chuckle.

"You sound like your dad. Mr. Kane went on and on about her sleek unblemished coat and silk mane and tail, said she was the epitome of coal black perfection."

"Yeah, with one major flaw."

"What's that?" he asked, humor driving the question.

"She doesn't know I'm the boss in charge."

Maybe she was mesmerized by the animal earlier but things changed after a few hours. Several times Bitch started toward her, pursued her slowly, and then dodged around her, kicking up her legs and neighing. She earned her name, without a doubt. She also earned Sydney's respect instead of the other way around.

"Sounds to me like she understands precisely who wears the saddle over there," he said, chuckling. "Hmmm, I never took you for a quitter. Are you sure you're not up to somethin'?"

She didn't think fast enough once her teeth started to chatter again. She only managed an "uh-huh" and then wanted to kick her own butt with the heel of her icy boot. So much for conversation, her words were frozen solid and stuck in her chest.

"I'll be right over. Besides, I've been meaning to stop by and see you, planned on it today, actually. After I heard you were back, it's the only thing that's been on my mind. I'll see you in a few."

He hung up before she responded.

He'd heard she was back in town? Did such a statement mean he liked hearing the news? No, she'd been there before with the Donovan men. They were players to the bone and they would, if she gave any of them a chance, play her to the bitter-sweet end. Undoubtedly, a finale with the Donovans meant ending up in one of their beds. Nothing to complain about there except from what she'd heard, one trip and that was pretty much it.

She primped in front of the office mirror, which was broken and tough to use but served the purpose. By the time she finished, Kevin's old blue truck rolled through the last of five gates.

Taking a deep breath, she poured a scoop of grain in the bottom of a tin pan, one they used for the sole purpose of getting a horse's attention and she started for the field. She might as well let the Donovans think she wasn't completely defeated.

Riley and Kevin met her at the fence. She easily translated both of their expressions. They thought she pulled some sort of stunt to get them over there. It wasn't beneath her.

Years before, she'd attempted it, but a lot had changed since the last time she'd been home. For starters, she somehow lost her zest for life, something that happened after her father moved her from one remote location to another.

When he finally allowed her to stop running from whatever he had her running from, she'd been so busy with school that she had little time to think about the Donovans. On occasion, she even dated a nice fellow or two. Lately, she stopped comparing every man alive to a Donovan and sometimes, she didn't think so much about her Master, even though at times she still craved him.

"Hiya Sydney," Kevin said trapping his bottom lip under his teeth like he had to do it so he wouldn't eat her alive.

Riley made some sort of grunt and then shook his head. "I swear you get better looking with age."

"Thanks for coming, guys," she said, lowering her eyes.

Kevin slapped Riley's chest with his hat probably because she walked right into a completely innocent statement.

Riley's salacious expression held. He dropped his gaze over the length of her body. His stare left an impression at every curve and her nerve endings danced with new life.

"Don't thank me yet," he replied, nudging Kevin in the ribs before quickly adding, "Besides, you'll thank me soon enough and when you do, I'll make sure you come too...maybe even several times."

Her eyes were wide in an instant, but not from surprise. Riley always cut up with the opposite sex and carnal implications were his specialty. Most of the time he directed them at the girly-girl kind of woman, and Sydney didn't fit into the category.

"I see you haven't changed much," she quipped.

The differences she noticed were a vast improvement. The way he studied her now was a far cry from how fast he used to run from her as a teenager, and his explicit comment heated her in just the right spots.

Riley awoke a sudden awareness she needed to dismiss. After she returned to Virginia the last time, she swore off the kind of men who reminded her of her Master. While she didn't know if she'd ever see him again, to show him respect, she stayed away from his type.

Riley apparently felt pretty good about his sexual skills because generally, he turned everything into a bedroom challenge. Only, Sydney couldn't remember when, or if, he ever directed them at her. Under normal circumstances, she watched and listened as someone else became the intended target of his delicious promises.

"For a guy who spent the better part of his life running away from this ranch, never mind the woman on it, I imagine if you grunt or groan, it'll happen when your hand is wrapped real tight around that joy stick you like to talk a lot about."

Riley stared at her blankly. "That was a mouthful."

Kevin smiled at his brother. *"Told ya."* He then turned to Sydney. "You're looking good, Sydney. Life treating you all right?"

Before she answered him, Kevin draped his arm over her shoulder. Noted as the touchy-touchy kind of guy, every woman in Abingdon knew Kevin. He was likeable enough to run for public office and win by a landslide, unless of course someone dug into his past indiscretions. Plenty existed and they proved easy to find. Most women boasted if they spent the night with a Donovan. Kevin made sure he kept the tongues wagging.

"Sure, life's grand. It beats the heck out of any other option," she said, bending down and squeezing under the split-rail fence. "You should listen to your brother, Riley. Whatever he told you, he's probably right."

She shot them a saucy grin and then said, "And I hear he gets it right a little more often than he gets it wrong."

"You heard some of that beauty-shop talk, I guess," Riley said, looping Kevin around the neck and rubbing his head with a closed fist.

"It's all true," Kevin relayed. "Every bit of it."

She thought about telling him some wild and crazy tale just to get him going but then changed her mind. She tossed the halter at them and started shaking the metal bucket. They headed into the heart of the field.

In the distance, Bitch's ears twitched but she didn't move, she only stared at the obvious. She was outnumbered. Sydney felt certain horses, especially contrary ones, noticed these things.

"Heard your Dad is out of town," Kevin said, showing too much interest.

She shot Riley a knowing smile. "Wonder where you heard such a thing?"

"Bet this is the first time Mr. Kane has ever left you alone on the ranch. You must be over eighteen now," Riley teased.

He knew damn well she was legal. "Yeah…five years ago."

"*Really?*" Kevin asked. "We've missed out then, huh?"

"Yep, time flies when a girl is having a ball," she replied, rattling the pan in Bitch's direction again.

"Are we talking about *you* and a good time in the same sentence? Surely not. Are you teasing me and talking about *balls* as in what a man closely guards or—"

"Good Lord, Riley," she complained. "Are you always this crude?"

Kevin laughed. "I'm sorry to say, he is like this all the time."

"Riley, don't you ever think about anything other than sex?"

"Rarely," he admitted. "I mean what else is there to talk about with a good looking woman, ya know?"

"For starters, you might find a better way to sneak up on the subject."

"I doubt it. I want your attention."

He had it. Oh Lord have mercy did he ever earn it. She'd never known Riley to openly flirt with her, even if his way of doing it bordered along the perverse. She turned toward Kevin. "And he's always like this?"

"You better believe it," Kevin replied, studying her with too much focus on her legs. "Besides, he's been saving up for you. Since you've been back, you're all he talks about and if you want to know a secret, I'll tell you one. He stands in front of the bathroom mirror rehearsing the lines he plans to use on you."

"That's not all I do in the bathroom when I'm thinking about our pretty little neighbor," he said, peering over at her. "I heard about your recent birthday. That makes you what, about twenty-three?"

She lowered her eyes and then quickly looked up again. Those who knew anything about the lifestyle, most likely recognized submissive practices and these two probably caught on fast given their reputations. The second he came on a little too strong, she acknowledged him as a Dom and couldn't help herself.

He snapped his fingers in front of her face. "Earth to Syd?"

"What are you doing, Riley, counting off years?" she asked.

"Nope, just keeping a mental tally for my own amusement," he chimed. "You know, I had it figured, a while back," he said as he took a step or two closer, "that me and you would somehow get it together by the time you turned twenty-four. We're running out time and it suits me just fine."

"What'd I tell ya?" Kevin warned. "Brace yourself. He's just getting warmed up."

Sydney felt her skin heat but the burn on her cheeks wasn't what concerned her most. Further south, in the juncture between her legs, a pool of excitement formed.

Kevin let her off the hook. "So tell me about this birthday we missed. Did your dad take you out and get you drunk? Sam's a party animal," Kevin said. "Trust me, we know. We've tossed back some moonshine with your daddy."

"Uh-huh, that's what he needs. Guys in their twenties and thirties around to make him think he's still young enough to chase wild women. I don't want another step-mother, for the record."

Kevin approached Bitch at the flank with his hands out. Naturally, she ran. "So besides making sure your dad didn't spot another candidate for part-time wife, did you have a good birthday?"

"Yeah, just another day."

"What did you get?" Riley probed.

"He's hoping you'll tell him sex toys."

"Nice thought."

"Told ya twice," Kevin teased, smacking Riley on the back of the head.

"You told him what twice?"

"Nothin', it's kind of an inside brother joke-thing." Riley replied, whistling for Bitch. He inched closer to the animal, quickly reached for her and she galloped off at a wild pace.

"I swear, if Daddy wouldn't miss her, I'd open the gate and let her run the hell on at this point."

"Yeah, but then Mr. Kane would know that you didn't mind him, now wouldn't he?" Riley's voice dropped an octave. "Men like Mr. Kane probably expect a woman, particularly a daughter, to do what they're told."

"I guess," she said reluctantly. "And what about you Riley," she went on a self-dare. "Do you like your women to *mind you*?"

If rumors were true, she bet he did because she'd heard about the sex games the Donovans liked to play, or at least, three of them. She rarely heard anything about their youngest sibling. Luke must have kept things to a low rumble when he closed his bedroom door.

Now, with the mere mention of something more explicit, Riley couldn't look at her. He walked ahead of them and she watched him closer while bracing for his rebuttal.

"Riley, I asked you a question," she chirped, but she didn't dare repeat it. She was already wet thinking about it. From handcuffs to riding crops, she'd discovered her neighbors made a few strange purchases at the local kink shops. Bondage seemed to really get the

Donovans going and the girls working at the local stores told tall tales.

Riley turned around and she saw his hard erection bulging in his jeans. In fact, she might swear to a visible twitch, maybe even two. "Careful, Sydney, you don't know what you're inviting."

"I think I have some idea," she cooed. She threw her hands high when Bitch charged her and thanked the good Lord above that the darn animal missed plowing her over. Her heart raced and she understood the reason for it.

She entertained the idea of sex again and the games she used to play with her Master. It was the thought of having a similar experience with Riley or Kevin—better still, both—driving her forward.

Riley and Kevin turned her on and they didn't have to try. A few underlying suggestions in their conversation and her body parts responded. A sudden eagerness encouraged her to go with it and learn all she could about the men she once fantasized about.

Maybe it was the cold weather. No, not likely. After a few lip smacks and a head to toe evaluation from each Donovan, she didn't think so.

Her pussy clenched with a smoldering hot sensation and her nipples pressed hard against her shirt. Oh yes, her neighbors always captured her attention. Only now, things were different. At twenty-three she'd craved a feeling, some kind of something to let her know she wasn't weird.

She wanted to feel like a woman. She longed to know what it felt like to have a man desire her and for some reason, the Donovan brothers made her feel sexier than she had in quite some time.

They aren't coming on to me. She tried to convince herself. Sure, Riley added a little spice to life in the way he talked to her but it had been a long time since she'd been around him. Maybe he always used a suggestive language with her and she failed to notice. Age made a difference in translation. As a teenager, she didn't understand his lingo but as a woman, she took everything he said as a rich temptation.

"Why don't you go in the house and let us round her up for you?" Riley suggested. "She might relate better to men and you look like you're plenty cold. You're uh...cheeks are blue."

He stared at her chest and then puckered his lips. "Not that I object. I like the company of a pretty woman, but I think you've probably got a thing or two inside to keep you busy." He continued to stare at her breasts and then said, "Besides, I'd hate for important body parts to freeze off altogether."

She ignored the very pointed remark but decided to even the score. She stared at his cock and continued with normal day-to-day conversation. "I should've gotten some supplies in hours ago."

Riley was ready to play. "What kind of supplies do you need, exactly? You never know, I may have precisely what you're looking for."

She never doubted it for a second.

Kevin broke the sexual tension before it got out of hand. "The local weatherman says there's already five inches on the ground in Saltville. What do you need from town?"

"Do you have kerosene heaters?" Riley asked.

She shrugged. "I guess so."

"You don't know?" Riley probed, frowning. "You can't just depend on a fireplace if the bedrooms are upstairs. You need to think ahead, Sydney."

She tried to gauge the way he mentioned bedrooms. Sometimes it was hard to tell when Riley wanted to leave a hint of sexual flavoring here or there.

"How about flashlights? Got any of them on hand?" Riley continued his neighborly interrogation.

"I'm sure we do somewhere."

Riley dodged Bitch when she ran by them. "Do you have batteries?"

"Probably," she replied. She might pick up a few extra for her vibrators, too, now that she had motivation to use her toys again.

"How about logs for the fire?" Kevin asked.

"We don't use the fireplace and–"

"You will." Riley interrupted. He looked at his brother and then pointed toward the driveway. "Run back to the ranch. Tell Jett and Luke to bring some kindling over here while you drive her into town."

"Riley, really. I can manage."

Kevin took her by the arm. "Come on, let's get going. By the time we get back here, I bet we'll find five or six inches."

"Speak for yourself, Kev," Riley scoffed. "I hate it for you brother but I don't feel your pain."

"Cute, Riley. I guess you're swinging fifteen, huh?" Kevin said, laughing.

"Ouch!" she exclaimed. She shouldn't have said anything. Her outburst implied she knew what it felt like to have something inch between her legs. Besides, she should've just let it slide and allowed them to keep all private jokes between them. They were talking snow at one point. Playing dumb might have worked.

"Sydney, how would you know?" Riley asked, narrowing his gaze. "Mr. Kane would kill someone if he thought for a minute you had some guy romping around in your bed."

No, he'd murder the Dom who'd tied her up and wired her pussy for means of control. If her father knew he hired someone to protect her and he took care of her by keeping her sexually aroused rotating on a Catherine Wheel for punishment and pleasure, he'd have a fit. Maybe even the man's life.

She shivered with the memory. Suddenly, she was completely drenched with desire. She needed what her Master once gave her all over again. Could she find it in the Donovans? Probably not. The relationship she had with her Dom wasn't something she'd find twice in a lifetime.

Kevin shook his head rapidly. "Change the subject, Riley."

He didn't have to. She did it for them.

"Guys, I just needed help with Bitch. Really, I appreciate what you're trying to do but I can manage."

Maybe so but why put up resistance? The chill in the air and the wind whipping up around them continued to stir up more than dust. She saw little reason to refuse the handsome company.

"Ever driven on ice, Sydney? These roads will turn treacherous in a few hours," Riley pointed out.

"No," she answered, truthfully.

"Didn't think so. Get going now and please, no lip today. I can turn you upside down and paddle your behind."

Her mouth dried with the mention. Her bottom clenched right then and there. "In your dreams."

Mine too, she thought.

"And he'd like it," Kevin advised.

"A lot," Riley added before he approached the horse Sydney might later thank for being such a bitch.

* * * *

Brock watched them through the binoculars. They were working her over. Riley, at least he thought it was Riley, kept putting his hands in his pockets. The way he did it allowed him to shift the weight of his cock. It was pretty obvious what he wanted to accomplish. The little shit wanted her to see his hard length.

For a few minutes, he wondered if Sydney noticed. Riley tried to draw attention to his erection. Brock had to give the guy credit. He sure thought he had it going on below the belt.

Sydney kept her head down. Brock suspected she never noticed the bulge in Riley's pants. Hell, who was he kidding here? He saw it when he moved the field glasses downward so naturally, she did, too.

He zoomed in on her. He studied her face, her expressions, even her body language. Then, he tossed the binoculars aside and quickly changed the lens in his camera. His fingers itched as he pushed down on the shutter release button and made a few pictures.

"You're still my beautiful little slave, Sydney," he said with a growl. "I wonder if you still think of me."

One day he planned to ask her. One day soon.

Chapter Two

Jett walked up to Kevin's truck with a smug look of satisfaction. "Wowee," he drawled. "I didn't expect to see this pretty little thing with the likes of you."

"Hi, Jett," she said refusing to look at him. He was the one Donovan rarely spotted around town or even at the ranch. He ran from farm work and his brothers let him get by with it.

Jett was the wild card of the bunch, and the one who chased a good time. From what her father once told her, his shenanigans led him overseas a lot. Often, he disappeared without a trace and reappeared again like he never left in the first place. It never seemed to bother the other Donovans when he went missing.

"Ah now, you don't sound too glad to see me," Jett complained, adding a wink. He tapped her on the knee with his index finger. "I was hoping for one hell of a homecoming, pretty lady."

She held her breath and thought of the last time she set eyes on Jett Donovan. It was at a local fair. He ditched his companion and followed her around all night. In the end, she didn't remember much of the festivities but she knew one thing for certain. Jett Donovan kissed and groped a woman right into an orgasm, and it didn't take much.

He was the care-free Donovan rascal. He stirred a lot of commotion with the ladies—some said many of them had husbands—and the local authorities knew his name. The man was over six feet tall and every inch of him spelled out trouble.

Luke approached on the driver's side. "Where are you two headed?"

Sydney waved at Luke. "Good to see you, neighbor."

Kevin waggled his eyebrows. "We're going out on the town."

"In this weather?" Jett voiced his concern and looked over his shoulder. Sydney's eyes followed his to a barn already hanging in icicles.

"That's smart, bro. Real smart," Jett said. "Winter advisories are out everywhere. You can leave the country roads in fair enough shape but you two will never get back in here tonight."

"He might have a point," Sydney agreed. The roads leading to their farms were hairpin curves and fairly steep in some places.

Luke leaned inside the cab of the truck. He put his face in front of the heater and his cologne filled her senses.

"What are you wearing?" she asked, wishing almost immediately she'd kept her mouth shut.

Jett laughed. "You mean outside of a hard-on?"

She swallowed. "Oh God, here we go."

While Jett wasn't as provocative as Riley, on occasion he had a few outbursts. Sometimes she thought it was genetic.

"Sexy Cowboy," Jett quickly added. "Got your attention though, huh?"

Oh yes, he definitely had it. He always captured and kept it.

"And how would you know what he's wearing?" she chirped and sounded more like a girl than she ever had in her life. Grief, it was official. She lost her balance whenever she shared air with anyone by the last name of Donovan.

"Cause baby I'm wearing the same thing. Wanna move that little button nose a little closer and inhale a good whiff of me?"

"You wish," she said.

"Knock it off," Kevin warned them. "Riley said you and Luke need to take some wood over to her place. She's not prepared for this storm moving our way."

"What kind of wood are we talking, Sydney?" Jett asked, his lips curving into a wicked smile. "Anything come to mind?"

"No, Jett," she stated. "Not right off." Adding the last tidbit was unnecessary. She looked away, scared she might start breathing hard if she gawked much longer.

Jett didn't miss the opportunity to rib her. "You and I both know that's not true."

He tucked his hair behind his ear. She wanted to reach out and take care of the other side.

Luke bit his bottom lip and studied her with fierce, hungry eyes. "I'll gladly help you out, Sydney."

Did he just try his hand at sexual implications as well? Surely not. Then again, his brothers had the art of seducing women down to a perfected science.

"Thanks, Luke." Oh no, she said two words and they spilled from her mouth like a breathless damsel in distress spoke them. Did she bat her eyelashes too? Maybe, probably, sure she did.

Sydney always liked Luke. A true good guy, he had the bad boy looks but his demeanor prevented him from using them to his advantage. Most women would cream on contact with a man like Luke Donovan.

Luke was—as her grandmother used to say—a looker, a real looker. His blue-green eyes made a woman want to stay locked in his gaze and lose all control. The real enjoyment, Sydney decided a long time ago, existed in his body. She was sure of it, even if she lacked the experience of trying him out for herself.

Luke possessed God-given six-pack abs. He endured a lot of hay tossing and it showed up in his belly—the one he kept bare in the summertime so all the ladies in the county could drive by with binoculars and gape. Stare-worthy, the man earned the right of a woman's praise. Where his brothers probably worked a woman into an orgasm, Luke just had to look pretty and stand still.

Jett walked around the truck. He mocked her with the curve in his lopsided smile. When he reached the driver's side, Luke moved over.

Jett opened the door. "Get out."

Kevin reached for the top of it and missed. Jett grabbed Kevin's arm and physically moved him.

"Hell no, you're dreaming, little brother," Kevin said, glancing at Sydney.

"Maybe so, but you and I both know a fella's gotta wake up sometime," he said, refusing to move or further acknowledge his brother.

His focus remained somewhere else—on Sydney. "Yeah, I believe it's time to stop fantasizing. I want to play house in the real world. What do you think, Sydney?"

Play house? She started to ask but decided against it. Riley and Jett had the ability to keep her tongue-tied. They obviously recognized their impact on the female population. Most of the time they wore around satisfied smiles.

Kevin studied Sydney before he moved away from the truck altogether. "Are you okay with this?"

"It's fine," she said.

Not really but why fight it?

In some ways, Jett and Riley reminded her of her own father. A woman didn't waste her breath arguing with men like them. They were the alpha males that romance writers liked to write about, the kind of men who lived each day in living color.

"You really are a true legend in your own mind, aren't you?"

Jett took a deep breath, tossed his arm over the seat and stared deep into her eyes before he supplied an answer. "You of all people ought to know. Legends are the kind of guys who make their mark on a woman. I assure you, I'm more than a legend in my own mind. Sugar, I'm instant recall. You think about me a lot, don't you?"

She gulped. He must've told his brothers. They pretended to ignore his theatrics but she knew better. Why would he carry on like this if he didn't? She stared straight ahead and watched it snow. For a wintry afternoon, things continued to heat up.

Jett and Riley, maybe Luke and Kevin too, most likely believed they offered a woman more than any other man walking. Yes, from what she'd heard, they had reason to believe they possessed certain alpha rights—size mattered, after all.

The brothers made some additional small talk. They discussed what they needed to pick up from the feed supply and hardware store, which was one in the same in their small southern town. While they chatted, Jett shot her a few sideways glances. It started a whole chain of emotions and brought up some fiery memories.

Instant recall, she reminded herself. Why the glass didn't fog with what she remembered, she wasn't sure, only thankful a thin film never appeared.

The defrost setting wasn't necessary yet, but it might come in handy later if Jett picked up where they left off three years ago. He wouldn't dare. A lot changed in thirty-six months.

Sure it did.

She thought of the last time she saw Jett. No one had ever made such a hard play to screw her before their time together. No one tried since.

Good grief, she sat in wet panties just thinking about it. The way he'd taken control over her body that one hot summer night left her forever ruined for any other man, maybe even her Master.

After her time with him, she cursed herself for letting him use her like she did. Lucky for her, or so she tried to believe, her Master trained her to remain a virgin. It was the discipline she developed through her Master's training that prohibited her from screwing Jett in a very public place.

Her Master expected her to remain pure. It was important to him and what he cherished most about her. Otherwise, she wondered sometimes what might have taken place in the few short hours she spent with Jett Donovan.

Luke backed away from the truck. Kevin shot her a wink and then pointed his index finger her way. "Behave," he mouthed.

Oh yes, he knew. More than likely Jett told everything right down to the dry humping. She swallowed stiffly and cursed Bitch under her breath. She was in for one hell of a ride now.

* * * *

Brock glared through the scope. What the hell was going on over there? Why the sudden change of plans? What was Jett doing? Why did he have to get in that damn truck with Sydney?

Brock swallowed back the heartbreaking memory. He remembered how Sydney reacted to him when he once asked for information about her time alone with Jett. Three years ago, she refused to tell him everything he wanted to know. It angered him but he kept his rage intact.

Even after he restrained her and delivered the appropriate punishment, Brock realized a certain truth. Jett Donovan possessed intimate knowledge of his slave. No, maybe he didn't go as far as he wanted with her, but only because Brock wasn't there to grant or deny permission.

He dropped the field glasses and snatched his camera. He zoomed in on them. He saw both heads in the truck. Sydney stayed on her side, Jett on his.

The vehicle moved up the driveway. Then, his worst fear materialized. It stopped, the brake lights dimmed.

Shit. Now what? The sick sensation rumbled in his gut. *No, Sydney. Not here in front of me, lover.*

A lot of time had passed. Now, Brock wondered, if Sydney would reach for temptation, invite and embrace it. Jett, from what Brock knew about him, would give her everything Brock once withheld from her.

He closed his eyes and remembered their time together three years ago. After he punished her, it took him a long time to manage her body appropriately. It was only after he promised her the toy she loved most, that she described her feelings for the young rogue. In fact, she told him more than he wanted to know about all of them.

Sydney confessed a strong attraction for her neighbors. She genuinely cared about each and every one of them. Now, she was there alone with the very Donovan who might use it to his advantage.

* * * *

At the end of the driveway, Jett slammed on the brakes and pushed the gearshift into park position. He casually extended his arm across the seat and turned to face her.

"What are you doing with Kev, Sydney?"

The question took her by surprise. "What?"

"Answer me. I want to know what you're doing riding around with my brother."

"We were going to the store to get some supplies." She stopped chattering out excuses, but only for a second. "Riley told him to give me a lift. I guess he thinks I'm incapable of driving in the snow, who knows."

"Is that right?"

She wasn't sure why she felt compelled to explain anything to Jett Donovan. "Yes. Sure it is."

"Tell me something, little Sydney. If you'd gone to the store with my brother, would the two of you have stopped long enough to do this—"

Before she even saw one coming, Jett's kiss invaded her lips. She felt the heat pass between them while some sort of magnetic current held them together.

His mouth covered hers while his tongue led her into a wet tunnel of pure bliss. Her heart raced and her nipples burned for a touch, not just any caress, but a Donovan hand. The kind of fingers she felt certain were fully trained to manipulate a woman.

If she imagined the bolts of electricity between them, it didn't matter. This was what she'd read about. This was what she'd dreamt about. She realized when she looped her arms around his neck that what they had between them defined sexual chemistry to the extreme. Jett wasn't a man who aroused a woman and then refused to screw her.

Jett framed her face with his large palms and kissed her breath away. In that one moment, she fell back in love with a Donovan. The kiss he robbed did more than snatch her lips. He stole her heart all over again.

A few times, she tried to break free from his mouth but he weaved his fingers through her hair and drew her closer. She felt his pulse pounding against his wrists and her ear. He stroked her tongue with his and nipped, oh how he bit and sipped at her lips before kissing her whole mouth again.

He ran his fingertips along her neck, adding a little pressure to her collarbone while his lips moved lower. At the same time, a loud peck on the windshield stilled their moment. Jett slammed his fist against the steering wheel and then used it to pull away from her.

Before he rolled down the window, Kevin opened his door. "What 'cha doing here in this truck, little brother?"

"More than you've ever done," he growled. "You need something?"

"Yeah, I do. Riley called after you left. He told me to stop you. If her daddy finds out we put her in a vehicle with you, he'll have a fit."

She released a tortured, but satisfied, sigh. Tormented, because she most definitely wanted more from Jett's lips and if she found it, heaven help her. She might take everything he offered and provide him with more than she had the right to give.

The guilt returned without warning. She immediately thought of her Master.

It took her a minute but she shook the sensation. Her Master only came to her when he was summonsed by her father and for no other reason.

Jett was there with her because he wanted her and he kissed her like he meant it. His kiss led somewhere and it wasn't to a large seaside home with a room full of stimulating toys and promises never delivered. If Jett ever took her to his bed, he wouldn't leave her with unfulfilled fantasies and shattered hopes.

A quick memory returned. It was one where her Master towered over her but unable to give in, restricted by his own rules and guidelines, he forced himself back before penetration. In some ways, she resented him for it. Sometimes, when she thought of how close they came, she viewed his act as one of betrayal. Why he refused to make love to her never added up and he left her with a feeling of tremendous loss.

Even with their scattered memories, a small measure of satisfaction tugged her lips into a wide smile. She knew Jett still wanted her and because he did, a sigh of relief hung in her lungs. She needed someone to stop them before they revisited that hot July night where everything changed between them.

Kevin was right. Her father would have a dying fit if she even thought about going into public with Jett. It went far beyond their one-time attempt at public exhibitionism, too.

Her father had his reasons for wanting her to keep her distance from Jett. She'd love to know more about those. The men keeping her company probably wouldn't offer much insight.

The youngest Donovan made his way around the front of the vehicle. Once Luke reached the passenger's side, he opened the door. Methodically, he reached for her. He swiped her hair away from her face and gently touched her cheek.

"She sure is pretty," he said.

Her pulse raced as he studied her. *Pretty? He said pretty?* She wanted to ask him to say it again, just to make sure she heard him right the first time.

"She's also had my lips all over her mouth, in case you missed that part," Jett mumbled, sliding away from the wheel. Kevin reclaimed his seat.

Cupping her neck, Luke looked deep into her eyes. His attentive gaze warmed her to the bone and she barely noticed the cold gloves at her nape.

"We saw what happened from the barn," he said, ignoring his brothers while staring at her mouth. "You took these lips by default."

She swallowed tightly. *Oh God! He's going to kiss me. I have to stop this. No, you can't kiss me, Luke!*

Oh why not, she countered when he drew her closer. As quickly as she debated whether or not she wanted his kiss, if delivered, she focused on his thick lips as if she planned to entice him. If any man had lips designed for kissing, Luke Donovan did.

He leaned in the truck and slanted his mouth over hers. "That's right, isn't it Sydney?" The question fell into her parted lips. "He embezzled that smooch, stole it before any of the rest of us had a chance to ask for one."

Over and over again, she swallowed. She stared at his luscious pucker and then grinned when she realized Luke was deviling his older brother. He wanted to make Jett crazy and as Jett started around the truck, she realized it worked.

"So *are you* asking?"

Luke nudged her with his hip. "Scoot over."

Kevin shook his head. "Hell no. You boys agreed to help and I'm telling you, we've got work to do over at her place. Now get out of here and go help Riley. By the way, Riley said to tell you to pack your toys."

She opened her mouth to say something, but Kevin quickly warned against it. "Don't ask. You'll find out soon enough."

Jett tried to move Luke out of the way. His large leather-covered hand tapped Luke's shoulder. "You heard him."

Luke licked his lips with a slow moving tongue. "Yep, sure did. And Sydney, I'm asking for my turn *right now*."

Good heavens, he moved his tongue all the way around his mouth like he wanted her to watch every inch he swiped. She had a few intimate places she'd love to introduce to a tongue like his.

Offering her a quirky smile, he patted the same hip his own pressed against in an attempt to move her. "You know, I have a solution to all this," he said changing the subject from smooching to the potential for something a little cozier. "You could stay here with us. Dad wouldn't mind. Then, we don't have to worry about you in this brutal weather."

"That's uh...very generous of you but as you can see, I'm fit as a fiddle and ready for anything. Besides, the two farm hands Dad hired quit after the holidays, which is why I'm home in the first place. Dad had some kind of secret trip planned. He needed to turn the ranch over to someone he trusted."

"Is that right?" Jett asked, shooting a suspicious smile Kevin's way. "So you're prepared to take on the world now?"

He obviously read too much into her statement.

"Sure. Jett, in case you haven't noticed, I'm not a young girl barely out of my teenage years now. I can take care of myself. I could've easily driven myself into town for supplies but you know Riley, always worried about this or that."

Jett snickered. "You don't know Riley too well. He's never worried about a woman."

"Never," Kevin confirmed.

Luke shook his head. "You're the first I've heard about."

After Luke worked his mouth into another delicious smile, she saw the next move. He lowered his head and kissed her with soft, gentle lips.

"Damn it, Luke," Jett pulled him away from her. "The kissing is reserved for one Donovan—me."

Feeling frisky, and just entirely too full of herself, she yanked Luke's collar and planted a good kiss, a woman's smooch right on him. She put some effort in it. Jett deserved it and he stood there in utter amazement while she made out with the youngest of the lot. Luke responded even better than expected.

His mouth sank against hers and he loved on her lips with a soft stroke and a whisper of something sweet here or there. She couldn't make out the words, but she thought he said something to her in French. God, she hoped this wasn't a dream.

"Ahem…" Kevin cleared his throat. He stretched his legs forward with both palms caressing over his denim-clad thighs. "You two think you can knock it off until we get back?"

"Let me go with you?" Luke pleaded, pulling away slightly but still nibbling at her lips and jaw while he asked for the permission she realized Kevin would refuse.

"Nope," Kevin objected. "Riley said me. M-E."

Luke took off his glove and brushed his knuckles over her cheekbone. "He only said you because of Jett's driving record, never mind the fact he doesn't have a driver's license at all now. He won't mind if I go instead."

Kevin laughed. "You're probably right. But I mind, little brother. I promise you," he said, slapping the back of the seat a few times and adding a wink. "I can't wait to drive Miss Sydney."

"I just bet you can't," Jett growled. "Did you like that kiss, Sydney?"

"Yeah, Jett. I did. Thanks so much for asking."

"Not a problem," he said, sounding rejected. "I plan to spank your bare bottom for making me watch. What do you think about it now, sugar?"

She shuddered with excitement, or was it fear?

"Oh, you like the idea, huh?" he teased.

"Step away from the truck," Kevin said. "I told you boys. She's off limits for this until I have a talk with her."

"Off limits for what?" she quickly inquired.

"I'll explain later," he snapped before reaching for his seatbelt.

Jett acted amused. He stood back and crossed his arms. "No, why don't you start with it right here because I'd love to see her expression."

"I told you," Kevin growled. "I'll handle this part, alone."

"This part?" she asked again. "Let me guess, you all think I'm some sort of—"

Luke covered her lips with his again. "Shh...no...we think you're beautiful." He barely whispered his sentiments before he licked beyond her teeth for another sensational kiss.

Shifting into drive, Kevin allowed his foot to ease off the brake. Luke shuffled with the forward movement and then moved away.

"We gotta go," Kevin told them again.

"I'll see *you,* later," Luke promised.

"I'll be waiting for you, too," Jett added with a hearty grin. "Count on it." He smacked his hands together. "You know what I'm thinking, don't you, sweetheart?"

The door slammed and Sydney waved goodbye but not without noticing the obvious delights packaged tight in denim blues. Both men were hard and the bulge in their jeans made her own center thicken with a woman's lust.

Kevin drove through the gates of the Donovan property spinning out on the gravel before they hit the paved public road. He didn't stop to allow her a nip of his lips until they were four or five miles down the road. It was a good thing too because after Jett's intoxicating promises, she wasn't ready to take on anyone, especially Kevin.

Chapter Three

After some heavy groping, and a tongue battle she wanted to lose, Sydney moved away from Kevin's mouth. She touched her lips.

"They're still there."

"Good," she let go of the lone word and quickly added two more. "I wondered."

"Guess you have some questions."

"I get what's going on here," she remarked.

"You do?"

"Yeah, I understand," she whispered.

He chuckled. "I doubt it."

She tried to readjust her clothes. Kevin remained a gentleman during their kiss, with one exception. At one point he mimicked the sex act with his tongue and she went from bake to broil in about two seconds. She even stretched her hand and touched the meaty part of one hell of a man.

During their moment of well spent time and too much fondling, she flipped around enough to straddle his middle. At one point and after a few grinds up and down, he pushed her away and asked her to give him a minute.

Now, she decided, it must have been enough to make her look like a complete mess. After she patted her hair down in the back, she faced him.

His thick arm draped across her shoulders. "You okay?"

Confusion set in. Why she allowed things to go this far with Kevin when she had other Donovan attractions, she wasn't sure. Maybe she trusted him more than the others.

Dark eyes stared back at her. He looked eager, hungry for more.

She couldn't trust any of them. No, correction, she couldn't trust herself.

His hands played in her loose curls. "Sydney?"

All of the Donovan men possessed extraordinary good looks. They knew it, too. They had sex appeal programmed in their veins. They didn't have to practice come on lines. Any one of their bodies offered enough sweet temptation to lead a woman right into their arms, straight for their beds.

"I'm fine and," she reassured, pointing outside, "It's snowing."

Kevin put the truck in drive and pulled back onto the state highway. He leaned over the wheel as he drove, glancing up at the sky.

"You know, I told them from the very beginning, you're the one for me. Riley just came up with a better plan," he advised, cocking an eyebrow. When she didn't say anything, he reported on the weather. "Darn. I think we're in for days of this stuff."

She hated it when a man changed the subject. She especially loathed it when the one in question held a lot of insight, the kind of explaining she wanted explained, and deliberately danced around providing it.

"About the Riley plan, go on," she encouraged.

He tapped his brake and looked over his shoulder, waving to an older fellow who allowed Kevin's truck to squeeze into the downtown traffic. "Look, I know what you're thinking and it's wrong for you to jump to conclusions. We don't think you're a slut or anything."

"Uh-huh. You sure fooled me."

He pulled into a parking space in front of the hardware store. "No, not at all," he said, shoving the long gearshift into a parked position and yanking the keys from the ignition.

"In fact, it's just the opposite. We've decided to share you," he advised, his eyes dancing with mischief. "Sometimes, we'll share you at the same time, if you're up to it, and I think you are. Other times, you'll have some one on one attention. Whatever works for you, will work for us."

At the moment, nothing *worked* at all. Sharing air with Kevin Donovan suddenly became a chore. Her mind churned in a few too many directions. What would her father think? What would Mr. Donovan think? What would her Master do? Would he reappear in the middle of the night and tear down the walls just to get his hands on her?

He might.

She tried breathing again. This time it worked. "Now, that was unexpected and uncalled for."

She watched a little old lady toddle up the front steps of the hardware store. Waiting patiently, she thought Kevin might correct his slip or throw in some sort of punch line, assuming this was all a joke.

He didn't say a word. He only waited for a reaction.

She found one quickly after she realized he wasn't kidding around. She released a guttural groan.

She pursed her lips, gripped the door handle and then shoved it forward. "Why you...you...." She didn't know what to say. At least, not at first, but she quickly came up with a few choice words after the shock wore off.

"You have some nerve, Kevin Donovan," she said, insulted. She hurriedly slammed the door behind her and headed for the store.

He stayed right on her heels. "Hang on there a minute, Sydney. It's not as if you have a dislike for any of us."

No, she actually felt something more along the lines of love for them—all of them—or she did about three minutes before Kevin opened his big mouth.

They must've known how she felt and there existed the first of several lingering problems. They wanted to take advantage of her feelings. It wouldn't be the first time a man tried it.

Where the Donovan brothers were concerned, Sydney possessed a lust gone wrong. When it led her astray, it spun into something unexplainable and terribly wild. Apparently at some point, long before she came back to Abingdon, they realized how much she cared about them.

She grabbed a shopping cart and pushed it through the store. "Get in the truck. Go back to the farm. I'll find my way home."

She threw various items in her buggy. Flashlights, batteries, extra heaters, more batteries, horse blankets because they were on sale, and anything else she found she might need.

When she reached the cashier, she noticed half of her loot had disappeared. "What did you do with those small space heaters?"

"You don't need them. We have plenty of kerosene heaters and besides, we're going to put those fireplaces to good use, too," he told her, waggling his brows with a deeper insinuation. "Especially the one in your bedroom."

She gasped. Immediately, Sydney's mind flashed with an image. Four hard bodies wrapped her up in a blanket and carried her to the hearth where they towered over her with their cocks hard and ready.

"No!" she exclaimed, burying her face in her hands. "This can't happen!"

Kevin looked around at the attention she easily gained. He smiled at a few of the patrons, waved at a farmer who looked familiar, and then gently nudged her arm. "I'm sure you're having all sorts of wicked images form in that overactive brain, but please keep the outbursts to a minimum until we're alone."

She looked up right away. "Don't you use a stern tone of voice."

He grabbed her upper arm and forced her to look at him. His grip was firm. "Sydney, I don't want to discuss this right now but I want you to listen to me. You're Sam Kane's daughter. I'm Mark Donovan's son. Everybody in this store knows that much if nothing else. Now, I want you to straighten up and walk out of here with a smile on your face."

She blinked a few times. Who the hell did he think he was all of a sudden? No one dared to talk to her like this. She gasped as soon as she thought it, no one except her Master.

"Oh no you don't," she exploded, tugging her arm away from him. "You and your brothers do not get my permission to step in and take over where my…my…my father left off."

Her dad wasn't the man she wanted to accuse right then.

He winked. "If that's what you really think, Sydney, then you already know I don't ask for or wait on a woman's stamp of approval."

Before she stopped herself, she pushed by him and he whirled her around by grabbing her by the waist. He pressed his erection against her center.

"See, Sydney, part of the war you think you have to fight is already won for you. Most women would kill to be in your position. Four men want to take care of you and protect you. You don't have to make decisions or choose one of us over the other."

"How thoughtful of you. Thank you for letting me know," she spat, wiggling away from him before he felt the rapid beat of her heart.

Oh heavens. She'd lost her ever lovin' mind. At least the earlier mental clip only lasted a few seconds. A few more and she'd just leave her clothes in Kevin's truck once they returned to the farm. Even the way he talked to her turned her on. Good Lord, she'd truly forgotten what it felt like to want a man until the Donovans stormed into her afternoon and took her by sweet surprise.

A few minutes later, Sydney unloaded her selections at check-out. The cashier held her hand out. "Ma'am?"

Sydney shook her head and stared at the palm in front of her.

"Cash or charge?"

"Oh, I um…I'm sorry about that," she said, pulling out her identification. "Just bill it to the Kane ranch."

"No problem," she grated out, glaring at Kevin. "How are you doin', cowboy?"

"Good," he snapped. "You okay, Lori?"

"Doing better now that I've seen you," she flirted. "You two seeing each other now?"

"Yes," he said.

"No," Sydney chirped simultaneously, slapping two bags against his chest then stomping out.

Before she reached the truck again, she was bitching. "You had no reason whatsoever to outright lie in there."

"It's not exactly a tall tale, is it? I mean, after what I told you?" he asked, opening the door to the truck. "It is now, of course, because we aren't seeing one another yet by true agreement but why bother explaining all of this to an outsider when things are likely to change in a matter of hours?"

"I don't think you, or any of your brothers for that matter, are as good as you've obviously been told one too many times."

"You don't, huh? I can prove you wrong."

"The hell you can."

He leaned over, grabbed her around the neck and kissed her hard on the mouth. "I had to do that, Sydney. If I hadn't, she might find our *pairing* unbelievable," he said, pointing toward the hardware store where little Lori stood dumbstruck at the window.

"Oh, so now orgies are called pairings?"

He playfully bit her lower lip. "Call it whatever you want, babe, but acknowledge it as something. Just know that I belong in between these legs, and my brothers have assured me, I'm not the only one," he grunted before he squeezed her inner thigh. "And once I get them wrapped around me the first time, I'll slide in again for frequent visits."

"I'll take your words as a warning," she huffed and puffed for a minute, then buckled her seatbelt. When she looked up, she narrowed her eyes on Lori, who now pressed her nose to the glass.

"She looked at you like she wanted to take you home and introduce you to her momma."

"We've already done that," he admitted. "It wasn't pretty."

"Oh," she whispered. Then, suddenly she remembered something. "Yeah, you did meet her parents, didn't you? Uh-huh, I think so. You two were the talk of the town for a few weeks."

He poked her in the ribs with a few fingers crawling up her side. "What did you hear exactly?"

"You met her momma *and* her daddy coming out of her bedroom one morning, or at least that's what the local gossips around town report."

"Hear that all the way up in Wyoming, did you?"

"For the record, I was in New York. Not Wyoming. Where'd you get Wyoming?"

"Your daddy said you were in Cheyenne."

"Huh?" Oh right. She forgot. How quickly she screwed up when she was off her game. She hung her head in shame.

Her father never mentioned how much she could divulge to the Donovans about her sudden trips. She was always a little curious about what he told them when she vanished.

"Oh well, it really doesn't matter where I've been. I'm back now," she said flippantly.

Kevin brushed her cheek. "Actually, for the record, it's always mattered to me."

His sincerity took her by surprise. For a second, she saw husband material, but by the time she pondered it for eight seconds more, she remembered his plans varied slightly from hers.

They wanted to share her. What a wicked concept.

Kevin stared at her blankly before changing the subject altogether. "I'll take things slow. These roads are bound to get treacherous."

She wasn't worried about the streets in front of them. Instead, it was the obstacles they might encounter along the way if she decided to consider Kevin's offer.

Wait, she thought. *Am I considering this?*

They drove back to the state highway in silence. A few miles outside of town, he reminded her that they missed an important item on her list. "You left without the sweet feed. Do you need me to turn around?"

"Uh-huh," she said. She left her good senses somewhere too but that was beside the point.

"Syd?" he asked again, "Did you hear me?"

She swallowed tightly. "Forget it. I have enough grain to get by."

"If not, we'll bring some over from the farm. We probably need to get home," he said, pointing toward the road. "As much as I'd love to stop off at the Martha Washington Inn and hold up there until the storm blows over, I have a feeling two or three of my brothers might come looking for us."

"I imagine so since you four seem to do everything together," she snapped. "Now, why don't you start at the beginning and don't leave out the best parts. I like a good bedtime story."

Kevin stopped on the side of the road again, something she decided he liked to do. "It's not your bedtime, Sydney," he said before he sealed his words with a fiery kiss.

No, but the way he slipped his tongue inside her mouth made her all about finding a bed and landing there soon.

She backed away from him but before she broke the kiss completely, bit at his lips one last time. She savored his taste and greedily wanted more. "Maybe not, but I believe whatever you want to tell me has a lot to do with a bed, doesn't it?"

"Oh, I don't know. From what Jett said, you manage just fine up against a solid wall."

Now, she wanted to hitch a ride.

* * * *

Mark Donovan stared at his sons. They rushed around the Kane property in a hurry to prepare the barn area for the worst of storms. They rushed in and out of the sheds and outbuildings before any of them spotted him.

He frowned as he watched them. They weren't his boys anymore. They were his men, a strong division of skilled operatives he trained along with Sam Kane.

He still worried about them. They were his sons and while they made him very proud, their business involved risks and often required sacrifice.

He worried Riley had paid a price too high for any father to contemplate. Riley was running from something and it troubled him. One of the oldest, he was a natural leader and not one to take any relationship lightly.

After Riley returned from his last mission, he used humor and women to cover up his inner pain. Sam had suggested that he press for answers, but now wasn't the time. If Riley was dealing with something personal and it was what he suspected, then there would never be a right time.

He had just spoken to Sam and he needed to make a few decisions now. He gave thoughtful consideration to the risks and what they all stood to lose and hoped to gain. Then, he decided how to proceed. They needed to stand ready whether they stayed there with Sydney or at home.

Riley saw him first. He stepped inside the barn, hollered out for the others and then made his way down to the SUV.

Concern washed over Riley's face. "Dad?"

"Riley," he acknowledged him, cranking up the heat the second all three doors slammed around the vehicle. "Jett, Luke. Afternoon, boys."

"What's up?" Jett asked, grabbing him by the shoulders and shaking him in a playful gesture.

Mark glanced in the rearview mirror and held Jett's gaze. He had a glassy look in his eyes when he anticipated new orders. He must've thought he had some headed his way. His shoulders squared and there was a certain edge to his voice. Mark recognized it. He used to possess the same enthusiasm.

All of his sons looked forward to a good assignment but Jett was different. He had the itch. He wanted a real hard battle to fight, and a superior cause to support.

"Trouble as always," Mark said.

"Before you go blaming me for crimes unsolved in the murder capital of the world, tell us what this is about. Kevin just called and he'll be here any minute with Sydney."

"How many men did we lose in South America two months ago, Jett?"

Jett shifted uncomfortably behind him. Riley coughed and then sniffed like he was too preoccupied with both to answer. Luke stared out the window.

"I asked you a question." His deep authoritative voice pulled few punches. He was working his sons for more than official business. He expected them to disclose what they refused to place in their reports. They probably suspected it, especially Riley.

Mark Donovan had a little information. It was enough to worry the hell out of him and convince him danger moved too close for comfort, too close to home.

Riley took a deep breath and Mark shot him a sideways glance. "Do you have any idea?" Mark asked.

"No sir," Riley said, unable to look him in the eye.

"Luke?" he asked, turning in his seat.

"How would I know? I'm not permitted off the farm."

"Count your blessings," Riley growled. "Not the trips you miss."

If circumstances were different, he might pat his son on the back and tell him how proud he was to hear him quote the same words he often said to all of them. Instead, he slammed his fist against the dashboard. "Jett, did you leave some of our men behind in Venezuela?"

"No. Hell no," he blurted out, peering at Riley.

Mark didn't miss the secrets they tried to hide when they glanced at one another.

"What happened in Caracas, Jett?" he pressed. He wanted Jett to tell him what he already suspected. Something went wrong, something happened they didn't detail in their reports. Death was everywhere and violence followed him, and maybe even Riley, all the way home. He expected a good dose of the truth.

"Jett, you and Riley seem to forget one thing. I know what kind of people wait for us whenever we venture beyond our gates. Southwest Virginia doesn't protect its own from the worlds we try and save when we leave here.

"Now start talking. One of you better tell me what happened in Caracas, and the other one better start thinking about how we can fix this without casualties here at home. Someone from Venezuela followed you back. I want to know who."

* * * *

Brock squinted and raised the binoculars. Even at a distance, he picked up on it. Mark Donovan was shaken. He had cause for deep concern. Brock could only guess why.

Venezuela.

He shuddered when he thought of the few times he'd visited Caracas. He didn't bring back memories to cherish from South America.

Before he jumped to conclusions, he raised the binoculars again and focused on the older Donovan. Sam Kane and Mark Donovan went way back and Brock was aware of the problems facing Sam. Based on body language and alert eyes, he didn't think the news relayed in Donovan's SUV had anything to do with Sam or his illness.

He dropped the field glasses to his side. Whatever had them upset, he prayed it didn't have anything to do with Sydney.

He heard a vehicle and looked toward the main road. He saw Kevin's truck moving closer to the Kane property. Quickly, he rested the binoculars against his forehead again and peered down the hill.

Brock snarled. He sensed the danger and he recognized the gnawing sensation. His instincts, the sixth sense he developed through the years always worked overtime. He never questioned why.

This, whatever it was, had everything to do with Sydney.

* * * *

Kevin parked in the vacant lot in front of the barn. Over the last hour, the weather drastically changed. She hopped out of the truck the second Jett opened the door for her.

"Thank you," she said, batting her eyelashes.

"No problem," he replied, turning around in time to watch her bottom. Oh yeah, he stared and what she would give to really work her shake about right now. She feared it might freeze in one direction or the other so she decided not to tempt the devil.

No thanks to Kevin, she now wore wet panties and her nipples were rock hard something she felt certain every Donovan man there knew. They took the time to lick their lips and stare at her chest before looking into her eyes.

It took everything she had to hold Kevin off only because she wanted his hands everywhere he put them while they were on the road. Everywhere except the one place she wanted them most—inside of her.

As if he knew he toiled with a virgin, Kevin never crossed the boundaries clothing provided but she almost did the unthinkable. After she rubbed her hand over his denim-covered dick, he started to unzip himself. If the snow had stayed in the sky just a few more seconds, she would've wrapped her hand right around his size, maybe her mouth too.

Riley towed everything he picked up straight into the tack room. The guys unloaded a few bales of hay and salt from the back of one of the Donovan trucks.

The wind whipped and churned around them. Sydney felt a strong gust at her back as she hurried through the barn dumping grain in the fancy feeders connected to each stall.

"You boys went above and beyond. Riley, thanks for getting Bitch in for me."

Riley pulled his coat around his neck and through chattered teeth, gave her a song and dance. "If you'll offer us a drink and let us come on up to the house, I'll keep you entertained with Bitch stories. It wasn't easy rounding her up, I'll have you know."

"You guys will do anything to get inside my house, huh?" she teased.

"Nope," Jett replied, following her to the office.

She hurriedly flipped the row of lights to the off position.

He said a little too much when he added, "But we'll do just about anything to get in a good looking woman's pants. You should know that better than anyone, Sydney."

The chuckles rippled around them and she narrowed her gaze on nothing more than cowboy sex. "For the record, I don't remember you getting in my pants."

"You're right. I did not, but damn woman, I sure tried."

"Knock it off you two," Riley instructed, and then pressed for the invitation. "How about that drink?"

"Sure, come on up to the house. The least I can do is feed you some dinner and offer you a beer or something."

She grabbed the metal barn door and pulled it over the entrance. With the snow whipping around her, it was hard to tell what dropped faster, the snow or the temperature. Her fingers were too cold to grasp much of anything.

Luke stepped in front of her. "Here, let me get this. We'll seal off both ends."

"I can get the back sliders on the way to the house," she shouted over the maddening sounds of winter.

"No! Go on with Kevin! We'll meet you at the house. Let us do this!" Luke shouted. The damning winds prevented his words from sounding out with any level of high volume. The blizzard's greedy fight for attention won out and everyone scurried about trying to lock down the barn and make their own dash for shelter.

Sydney hopped back in the truck and by the time Kevin slammed it in reverse, Luke gave the passenger door a fling and jumped inside. Kevin turned up the heater and aimed the vents her way. Luke pulled her body on top of his. With his body heat, she didn't need artificial warmth.

Sydney wasn't sure if she froze in one place or just lacked the inspiration to shift anywhere else. She especially liked what she felt under her tailbone. Luke's thick erection gave her plenty to think about. He warmed her in the important places the instant he pulled her tight against his chest.

"Warm, yet?" Kevin asked, peering over at them.

"No, but I could get hot fast with you two," she said, pointing as a way of directing them. "Just pull around back and we'll go in there."

By the time they parked in front of her backdoor, Riley and Jett were driving onto the nearby carport. They brushed the layer of snow from their coats and then stamped around the patio before discarding their cowboy boots right inside the glass-enclosed porch.

* * * *

Brock watched the Kane house buzz with new activity. He sat in the control room with a tight fist formed under his chin. The weather forced him inside. He hated placing this much distance between himself and Sydney but thanks to old man winter, he didn't have a choice. He sipped on his whiskey and resisted the urge to pick up the phone and call her.

Over the last three years, there had been several times when he thought he couldn't stand another minute without her. Today may have been the truest test.

He watched other men hold her, touch her, grope and handle her with no regard for what might exist beyond their lust. By giving into their desires, they placed her at risk. They weren't aware of their surroundings, but he was on top of it.

"I'd like to call over there and tell her to send them home," he said, the guttural possession thick in his statement.

He wouldn't dial her number. If hell broke out in the middle of the blizzard, and it might, he needed to know she was safe. With her protected, he could concentrate and do his job.

"You love her."

"What?" he asked, noticing the concern etching its uncertain path into his father's wrinkled forehead.

"I've known it for awhile," his father added.

"I've loved her for as long as I can remember."

"I suppose you have son," he said thoughtfully. He paused like he needed time to consider the best way to issue a warning, and then he said, "She's your weakness, and because you have one, you're vulnerable and she's in danger. Even her own father didn't place her at such a high risk."

Brock stared at the computer monitor. "And you think I don't know this?"

He glared at the monitor, his new worst enemy. He saw Sydney and Riley. He had his hand on the small of her back. Brock moved closer, hit the zoom feature.

"You'll drive yourself insane if you watch their every move."

Maybe so.

"I wonder if they realize what they've done, huh?" Brock snapped over his shoulder.

"What do you mean?"

"She's in danger because of all of us. Her father, me, them...even you put her at risk. We've placed an innocent girl in harm's way."

"An innocent girl?" he asked, chuckling. "That's how you see her?"

"Yes."

"She's a woman, for God's sake, and considering what you've done *with her* and *to her,* I would think if anyone knows that, you do!"

Brock gritted his teeth and stewed on his father's words. There were few secrets between them but the one he wanted most to hide surfaced at the wrong time.

"You don't know what you're talking about," he said, peeved.

"Yes, son, I do. I know everything I need to and even understand some of the reasons behind what you did."

His father's words stung him, but he quickly moved passed it.
He tried to keep a clear head, stay focused and use what he had at his disposal. This mission required his strength and his training, and if all else failed, the trust and confidence he had in Sydney. At least, with her, he didn't have to worry about surprises.

Chapter Four

"Come on in, and I'll get something hot on the stove," she said. "You know where everything is, I guess. Washroom is at the end of the hall and if you want to relax in the family room, I'll start a fire in the wood burning stove. Just give me a minute. Let me get some logs on the fireplace in here first."

"Now that's my kind of woman," Riley commented. "She looks good enough on her feet for a man to imagine her on her back, and better still, she'll use her knees to squat down and get some work done."

"What kind of work are you talking about, Riley?" she asked playfully before placing a large pot on the stove top.

"You don't want to know," Luke warned. "Here's a hint, Sydney. When it comes to anything Riley says, always read between the lines and imagine the worst."

"Or spin it with a naughty twist from the beginning and assume there's always one there to find," Jett suggested.

Riley took her frozen hands in his and scrubbed his palms back and forth, providing friction to warm them. "I'm talking about the kind of work required to start the best of fires, you know what I mean. I'm the only one who missed the kissing party, but I'm not in the dark here, Sydney."

She backed up and immediately bumped into the kitchen counter. "Kissing party?"

"What would you call it?" Riley asked before he made a point to focus on her lips. "One of these guys said it's the kind of kissing that makes a man want a woman. From what I heard, I missed one hell of a good time."

"Oh, I see," she drawled, turning to the culprits who provided the play by play report. "And did it make you fellas want a woman?"

Jett grinned. "You know it."

"In a bad way," Luke said while his brothers laughed at some sort of inside joke.

Riley grabbed her hips and moved into her. "Honey, I've waited a long time to get your lips on mine and what I want to know is why you skipped me in the first place. I'm the one who rushed right over to help you with Bitch, remember?"

"I seem to recall someone saying they didn't have a way with bitches. Turns out, it was like bees to honey, huh?"

"Actually," Luke said. "He can't take credit. I did it."

"Then I owe *you*," she chanted. "Looks like you're skipped again, Riley."

He slapped her on the hip and watched her with too much amusement when she flinched. "Watch it, sweets. I'm the kind of man who gets worse with the wait."

"Riley, is there a particular reason you and your brothers like to smack my behind?" she asked, putting him on the spot.

Kevin grunted. "You mean besides the fact that you have a great one? Nah, I doubt we have a good excuse."

"He didn't slap your shapely ass, sugar. Trust me, I would notice. Now if you want one of us to do it, then I'll gladly volunteer."

"Shush up, Jett. You had your chance."

"Burn," Kevin replied. "Speaking of, there are few details I can't wait to hear from your point of view concerning your romp with Jett several years back. What about it? What happened?"

"Ah," she purred. "Nuthin' much."

"I'll show you nothing," Jett said, grabbing his front bulge. "Better watch it, sweetheart, or else I'll flip you over and spank that pretty behind right here."

She blushed.

"Lookie there what you boys have done to our girl," Kevin drawled. "She's as pink in the cheeks as I'm willing to bet a few other parts are under the sheets."

Riley snorted. "How poetic."

Kevin's words were about all it took to stir a little hot pudding. She squeezed her legs together and focused on the water she wanted to see churn with a bubbling boil. Maybe if the water heated as fast as her pussy, they'd have dinner served within the next few minutes.

"She's right. I had my chance and I took it too. You want me to give you a few oohs and ahs to refresh your memory, Sydney?" Jett asked, biting his bottom lip. "How about this? Does 'lower, Jett, ah please go lower' ring any bells? I also remember something about being good at it too but I won't quote verbatim."

"Oh why not? Don't hold back on my account," she said, fidgeting. *Oohs and ahs?* Oh sweet heaven, he was right. She remembered everything in a flash with vivid images to boot.

She grabbed onto the doorjamb and gripped it until her knuckles turned white. She moaned? Probably so, and now with the recent memory, she wanted to feel his hard cock against her once again.

It was the details. That's what did it.

The ridges of his cock particularly interested her when they were together. She gave him a hand-job that night because after he pressed against her, she wanted to hold him in her palm and wrap her fingers around his size.

Maybe it was exactly like he said. She bet it was worse. She did have a few drinks in her. She probably cried and begged. Oh heaven help her, did she plead? She wanted to ask him to fill in the blanks. There were a few grey areas, like she didn't remember his reason for walking away right when she thought they might fuck.

She cleared her throat and thought about it. Then, she wiped the bead of sweat from her brow.

"You okay, Syd?" Riley asked, amused. "I mean, do you need to lie down or something?"

"I'll carry her," Jett teased in passing. He cupped her neck and whispered in her ear. "I can make you cry out for me again, sweetheart. I swear it." He lowered his voice another octave. "Sometimes, I can still feel you working around my fingers."

"I believe it," she whispered before her own hand covered her mouth. She remembered how it felt to caress him also and sweet mercenary, the way he thrust his hips against every tug.

"No secrets here," Riley reminded.

"Remember, Sydney, you do owe me." Luke stated with moist lips trying to steer the conversation in another direction. "And I'll love any payment you offer so long as it involves me and you, one on one."

"Whoa now," Jett said. "Take it easy there Luke. We don't want to scare her off and—"

"I'm not scared," she interrupted.

"You were *something* a moment ago," Kevin reminded. "It didn't take much. Whatever Jett said to you, it must've been good."

Whatever he did to her three years ago was damn good.

"Tell me what I can do to make you shiver." Riley's statement matched his wicked expression and he made a play for her again. This time, he popped his lips and she wanted his kiss. Unless someone spoke up to object, she planned to do it there.

She rubbernecked it around the room and looked for Kevin. He immediately informed her he wasn't going to stop it. "I don't mind, Sydney."

They laughed and she shuddered at once. Her Master made her tremor with anticipation, with a lust so intense she ached for sex and she liked it a little rough. Sometimes, she wondered if that's why he continually denied her. She believed he was afraid of their intimacy and terrified he might harm her in some way if they formed a deeper connection.

"I didn't get very far in explaining things to Sydney," Kevin said, apparently amused by his confession.

"You didn't?" Riley asked, gathering Sydney in his arms, like she belonged there. "Why not?"

"We had to prioritize," he explained.

"I bet," Jett said. "Elaborate."

Sydney backed away from Riley. "Do you always pursue a woman like this?"

"Like what?" Luke asked.

"You think that's what we're doing?" Riley inquired, taking a sidestep and closing the distance between them. He tilted her chin and looked into her eyes before he shot her one of those Donovan signature smiles. "No, honey, you got that part wrong. We're not here to chase a woman."

Riley dropped his arm and held onto the belt loops on either side of her waist. She almost swooned when he pressed his hard cock into her center. She felt his length all the way to her belly, or maybe she imagined it.

He pressed again.

She gulped. Maybe not.

She cleared her throat. "You might want to inform your brothers if you aren't game for the chase, Riley. They gave me the impression they were in hot pursuit."

"Then I'm going to have to teach them some manners. Besides, how do you chase someone you've already caught?" Riley asked, smiling so big that all she saw were dimples and teeth.

"He's right. All we have to do is claim you," Jett said. "We're looking forward to that part. Ask Luke."

"Oh yeah," Luke agreed. "I am."

She loved Luke's boyish ways. Even though he was the same age as she was, he acted like he was a horny eighteen–year-old with hormones raging out of control.

"I like the view back here," Jett said, positioning his hands on her torso and gripping her body from behind. "I could keep you grating against a shower wall, would you like that, Sydney?"

Very much.

Riley smacked his lips. "You'll have to wait until I'm through with her sexy little ass. I plan to spank it first."

Sydney gulped and then stood there dumbfounded. Unable to move, she lowered her eyes. The feeling of submissiveness so overwhelming that she wanted to ask Riley to make good on his threat of punishment. Preferably, right now.

Had she done something to deserve a good paddling? Yes, she decided. She should've left her dad's damn horse in the barn.

On second thought, maybe not. If Bitch remained in her stall, she wouldn't have the pleasure of watching Riley's grin widen with the promise of his hand coming down on her bare ass.

Jett kept looking at her like he tried to envision her in a thong. His lust-filled expression made her antsy. "Sydney, I have a pretty good idea of what I missed three years ago. I've had one sleepless night after the next and plenty of time to think about it. I'm ready for you when you're ready for me."

"Goes double over here," Kevin said.

"Ditto," Luke added.

"I...I'm...still not sure what's going on here," she admitted, scanning Jett's handsome face.

"You want me," Jett reminded her.

"Now where did you come up with such a notion?"

"That public display the two of you had went straight to his head and I'm not talking about the one you see right now," Riley motioned to his brother's tented pants.

"If Kevin had kept his lips off of yours long enough to explain, maybe you'd understand everything," Jett pointed out. "And Kev, don't deny it, you jumped out of the truck with a rise anyone would notice."

"And what did you want Kevin to tell me, exactly?" she asked, waiting for their responses with her palms planted on the stainless steel sink.

"Everything," Luke said from across the room.

"Like?" she fired back.

Riley wrapped his arm tight around her waist. "I'll explain, but first, I wanna see how wet those sweet lips can get."

"Remember, Sydney, read between the lines." Luke advised, briskly rubbing his hands together.

Oh sweet thunder, he meant the southernmost region, not her mouth! Immediately, she trembled with desire. Her body swayed and she suddenly stumbled drunk, no doubt, with new lust.

Riley steadied her with a heavy hand on her hip. "Luke, I think she likes the idea."

Yes, she liked it very much.

The kiss on the way snapped her into reality and her hands flew against Riley's chest to stop the one already in motion. His mouth barely brushed hers by the time she gave him a quick push.

"Oh no, you don't."

He snapped her wrist and held it to his side. "Try and stop me," he growled, slanting his lips over hers again.

A few low cheers made her dizzy from the excitement. She wondered if they stood around and clapped while one of the other brothers fucked. She gasped. Had they shared other women before?

She pressed her palm to Riley's gut this time. His belly was washboard perfect and she wanted to see what her fingertips touched. "I've had three Donovan kisses so far. I don't want another one before the four of you tell me what's going on here."

"It's pretty simple. Call it lust, maybe even a pursuit for the finer things too, like the potential for love. Call it whatever you want Sydney. Hell, I don't care," Riley bit out, turning to Kevin. He shook his head and tapped his chin with three fingers. "You really screwed up, Kev. You know I believe in plain English. I don't have a problem blurting it out like it is."

Kevin took the dare. "Have at it. I told her what she needs to know and she didn't act like she wanted to hear the rest. After my lips met hers, it was all over."

Riley stared at him blankly. "Uh-huh, and I'm sure she made the first move."

She tapped her foot. "I prefer straight talk to macho gibberish myself. Keep talking."

"We want you and you're old enough to make the decision for yourself now. Seems your daddy is going to let you make it, too, thank God. I've waited years to get down to the good part."

"What is the good part, by chance, Riley? Sex?"

"Sounds like a terrific place to start," Jett said.

"Hush up, Jett. I'm asking Riley."

"I'm sorta wise to the idea, too," Kevin admitted.

"I'm not surprised, Kevin," she fired right back. "But for the record, I don't have any parents around to fix you breakfast when you sneak out of my room at six or seven in the morning."

After a few chuckles, Kevin retaliated. "As much as most women like it in my bed, I don't think you'll worry too much about pancakes."

"Don't," she put up her finger. "I don't want to hear any male wise cracks about pigs in a blanket. Not right now."

"I wouldn't dream of it, darlin'," Kevin said. "What the four of us keep wrapped up has a different name altogether."

"Please, let Riley speak," she said, searching Riley's eyes. "I want an answer. I want to know what you meant by the good parts?"

"You do?" he asked.

"Yeah, now."

"Sounds like a great idea. I like *now*." Riley said, giving her a half-nod. He slanted his mouth over hers and nipped at her lips. "Honey, the good part is the kissing and where those kisses lead depends on you. I like taking turns, even going last." He opened the laundry room door and gave her a quick push inside.

"Wait! I need to…boil water and…" she whined. "I have things to do, Riley Donovan!"

"Add me to the top of that list," he advised, laughing. "Boys," he said with a devious smile, "Can you handle things for a second and let me have a minute here with Sydney?"

Naturally, they said yes.

Riley slammed the door with his palm sliding down the surface with a dramatic swipe across the texture. He allowed his arm to fall at her waist.

He dragged her body against the flat panel and then eased himself right into their kiss. Riley kissed her like it was against the law not to do it up right. His tongue slid easily in between her lips and he moved it across the length of hers like he'd kissed her a thousand times.

He brought her arms around his neck and within a second or two more, her heart raced out of control. When his tongue darted in and out of her mouth with the insinuated act of a slow screw, she came unglued.

In an instant, his kisses were deeper and his hands traveled south and north and south again. The heated matching of mouths led into a lot of groping and good heavens, did they ever find new ways to grind.

"That's right," he growled. "Give it a name, Sydney. Brand it." He thrust his hips forward and slipped into another kiss. "It's good, isn't it?"

She moaned, arched, and loved every minute of it.

He licked around her lips. "So good."

Oh but he was right. It was the experience of her lifetime. An encounter she'd never forget, one like no other…except one. She suppressed the immediate need to bring her Master into the moment.

It didn't work.

Riley's hands propelled up and down her sides as his mouth let everything unwind in a simple kiss that turned too complicated too fast. When his mouth left hers, she knew she was in trouble, but she didn't stop him.

Removing her shirt, he tugged it over her head, and bit his lip fighting off a delicious and devious grin. He was getting his way and he damn well knew it. "We need to get these wet clothes off of you," he said. "*And I need*, listen to me Sydney, *I need* inside of you."

"Oh God," she gulped. A man who knew how to finish the process of arousal made her cream.

Alarms went off as if someone had a way inside her head and she knew who held the reins of tight control. Why wouldn't he let her have this moment? She placed her palms against the wall and arched her neck for Riley.

"Master," she whispered.

He stopped at once and held her hands tight against his thighs. Their breaths were uneven, shorter than before. "What did you call me?"

Her chest rose and fell. "I didn't say anything."

His mouth curved in a smile and he munched on her thick lips. "Sure baby, whatever you say," he kissed his way to her ear and then whispered. "I heard you call me by name, Syd. I want to hear you say it again. It was so sweet, doll."

She sank within herself and thought of Master Brock and how he'd punish her if he knew what she mumbled in a moment of weakness. What if she allowed Riley to take her? What would her Master think? Would he ever understand her needs, her deepest desires? Her servitude wasn't conditional but his love was. No thanks to him, she had a problem forming relationships and it wasn't fair.

For the first time ever, she mentally questioned her Master. He'd never know. She'd never tell him. Did he have other women now? Did he treat them like he treated her or did he let down his guard and love them?

She must've gone limp in Riley's arms. He caressed her cheek and studied her expression, tilting his head from side to side in mockery. "Stay with me?"

She puckered, stretched, and then took his lips on again. Kiss for kiss, she stroked his tongue with her own. She pulled him closer.

Riley's breathing changed, his cock grew harder and he was turned on more than before. "Tell me again, Sydney. Say it just one more time. Tell me who I can be to you."

He held her chin in place and waited. She felt the moisture gather in the corner of her eyes. "Riley," she breathed.

He closed his eyes and mashed his forehead to hers. "I've lost my mind," he said, running his hands behind her. He lifted her to him. "Let me feel you, Syd. Let me have you."

She gasped as the ridge of his hard length left its burning impression. It would've been so easy to beg him now. Simple enough to let him have her, and save her from a life of pure intentions. She wanted him to strip her of all previous experiences and let her know the raw quality of a man.

His lips crashed against hers once again, but she needed so much more than this. "Riley," she said his name over and over again realizing it wasn't enough for him and didn't provide her with the assurance she desired as well.

Her body jarred with his movement and he jerked her tight against him. "Sydney, let me make love to you."

She wanted to say yes. "I can't." But instead she said no.

God help her, somewhere along the way, no thanks to Brock, she became dependent on him and only him. Now she couldn't enjoy a man without his permission, his direct guidance and it had been three years.

Riley whispered against her flesh. "Let me have you, feel you. Tell me why you don't want this, Sydney. We're good together, let me make you feel good, would you like that, sugar?"

"I'd like it," she confessed before smacking his lips and wrapping her arms around his neck. "If you'd let me kiss you quiet."

"You would, huh?" he asked, grinning. "Will you let me punish you, Sydney? Slap your pretty pussy until it's hot pink?"

Her moist mouth felt dry. He tried to kiss her again and she turned her head.

"You like that don't you, honey?"

She agreed by muttering into his shoulder. "Yes," she said.

"Ah, Syd, that's right. Tell me what you like, what you want. I'll give it to you. I'll only ask for a few things in return. Will you give yourself to me?"

He drew back and held her forearms. "Sydney?"

Focusing on what he wanted or needed to hear became a jumbled mess of mental jigsaw puzzles. This time, he waited. He wanted her to respond. She was afraid. He made her tremble. She was afraid of what she might feel.

Riley moved his hands over her bottom and he pushed his cock against her center. "I've needed what we can have for a long time."

She convinced herself that she had lived long enough now to hear it all now. A man professing his need for sex on make-out session number one made her pussy clench with her own desires. She had plenty for Riley, but her inability to let her Master go, destroyed her.

Even after time passed, her Master still had his thumb on her relationships. Without a word from him, she sought his approval. She longed for one hard romp from a man she accidentally called her Master, but she couldn't let go of her own bylaws and set herself free. Master Brock still kept her from knowing the feel of a man's cock rather than just a vibrator's speed.

Or was it all an excuse? Maybe there was something wrong with her.

"Riley..." she said trying to resist, yet wanting to play, and needing a closer connection to the man driving her insane. "You wrack my nerves."

"I'm trying to do more than destroy them," he grated out possibly in tune with the pending defeat.

He always did it better than the rest. Between Jett and Riley, it was a toss-up but Riley pushed her, challenged her mind, and stroked her wits in a way none of the others did.

Riley and Jett were the kind of bad boys that made Stetsons look better and she'd love to find them tied up in her bed with nothing but their hats on their heads. They weren't the kind of men who let a woman bind them. If rumors were true, they did the binding and she couldn't wait to let them tie her up tight.

"Sydney, they got the first kisses. I want to be the first in line for the important stuff, the big things in life." He bumped against her.

"We have to wait."

"Why do we wait? I want to get closer to your untamed heart, that vixen living inside of you just dying to get free. Let me see that woman, Sydney. Kevin says she's there. He thinks you hide that part of yourself. Let me see the lover you want to be when you're with me."

His palm went to her forehead and he kissed her cheek to lips and back again. "Show me, Syd. Let me take that woman to task and show her the kind of man she needs. You need me, baby. You long for men like me."

"You've got it all wrong, Riley," she said. *I've had men like you!* She wanted to scream to the top of her lungs.

"I've got it right, Syd."

Yep, he nailed it without trying. She yearned for men exactly like him.

With his palms against hers, he entwined their fingers and kept them pinned close to her head. He gave her another heavenly kiss before his mouth traveled past her collarbone and captured one of her full breasts.

"I can't believe I'm doing this," her breathless words made her reckless but did she sound desperate? No, she sounded like a woman driven completely mad by white hot lust. God help her, her body reacted because she once begged for this kind of attention, Riley's kind of spice.

He lapped at her breasts in an erotic and tempting fashion. Back and forth, he ran his tongue and lips over her nipples until they were pointed and hard, pressing through the scant mesh-like material.

"You're doing fine," he said. He drifted down her belly and knelt in front of her. He watched her as he unhooked her pants. Then, he focused on taking care of those tiny metal buttons on her jeans.

"Syd," he barely squeaked out the nickname he gave her back when they were kids. "Why did you have to wear button-down jeans?"

"For times like these, and bad-boys like you."

"Good answer," he said, reaching behind her and smacking her bottom. "And the wrong one." He bit at the denim and tugged it with his teeth before he licked right underneath the waistband.

She held onto his shoulders and fought her inner wars determined to find peace, or at least temporary gratification. "Let me guess, real cowgirls zip up. They don't wear designer jeans, huh?"

"I don't give a shit what you wear. I wanna see you naked. Right now, I just want these babies loose. You might as well have a combination lock on it."

He continued to work at unhooking her buttons with little success. "Damn woman, I know you've got something worth protecting but seriously, how many buttons does it take to keep your little pussy safeguarded, huh?" he complained. Most cowboys would in a similar situation.

Riley's big hands slowly worked at the round metal pieces before moving them over and under the small slits. He didn't have an easy time of it.

Offering to help him was out of the question especially since he stopped every now and again to kiss tiny circles or suck her skin in.

Oh Lord, passion prints would trail from her breastbone to her waistband.

With three more buttons to go, she stopped him by placing her trembling hand over his. "I can't do this."

He tried to slow the quest but still wiggled the buttons this way or that in an effort to rid them of their obstacles. "Sure you can. I can do it. If I can, you can," he said. "Trust me."

"Oh God Riley, is that the best you can do?" she muttered against the back of her right hand. Her left fingers weaved a pattern through his natural curls.

He glanced up, parted his lips and allowed his tongue to move in and out of his mouth. "No doll, I can do better. I swear to you. It can get really good when I'm down here where a man belongs. *Trust me.* You want me right here before everything changes."

What did he mean? Why did he tell her this now? Was oral sex a one shot deal with Riley, maybe with all of them? Heaven help her, she hoped not because she forced herself to do the unthinkable.

She knew what it meant to have a man drive her crazy with lust and she wasn't sure she wanted a replacement for her Master. She had a lot of healing to do the first year without him. Every time the phone rang, she silently hoped her father would get that far away look in his eyes warning her that the car was on its away. Her time at home was over. What she used to dread, she learned to wait for. She watched the gates for the convoy of vehicles but no one came. Her Master must've forgotten her.

After she'd grieved all one woman could, she gave up. A few times, she started to ask her father about him but there wasn't a right time to ask him personal questions. He guarded his men and their privacy.

"Sydney?" he snapped his fingers. "I won't hurt you," Riley promised.

"You don't understand and I don't expect you to, but right now, you need to stop and all of you need to... go."

The hard part was convincing him to leave. The other part, he stopped instantly. Just as quick as she asked him this time, he halted his advancements but it took him a few seconds to stand up again.

He backed away and bent down to pick up her shirt. He handed it to her. His fingertips skimmed over hers. "That was pretty intense," he said before he ran his open palm over his jeans.

"Hot enough to trigger more than a memory later on," she hummed. She was thinking about Jett's philosophy. She'd love to be a hot flash for Riley, an instant recall for all of them, but right now she'd like a dry thong. She had a feeling all of the Donovans plotted against her and intended to keep her panties damp. It was a good plan because the moisture made her crazy.

"Are you sure I can't convince you? I know you're wet."

She gulped. "And you know this how?"

Maybe it was a dumb question. She had dumber...or maybe not. To ask Riley Donovan anything like that was outright stupid.

His about-face showed carnal hunger. There wasn't a doubt in her mind what he planned to do. Slowly, he rubbed his hand, even his wrist, against her covered pussy.

A soft moan fell from her lips before she parted her legs and changed her stance. Her knees buckled but he held her up with one arm supporting her, saving her from a true fall.

"Oh sweetheart, I know. It's hot and damp." He brought his fingers to his nose. "You already smell like sex, fruity and sweet, passionate and—"

"Riley, you can't do this," she whispered.

"Why not? Give me a good reason. Make me stop. Tell me all the reasons, the real ones, Syd, not something fabricated to make me want to stop. Tell me why I should stop *for you*."

"Because I...I...I...want you to."

"Like hell you do." he said, applying pressure and grinning as he watched. "Try again."

He rubbed harder, created a good sense of friction. "I can make you come, Sydney. Would you like it if I made you scream?" he cupped the back of her head and continued to work his hand under her cunt.

Oh, what she'd give to be in his arms without barriers, without her designer jeans with buttons secured. He stirred her passion and his hooded eyes barely concealed that twinkle of male satisfaction.

"I'm…I'm…going to…"

He latched his lips over hers and stopped moving his wrist against her. "No Sydney, remember you don't want this yet. We haven't established our boundaries, have we?'

She shook her head. He moved his hand under her bra and pinched her nipple.

"Riley!" she yelped.

"That's my sweet doll," he growled, looking deep into her eyes. "Now, let me feel you once more."

Her legs were pressed together and he moved them apart for her and for him. "Open your legs, doll."

She almost cried out his name when she shifted her weight. She had to make him stop this. Talk, she reminded herself. *Speak so fast he can't distract me.*

"You're a mess, Riley Donovan and you're driving me…away," she said it before she thought, and she then dismissed any notion of talking herself away from him.

"I'm not driving you away, Sydney. You're running scared."

His dark eyes darted with a challenge. Riley Donovan wasn't a wannabe. He was ready to go all the way here and now.

"Maybe you're right," she admitted.

There wasn't *a maybe* to it. He was right-on.

She grabbed the door knob and gave it a hard yank. She walked right out into the kitchen with her shirt in hand and an appreciative audience waiting for her.

"Oh my God," she exclaimed, holding the material to her chest and closing her eyes. "What the hell am I doing?"

"I hope you're stripping," Jett said. "You've got the boobs and I've got the time to give them a lot of attention."

"Thanks, I think."

She turned back to Riley and he moved out of her way while she stepped into the laundry area and shoved her arms through the fitted white shirt. While she was at it, she decided to button her jeans. They needed to stay right where they were—on her hips.

Maybe she should send the designer a thank you note later for making this particular style with buttons. It saved her from a dryer romp. She glanced at the appliance and quickly changed her mind.

If she hadn't said no, she'd be in the throes of a passionate fuck right now. Maybe she'd call customer service and complain. She might talk to Kevin and see if she could seek damages.

Surely to the coastline and back there was someone she could blame for her current status as virgin submissive. Worse still, she couldn't blame Master Brock now when he wasn't there to finger.

Her reasons for walking out were legit, she told herself. Riley would never stay anywhere long. He'd fuck her and go. Men always left her behind. Right now, she wasn't sure she could give herself completely and without conditions to the men she'd always cared about. They'd leave and she'd watch them say goodbye one by one.

When she walked into the kitchen again, she cleared her throat and looked at Kevin. "Okay, now that we have Riley out of the way, who wants to go next?"

"Me!" Luke yelled, excited for the perceived opportunity.

She stopped him by pushing against his belly when he was close enough to wrap her in his arms. "Then someone needs to talk and tell me everything," she said. "There's more to this than meets the eye."

"You're right. There sure is," Jett said. "Pull up a seat. Let's chat."

"Or, you can always bend over." Riley suggested, rubbing his chin. "I'm still horny as all hell and with what I have under these jeans, you'll forget you ever had the first question."

* * * *

"You'll drive yourself crazy."

Brock was already there. Thank God his father didn't walk in while Riley had Sydney pinned to the door. He would've had to pull the plug and truth told, he'd never seen her look sexier.

He couldn't wait to hold her in his arms again. He wanted to let her know that he had watched her, saw her when she arched for another man. He also wanted to know if it was his name echoing in her ears, his face she saw when Riley's hands caressed her.

He needed to go to her. If for no other reason, to let her know he was nearby in the event something went wrong.

"I know what you're thinking and you can't do it," his father said.

"Why the hell not?"

"You know why, Brock."

Their enemies didn't know he was there. He was the element of surprise, the one that might help save Sydney, maybe even all of them. He had to stay underground because he had guarded Sydney enough for everyone to know exactly who he was.

"How bad is it going to get?" he inquired, wheeling around to face off with his father. "I need to know."

"What you need to do is find religion and then say a prayer. There may be two different attacks and we're going to need all the help we can get."

Chapter Five

The men made themselves at home. She noticed it right away. By the time they made their way to her cozy den, they each carried a drink.

"I get the feeling you spend a lot of time here with my dad," she observed.

"Kevin and Luke do," Riley said. "I've had my hands full lately.

The other Donovans snickered.

"I see," she said. "Got a girlfriend, I guess."

"Several," he said, studying her for a reaction.

"Want me to act jealous, Riley?"

"Nope, you don't have to act. It's scribbled all across your face. You just romped my ass pretty good in that laundry room. It's hard to think of my hands on someone else now, isn't it, baby?"

"Don't pay him any mind, Sydney. You'll see, he's the one who orchestrated a lot of this," Kevin said.

She retaliated fast. "I don't care if you have one woman or a herd of them. I see various men, too. So at least we understand one another from the start."

They stared at her in disbelief. Then, they asked for proof.

"Give me a name and I'll call him tomorrow. We can take care of the breaking up process for you, Sydney," Kevin said.

"One at a time," Luke assured her.

"I think I can handle my own affairs."

Jett grabbed another log and stuffed it into the fireplace. "So you're calling them affairs, are you?"

"Sure." She sounded too flip, too nervous.

"You're winging it as you go, aren't you sugar?" Jett asked from his squatted position. His hands settled on his thighs before he stood up again. "It's okay, you know. It's part of your appeal. We know you don't see anyone on a regular basis. You don't have a serious relationship."

"I do date," she stated flatly. "Some."

"Sure you do," Kevin said.

"I do."

"Rarely," Luke stated.

"Seldom." Jett added.

"Try never," Riley offered the final punch. "Or at least it's been a few years, hasn't it Sydney?"

Riley saw through her then, straight through her. Only one man held that power over her. Only one earned the right. Was Riley trying to acquire the same privileges as her Master?

The way their gazes met made her uncomfortable. Earlier, he had heard her. She only whispered it but he listened closely when she called him *Master*.

It was a stupid mistake and something she had no right to assume in the first place. Even if she didn't feel so connected and loyal to Master Brock, she had no way of knowing what Riley—or any of them for that matter—expected.

She narrowed her gaze on Riley. "Snooping into my business?"

"Damn straight."

"I see. Find out everything you wanted to know?"

"Not yet, but I will. Give me a day."

"It might take you two," she warned.

"I doubt it. If so, it only gives us more time to run off the men we plan to make you leave behind anyway."

He studied her a little closer then. He knew. Without a doubt, he understood there had been someone very special in her life.

Luke walked over to the window and looked out. "It's coming down pretty good here, guys. Maybe we should get her settled in for the night and do this another time."

"I'm not leaving," Jett said. "How about you, Riley? Are you headed home soon?"

"Nope, not on your life." Riley informed, dazzling her when he took her hand and pulled her to the sofa. Kevin and Jett sat in two old matching rocking chairs while Luke continued to watch the sky open up with a cascade of falling flakes.

"I didn't get an invitation," Luke said.

"You won't get one," she stated flatly. "None of you will."

"I don't need one," Riley informed.

"You all aren't staying here tonight," she said firmly.

"What are you going to do?" Jett taunted her. "Call the sheriff and tell them we won't leave?"

"Yes, I will, if I have to."

"What are you afraid of, Sydney?" Jett asked.

Riley wrapped her tighter. "You scared, baby?"

Terrified.

Kevin narrowed his eyes on her. "Are you actually afraid of being with one or...all of us?"

"All of you?" she gasped like it was the first time she'd heard the offer. Then she asked, "At the same time?" She played the part of dumb broad to the hilt. Apparently, they liked her best when she gave them an astonished reaction.

Riley jumped at the chance to gain a little moral support. "What do you say boys, at the same time?"

"I don't see why not," Luke replied. "That's the plan isn't it?"

Her mouth dropped. Of all the things and of all the times, she certainly didn't expect to hear Luke suggest something so naughty. No, he was the good-bad-boy. The one who looked the part but never led anyone to believe he'd act on it.

"What is it, Sydney?" Luke inched closer. He stood in front of her and Riley. "Come here."

She felt a rush of a fresh flood pool between her legs. Oh yes, the Donovans had one goal in mind. She wasn't going to be an easy mark. If she kept them away from her tail and boobs, they'd tell her anything she wanted to know, in time. It always took more effort with them because they were smart men.

She stood in front of Riley realizing he now had her rear parallel with his face. Luke's body melded to hers. His cock pressed into her as he kissed her neck and released his endearments. "I like the idea of watching you with all of us."

He showered her neck with the kind of kissing that left behind marks and then he drew back and ran the pad of his thumb over her lips. "You like the idea too, don't you, sweet baby?"

Her ears would never hear another word spoken by a man if they didn't add something like 'sugar, sweet baby, darlin', or honey' when a man chose to speak to her. She liked living in this moment. A Donovan minute was one well spent and their endearments warmed her.

"My body will look like one big bruise when all of you are done."

"Where else are we going to find those love bites, Sydney," Jett glared at Riley.

"Lower, baby brother, much lower," he told him with a little too much pride.

"As long as viewing them isn't reserved for the one who put them there, I'm okay with it," Jett grumbled.

She pushed away from Luke but Riley cupped her bottom and pressed her forward again. She moved right into Luke's cock and this time, he bent his knees and challenged her with an unhurried sexual suggestion. "Remove the pants, Sydney, and I'm in there."

The others laughed and she felt the weight of the world in her knees. They almost snapped and if Riley hadn't supported her, she would've landed on the floor.

"Luke, stop," she whispered but it was too late. He brought her fingertips to his lips and after he kissed them, he released her hand and then pressed her hand against him.

"Feel me, Sydney," he encouraged, guiding her hand over his thick erection.

"This is crazy," she whispered.

"Tell me about it," he agreed, sucking her lip in between his teeth and devouring her mouth.

He continued to move his hand with hers, squeezing the back of it so her fingers would close around what she could reach on top of denim. "You taste so sweet, Sydney."

"She does, now. I'm a believer," Jett replied, watching with lust lingering in his gaze. He took a seat and allowed his legs to fall open. Her eyes followed his and with a wide, half-evil grin, he patted his cock. "All for you, when you want it."

Oh, she wanted it. Whether or not she'd take it was the question.

"I want all of you to quit," she said in a small voice before taking a side-step away from Riley and Luke. The first time, she failed but on the second try, she moved away from both of them and walked over to the window.

"You're right. It's getting bad out there, boys. Maybe I'll give you a rain check on dinner."

Jett brought his beer to his lips and tugged a long sip from the slender neck bottle. "You heard the lady, Riley. She said boys. That means you."

Riley chuckled. "Oh sure, you know I'm out that door."

Jett pointed to the window. "Sydney, what makes you think, that we have the first inclination to go out there now?"

"You can make it home," she stated. "I mean, come on now. You can walk from our place to yours. I can draw you a map."

Riley grinned. "Little smart ass, aren't you?"

Kevin shook like the sudden cold outside made its way inside long enough for him to feel the chill on his back. "Walk? In this weather? You're kidding, right?"

"No, why?" she answered, running her fingers lazily over the old ivory piano keys as she passed the family heirloom, her grandmother's baby grand piano. "Let me guess. A woman doesn't say 'no' to any of you. Have any of you ever heard the word before?"

"It sounds familiar but can't say that I've heard it much, if at all," Kevin admitted. "Is that what this is about? You want to be the first?"

Oh she wanted to be a first for them but not in the way they might think. She was considering Kevin's earlier proposal and it was the reason she had a problem with them staying the night.

Jett managed a quick smile. "Darlin' you know I've been turned down before. You were the first and only one to do it."

"Oh, then I see where this is going now," she chirped. "I turned one of you down and now it's a challenge to all of you." She paused and then thoughtfully, she added more. "For the audience, I didn't turn your brother down."

"Just because you gave Jett a kiss and tug doesn't mean I'm like my brother and will settle for the same. Trust me. I'm not Jett," Riley informed. "You know what I want, what I plan to have."

She lowered her eyes and he mouthed, "Good girl."

Then, he glanced at Jett. She saw them swap a meaningful brotherly exchange. They showed one another their middle fingers.

Riley studied her like he meant to commit everything about her actions and reactions to memory. "Let me ask you something, sweet girl."

"Go for it," she said with a wink.

"I gotta know something. Call it a man thing. If we asked you to choose just one of us right now, for a quick romp, who would it be?"

"Good grief, Riley," Kevin groaned.

"You don't want to know?" he asked.

"I do," Jett admitted.

"Of course you do," she said. "According to you, I turned *you down.*"

Jett grabbed her, caught her unexpectedly. "Little Miss Controlled, aren't you?" He held her in front of him with his hands clutching her waist. "And I didn't share *every* detail with these guys. I can promise you."

In an instant, she knew what he meant. He didn't tell them she came during their heavy dry humping session. She did it three times. Oh Lord, once should've been enough, but it wasn't. She assumed when he discussed the low moaning, he told them everything. At this point, she really didn't care one way or the other.

What bothered her most was the way she reacted to Riley. She was drawn to him more than the others. He was actually the one brother that frightened her the most, at least on some level.

"Jett, we all know what happened," Luke said. "No secrets exist in this town. With the crowds at the fairgrounds, everyone saw you."

"Uh-huh," he muttered, touching her hair. He withdrew his hand as if he feared he might pull it, maybe even yank it, and start a new wave of sexual implications. "But not everyone heard you, did they sugar?"

Sometimes she wondered. While he had kissed her during her first one, he'd watched her second and third. Who could say if she screamed or yelped or maybe even cried his name? She whimpered some. Oh yeah, she remembered the mewling.

"Jett, please."

He closed his eyes and took a deep breath before looping his arms around her middle and nuzzling her skin. "Don't beg yet. There's no need."

He brushed her hair to the side of her neck and in a low voice, he said, "I can't wait to bury my cock so deep that you swear you lose your virginity all over again." The raw passion made her womb clench, her thighs drew tightly together.

"Oh hell," Kevin said. "There you go. Trying to keep up with Riley and acting just like him in the process."

"I know one thing you boys will love. She likes having her hair pulled tight." He lowered his voice and pinched her leg. "I liked what it triggered. Do you remember?"

She did. God help her, it was what she screamed about first.

"Quit teasing her," Kevin said. "Her nipples almost pressed straight through her shirt. I can almost see them now."

Luke started pacing.

"What's wrong, Luke? Can't wait to get her up on all fours and grab a fistful of her hair, can you?" Jett teased.

Riley was almost as bad. He possessed about as much patience as a man in a strip club waiting for a lap dance. He wanted to get whatever was on his mind off of it as quickly as possible. Unexpectedly, he started with a simple statement. "We want you, Syd and we don't want you to doubt how much."

"Well, I sort of got that part," she said.

"Your dad already knows it too, Sydney," Kevin said and all eyes returned to her immediately. No one uttered a word after his unexpected statement.

Luke moaned. "Great timing, Kev."

"He does?" she asked, suddenly unable to breathe. She shook her head. "Say that again. I don't think we're clear here on this. I took you for smart men. That was a dumb move."

She started out of the room but then turned to ask the gnawing question immediately. "What the hell were you thinking? When did you talk to him? This doesn't make sense. I called *you* today, remember?"

"Sure, I remember," Riley replied. "One way or another, we were going to end up right here tonight anyway, regardless of who placed the first call. Bitch only gave you a legitimate excuse, if she's even considered one. I think you let her out just so you had a reason to dial our number. Luke walked right up to her and she came inside pretty as you please."

"I guess Bitches like him. Maybe you should pay attention how Luke works his females, Riley. I have a feeling you may need to understand how quick a woman can change her mind, her mood, or her taste in men."

He shrugged. "If you're going to be mad at one, might as well throw stones at all."

Kevin spoke up before the conversation turned toward the horse. "It really didn't matter how it all played out. Your dad is counting on us to keep you safe while he's away. We had his blessing before he left. He wants us to take care of you. He wanted one or all us staying here. We bargained for all."

"You had his blessing to keep me safe, you morons!" she exclaimed, looking from one man to the next. "You did not, and I'm pretty certain about this, have his nod of approval to fuck me."

"I don't know, Syd, it's looking pretty good for the home team," Riley mused. "What do you think Luke?"

"I think so, too," Luke agreed.

Of course he would, he's the youngest. He had older brothers to impress.

"You think Dad imagined something like this? Oh dear Lord, what are you thinking?"

She shook her head, walked into the kitchen, pulled open the refrigerator, and grabbed a beer. She twisted off the top and slid it into her front jean pocket. She stared at the roaring fire. It compared closely to her raging temper burning out of control. She was damn mad.

Kevin's lips curved in a cute, devilish smile. "Admit it. We turn you on, huh?"

"Oh yes and the idea of you talking to my father about taking me to bed just charms me right out of my pants. You know what? Moron doesn't quite cut it. You're suicidal and I don't have a thing for men with death wishes."

Riley swapped glances with Jett. He took a deep breath and started to speak. Kevin stopped him by going first. "Sydney, there are a lot of things we're going to tell you and some of them may even make you think we are men with—as you put it—death wishes. But we're also the guys who can take care of you and protect you. No one can do it any better than we can. No one has our training or our resources."

"This is unbelievable. You're talking about sleeping with me like I'm a job or something. Let me guess, you're the only ones with the appropriate tools to get it done right!" she exclaimed.

"How'd you know?" Riley asked enthusiastically.

Jett chuckled. "Yeah, we sort of believe we're blessed in that capacity, Sydney."

She tapped her nails against the mantle. "I bet."

She glanced up toward the window. Sure enough, the snow was coming down in buckets now ensuring her of one thing, if nothing else. She most definitely had overnight guests.

"Okay," she began. "So let me get this straight. You two," she pointed at Kevin and Luke wiggling her middle and index fingers, "discussed seeing me with my father and then these two," she indicated Jett and Riley only by nodding, "decided to include themselves in the mix somewhere."

Jett cleared his voice and when he spoke, it was in a tone she barely recognized, one of authority, as if he planned to negotiate business and that was Kevin's forte, not Jett's. "I see where you're going with this, Sydney. Basically, Kevin and Luke hang out here a lot but no, when we sat down with him, we all came over to discuss you."

"I should thank you now, I guess?" she asked, biting back fury.

"Anytime," Kevin replied sarcastically.

She dropped her jaw and shook her head. She was stumped.

Jett pointed to his cock. "First and only warning. Close your trap fast, and don't tempt the devil. I'm ready to find an angel and take a dip into heaven."

Luke laughed. "Jett, give it a rest. I don't think she's in the mood."

Jett shrugged. "It's true."

"No doubt," Riley agreed. "I've taught him well."

"Why wouldn't we talk to Mr. Kane? We've known your father for as long as you have. We're not going to run the other way if he tells us something we don't want to hear."

"How about him, Jett?" she asked sharply. "Did he run the other way? Because with what the four of you are proposing here, I imagine he didn't bring out the champagne."

Luke offered his interpretation of how well things went. "No, but he acted pretty cool with it. He passed around some moonshine."

"I'm sure he did and if he did, then it was for the sole purpose of getting dog drunk! What father wants to think about his little girl with four men?"

She shuddered as she realized more. What woman resisted the cowboys standing in front of her regardless of what anyone else thought? They certainly had balls if they talked to her father. She'd credit them that much.

Kevin decided to act as the voice of reason. "Maybe he's the kind of man who realizes his daughter will have the best of care with four men looking after her rather than just one."

She gasped. "You're serious about this." It wasn't a question. She clearly understood they were.

"Very," Jett stated.

"Do we look like we're kidding? Have we acted like it?" Kevin questioned.

Come to think of it, no. They'd pursued her like they meant it.

Riley added more assurance. "You know me, Sydney. I don't beat around the bush unless I know I'm going to find something pretty *and* pink underneath."

"Enough Riley," Kevin said.

Riley raised his eyebrows, set his eyes and jaw and shook with exaggerated fright. "You scare me little brother, truly."

"What do you say you just give us a chance? We're going to stay snowed in here anyway. We couldn't have planned this out better if we tried," Kevin reasoned. "Come on Sydney, a few days. That's all we're asking for as a trial run."

"A trial run for me is costly," she said.

"How?" Riley asked.

She didn't supply a response. Instead, she pointed as she stared out the window. She thought she saw a shape form out of the darkness but when she blinked it was gone. Maybe with so much excitement, her mind joined in and played a few tricks, too.

No one was standing in a foot of snow just to spy on her. Besides, they'd have to break the best security system in the south just to freeze in her particular yard, not likely.

"I think there's one hell of a storm coming," she completely changed the subject. "And I don't mean just outside. If you think it's bad out there, just wait until I give you the cool shoulder. Make no mistake about it. Until I get some answers, it's going to get downright chilly in here."

"Look at it this way," Kevin pointed out. "You'll never want for sex."

She closed her eyes and instantly thought of Master Brock. What would he think about all of this?

* * * *

Brock stared at the screen. "They actually did something that stupid?"

"You heard it when I did."

"Yeah, I'm sure they'd love to know they had an audience."

Brock reached forward and hit rewind. He watched Jett and Riley make their separate plays for his woman. Dumb-asses didn't have a clue.

"Brock, let it go," his father pleaded.

"I can't," he said, sliding a disc into a nearby computer and making a copy of the last clip. "I'm going to talk to Sam about this. There's no way in hell I'm going to let this happen."

"Son, you don't have a choice."

He pushed by his father and headed for the whiskey bottle. "Why?"

"They weren't lying to her. Sam Kane is a smart man. He knows what kind of danger his daughter is in and he's fully prepared to do whatever it takes to ensure she is safe long after he's gone."

Brock shook his head. "And you're supporting this?"

"It's not up to me."

"Look at her!" He exclaimed, grabbing his father's arm and pulling him closer. "Does she look like a woman ready to take on the likes of them?"

His father stared at the monitor. The last clip was frozen in time.

"She took you on. I imagine if she can handle you, she can handle almost anything."

* * * *

Sydney was still furious. The biggest problem she had was trying to process all of the information at one time. "I do not understand how four grown men can ask a man for his permission to mess around with his daughter."

They found it funny enough to burst into laughter at the same time.

"That's what you think we did?" Kevin asked.

She released a huge sigh of relief. "Well, wasn't it?"

"Not quite," Jett said, amused.

Kevin shook his head. "Sam might have mounted our heads, maybe even a few body parts, on the wall if we implied we only wanted you for sex."

She felt her skin heat and her belly turned back handsprings. "So what did you ask him exactly?" Did she want to know?

"We only told him what he needed to hear and nothing more," Jett said. "Riley, tell her the rest."

He took an exaggerated breath. "We want to fuck you."

"Great. Thanks." Backatcha, she thought.

Luke muttered. "You just gotta run that trap. There are better ways to seduce Sydney. I promise you Riley."

"We're playing for keeps," Kevin informed her before addressing Luke. "How would you seduce her?"

"Slowly," Luke drawled, flashing a provocative grin.

Did Kevin say keeps? What did playing for keeps mean to them? Did they mean some kind of forever or until her Master came back and retrieved her once more? Maybe they should start with first dates and work from there.

"We didn't tell Mr. Kane about the fucking, not exactly."

She wrinkled her nose. "Thanks, Riley."

He winked. "Don't mention it."

Jett watched Sydney. "He's a grown man. He knows what we want."

"Nothing like the truth though is there, Riley?" Sydney asked.

"The screwing around is important to us," Riley said, eyeing her breasts. "I assume you know what we're looking for, or do you want me to tell you all of the particulars?"

"He means the kink-factor," Luke clarified.

"And this is news to me? After one afternoon with you guys, I know sex is by far your favorite hobby."

"It's a perfect sport," Kevin agreed.

Jett pointed at Luke. "Before you think our youngest brother has only good intentions, think again. There's a reason he's in a big hurry to see what you're keeping underneath those snug pants. I'll let you use your imagination and figure out the rest."

Chapter Six

The intense conversation made Zaxby nervous. It was bad enough that he had to stand there in the yard and wait for those clowns inside to head home but dear God, the conversation he overheard was almost worth it.

He had a job to do on the other side of Sam Kane's walls. After hearing Mark Donovan's boys talk about taking Kane's daughter on a trip of a lifetime, albeit their beds, he was one horny man.

If his balls weren't frozen, they were certainly blue.

The cell in his pocket vibrated. He pulled it out.

Where are you?

Target. It took him five minutes to type six letters.

He hated text messaging. He wasn't paid to text. He was hired to protect, or in many cases, kill.

What's going on there?

Company.

Get rid of them. Focus on the target. Go.

Obviously, no one understood his current predicament. First, it was bitter cold. Second, he was staring into a window where there were four trained operatives-slash robo cowboys-slash playboys ready to risk their lives for Sam Kane's daughter. He knew all of them personally and wasn't eager to go up against any of them.

Then he had another problem. He was horny. Worse still, he was contemplating what to do about it.

He reminded himself of something else immediately. He didn't rape women. Then again, after the conversation he overheard, he wasn't sure if rape was necessary with a willing woman like Kane's daughter.

Do the job. Clean. Neat. Then get out.

He signed on for this mission. He had a reason for it.

For years he listened to Mark Donovan talk about his boys and how they all had the hots for Sam's daughter. He used to describe her as sweet and pure. Mark almost convinced him too, but Zaxby knew something no one else did.

Sydney Kane wasn't as innocent as they made her out. On the last mission, he listened to Jett and Riley ramble on and on about her. He almost felt sorry for the poor guys.

They wanted to love her, cherish her, and take care of her. They'd never had her. Zaxby realized it before they told him. They didn't understand they wished for a woman that couldn't possibly exist in the same Sydney he knew.

He planned to tell them the truth. If they'd all made it out of South America together, he would have. Instead, Jett and Riley covered their own asses and turned tail. They left the rest of them there to fight their way home.

Caracas wasn't supposed to happen. He shouldn't have been there in the first place. He went on a favor to Mark Donovan and Donovan's boys repaid him by leaving him there to die.

I need this job neat and clean. Got it? Another text.

Yeah, that's how he planned on doing it. Without being pushed.

This kind of show made the wait almost a necessity. If nothing else, it made things a little easier. The sweet, innocent gal they expected to find had certainly changed over the years.

Zaxby understood who transformed her. He stood by and watched as Brock changed her into something none of them—at least not those hired to protect her—recognized. He knew it from the first time he saw them together.

Brock and Sam Kane's daughter had one hell of a nasty good time.

* * * *

The sound of a blaring phone broke the tension. It rang out with a buzzing sound and everyone stared at it.

"Are you going to answer it?" Jett asked. "Sounds like a blasted bullhorn."

"Nope," she said. "You are."

"Uh-huh. I wonder why?" Jett asked, marching over to the phone but Riley beat him to it.

"Sam Kane's place," he said with a little too much amusement in his voice.

Riley propped his back against the flat surface as he stood next to the wall outlet. "Hey there! How are you? Yeah, it's Riley, Mr. Kane."

She raised her eyebrow. Right on time, she thought as she glanced at the clock on the end table.

"She's here. Yeah, we're all here. Just hanging out right now, sir." He stopped and listened a minute. "Sure, she's right here. Yeah, you take care too, Mr. Kane."

In a matter of seconds, he used the phone chord like a lasso and tossed it across the room. Sydney caught it and trailed down the hall in search of a little privacy.

"Hello, Daddy?"

"Hey, peanut," he said.

"Daddy, I need to know what is going on here."

"You do?" he asked with too much humor in his voice.

"Yes, I do."

"They haven't explained anything to you, yet?"

"No and I—"

"Put Riley back on the phone," he interrupted. "And Sydney?"

"Yes sir?"

"You have four strong men with able backs to use at your disposal. I expect them to take good care of you until I return home.

Sydney, don't fight me on this. I want you protected while I'm away. It's them or my team. I'd hate to drag my men out in the middle of the storm there, but I will if it's necessary."

"Yes, but Daddy, you see I don't think they're here for—"

"Sydney, I want to speak to Riley again or any one of them will do."

She walked back down the hall and stared at the Donovans. Good grief, she had a den full of sex appeal. Every woman in the county would like to wake up in her house tomorrow morning. Sure they would, if they made it through the night.

She shuddered and then tossed the phone high in the air.

* * * *

Jett just happened to have the good fortune to reach for it. He was standing the closest to her when she let them know Sam Kane wanted to gab a little. He could only imagine the topic on deck.

It wasn't a hidden secret. Sydney's father wasn't fond of Jett but he grabbed the phone and held it tight against his ear.

He showed him respect when he fought with him side by side as his own father's occasional replacement. He might as well tolerate him now. Although, he had a feeling he was easier to handle when they were on the same side. When it came to his daughter, he might view all of them as adversaries.

"It's Jett Donovan," he said reluctantly.

"Perfect." It sounded like he really didn't think so. "Listen Jett. I agreed to let you and your brothers stay there and when I did, I meant for you to move right on in the day I left. Your father assured me his sons were up for the task. He informed me today that all of you have been brought up to speed on the current situation. Right now, I'm not too happy to know Sydney has been all alone for the last few nights."

"Yes, sir, I understand," Jett replied.

Only he didn't. They'd stood guard over the Kane place since he left. Someone had watched her at all times. They were so good that she never suspected they were there.

"Now, you need to understand something. This is the *craziest something* I've ever agreed to in my life. Considering the businesses that your father and I are in, I trust very few people with Sydney's safety.

"After your dad talked to me and you boys made your intentions known, I see the advantages here. If this works out, everyone benefits. You do understand, right? I tossed in an 'if' here because it's up to my daughter. I want her happy. Your father seems to think she can find some happiness and maybe a little peace of mind with you and your brothers."

"Absolutely," Jett stated.

A pause of silence assured Jett of one thing. He should have taken a pass on grabbing for the phone. Riley had the personality to deal with Sam Kane's tantrums. Jett did not.

"So you will tell Sydney *all of your plans*, I take it? Am I right?" He asked gruffly. "I want her well informed so there are few regrets."

Few regrets? The warning came down like an evil and unnecessary reminder. Mr. Kane wasn't the only one who wanted his daughter happy. Jett wanted Sydney happy. If she had regrets, he'd accept it as a personal failure. After everything her father had put her through in one lifetime, he'd never forgive himself if he did the same. His brothers shared the same sentiments.

"We'll take care of it, sir."

"All right then, Jett. Tell the others I'm only going to be out of the way for a few weeks. I won't give you a year here. Besides, I'm not just talking about giving you and your brothers a chance to win over my daughter's affection. I want her guarded. You get comfortable and stay there until I get home or let me know right now. I'll call for reinforcements. My boys can be there in a few hours. Sydney knows them well enough to let them stay there until I return."

His voice carried through the receiver because every Donovan eye pierced through him. Kevin, Riley, and Luke all whispered their separate words of wisdom offering various ways they wanted Mr. Kane reassured.

"We won't need a year, sir," he said before he shot his brothers a glare. They were enjoying this. "And Sydney won't need your men," he quickly snipped.

She looked relieved, but she arched an eyebrow like she questioned motives. It was cute more than inquisitive. She probably didn't like anyone speaking for her. Too damn bad. He never liked having his ass chewed by a woman's controlling father either. They both had a lot to get used to.

Riley reached for the phone but Jett turned away. He might as well suck it up.

"Jett, we both know you blew your first chance. Hell, the whole town knows it. Let one of your brothers have a shot at easing her into the crazy notion the four of you have."

"Yes, I'll do that, Mr. Kane."

When hell freezes over and not a minute before it's considered a new polar region with a nice ski resort.

"Consider it taken care of on our end," he added.

He never missed his chance with Sydney. He had the little vixen damn near begging him to fuck her three years ago. Instead of screwing her, he'd done other things to get her going and she'd clawed at him like a wild little woman ready for it.

He remembered stopping her once, making himself back away and then watching her shudder from one orgasm straight into another. After the dry humping and kissing, he'd wanted inside of her bad and he almost earned his chance. Then, she grabbed some kind of conscience or something. Right when he was ready to sink and swim, she uttered every man's worse nightmare, 'I said no' and he stopped.

He swallowed tightly as he thought of his alone time with Sydney. Her hot little body shook for a good few minutes when she jerked against him. Oh yeah, the little minx climaxed with him driving her to it. She begged for his cock before, during and after their dry humping session. Then, her confined channel closed around his fingers and heaven help them all, he still remembered how wet she was, how quick she gripped his shoulder and encouraged him to pamper her cute cunt until he left her helpless, plain helpless.

On that hot July fourth night, Sydney Kane almost knew every inch of him. Then, the crowd divided and she worried someone might see them. She forced him to stop because after she let him know she wasn't ready, he couldn't bring himself to persuade her. Now, he was hard again just thinking about it.

"If I come home and she doesn't like the idea of spending time with any of you, that's it. Do we understand one another?"

"Yes, sir."

"And if one hair on her head is harmed—"

"It won't be, sir. You have my word," he said solemnly. He'd kill any man who tried to hurt her in the first place.

They faced a serious threat but they were ready for it. Their father paid a hefty price and received details about an occurrence of extreme portent. It looked bad, even for strong cowboys who played war games.

With the weather, it was too dangerous to make a quick decision or plan a fast move. If Jett had received clearance, he would've flown her out of the country and taken her someplace safe. There wasn't enough time to get everything in order.

Jett and Riley realized who was behind the latest threat and they discussed their options. They had a better chance of beating these guys from home. Their father supported the decision.

Sydney was in danger, but they were prepared on the home front. Her father once again pissed off the wrong cartel. He played a significant role in placing three drug lords behind bars in Miami. Little did he know, they were well connected to the madmen Jett and Riley encountered in Caracas. These were the kind of lunatics no one wanted to find on the other side of their fences, let alone a pointed gun.

The Donovans expected company. When their guests would show face, proved hard to speculate with the poor road conditions and snow continuing to fall.

The Donovans realized Sydney's dad expected them to remain close in proximity to Sydney and for good reason. Mr. Kane and their father wanted them working from the inside out and not the other way around on the chance someone found a way inside the house.

"I'll call again tomorrow," he muttered. "And Jett? I hope to hear laughter and see smiles when I get home or else the four of you will answer to me."

The phone immediately went dead and Jett held it out and glared at it. "That's it," he said, walking over and slamming it into the cradle. When he turned back around, Sydney looked half tickled too death and half frightened.

"Did it go well?" Riley asked.

"Smart ass," he muttered. He had a right mind to slap Riley upside his ugly head. "Yeah Riley, terrific."

"Sounded like it," Kevin noted.

"I don't want to hear the first word from you," he began, pointing at Kevin. "This is your fault."

Sydney blinked. "How can you blame him?"

"Easy," Jett said, grumbling.

She regrouped and tried again. "*What* is his fault exactly?"

"For starters, your father doesn't want to explain anything at all to you. He wants us to do it. I can't blame the man. Naturally, it's *our* responsibility since he failed to take on *his* all these years."

Sydney dropped her jaw, and then set it. "Yes, I see. Well, if you four can stop dancing around this, and tell me what you want exactly, then maybe you can leave at first light tomorrow. I'm sure you have women tucked away somewhere. *My father* never did, but then again he didn't walk around like he was God's gift to the opposite sex either. With any luck, you'll be ready to make off like a good guy and find a sweet little gal who likes to build snowmen. You never know."

"I was out of line about your dad," Jett began. "I'm sorry."

"You should be," she snapped.

"Do you like to build snowmen, Sydney?" Luke asked trying to change the subject.

"I...don't know. I've never tried it."

Jett narrowed his eyes. "While we're stranded, we can build snowmen, igloos, or make snow angels. Whatever turns you on, we'll do it if it puts a smile on your face."

Spoken like Sam Kane. His brothers wouldn't let it slide.

"Ah...that's touching, Jett," Riley said, placing his open palm over his heart. "I mean, I'm choked up here. I feel a tear forming at the back of my eye now."

Jett tossed a small pillow at his brother. "Shut up. You're not far behind me and you know it."

"I don't have it as bad as him," he blurted out, indicating Luke.

Sydney acted uninterested in the conversation at hand and moved on to the next topic. "My bed isn't big enough for five."

They stared at her blankly. No one made a move.

What the hell was she thinking? Where did that come from anyway? She didn't have room for five? Shit.

Certifiable didn't quite cover it now. Someone should clone her mouth and her mind just to run experiments on both, and find out how those who hang themselves out to dry truly survive. While they were at it, maybe they could figure out what makes a woman in heat tick. On second thought, she knew. The Donovans, and men like them. *Brock.*

She closed her eyes and captured her Master in her mind's eye just for a rare indulgence. When she opened them again, they were watching her.

She stood up and walked over to the door. "Fine, if you stubborn men aren't going to leave, then I will."

"You aren't going anywhere sweet thing," Luke said, stepping in front of the door.

"Move, Luke."

"No way. I didn't stay a..." he stopped himself.

Riley and Jett roared with laughter.

"Man you can dig yourself deeper than she can," Kevin observed.

"You didn't stay a what, Luke?" Jett couldn't wait to hear his confession.

"Forget it," Luke replied. "You're not going anywhere, Sydney. That's final."

"So now what? I'm your hostage?"

"Shit, Sydney, you're really going to cry wolf now? Come on, baby. You're fooling yourself. You've been after my ass since you were able to walk." Riley expressed what Jett sort of thought, too.

Jett had time to think about their time together. For three years, he'd craved her, looked forward to the day when Sydney would come home and stay. They never really discussed what happened between them, but he never forgot it.

They romped around for one glorious night. The next morning, he picked a bunch of wildflowers, ordered long stem roses and walked over to her place with both. He wanted to make sure he approached her with what she liked most.

She was already gone.

He later learned he only missed her by a couple of hours. Her father barely looked at him that day and kept his fists balled at his sides when he instructed him to ask his father for details. His dad provided the same information he always gave them, 'she had to go away' and Jett had a hard time with it.

Now that he'd held her in his arms again and they'd taken things to the next level, he never wanted her to *go away* again unless he planned the trip.

She walked over to the fireplace and held her hands out just a few inches from the flame. "I'm frustrated."

She let her hands fall at her sides and backed away from the hearth. "You're right though. I've chased the four of you long enough so understand my confusion. For years, none of you noticed I was alive. Now, all of a sudden, you want me. Why now?"

The brothers looked at each other and then Kevin spoke for all of them. "Sydney, it's time to grow up. It's time for all of us to think about the future, start a family, and make a life together. That's the only answer I have other than to tell you that you belong to us. We've always known it. The question is, do you accept it?"

* * * *

Brock glared at the remote unit he installed in his bedroom. Damn Sam for not listening to him three years ago. The man was stubborn and evidently a little delusional, too.

Brock turned up the volume on the monitors. He could listen to her even if he wasn't able to hold her. The sound of her voice soothed him. If he had a better sound system, he might be able to drown out the others and focus on what she was saying, really tune in and cling to every word.

His father sat down on the edge of the bed. He stared at him with empty eyes. Brock knew those eyes well. They'd seen too much in one lifetime. He fought out of the pits of hell found in one decade straight into the fiery flames of another.

It never ended. Those scarred by it, those emotionally damaged by what they saw—perhaps what they were often forced to do— recognized those empty gazes.

"Do you remember three years ago when you called home and asked me to talk to Sam about the Cuban threat?"

"Yes, what about it?" Brock asked, mentally replaying the conversation.

"I was thinking about that the other day. The details of that particular threat always bothered me. I never could quite put my finger on how you ended up with the intelligence on it when Sam and I missed it."

Brock tossed a pillow behind his head and stared at the monitor. Sydney sure looked pretty. Her hair was longer than before. She still looked so innocent, like a beautiful porcelain doll with ivory skin and a painted on smile no one could turn into a frown. Even when she was mad, she didn't stay angry long. It was as if her lips didn't have the ability to form anything more than a smile.

Even in her current state of confusion, she was a real tiger when it mattered and she thought fast on her feet. Riley and Jett were putting too much pressure on her, Kevin, too.

She'll sharpen her claws on you boys.

His father rambled on and by the time he refocused, he realized his father was on a soapbox. "Sam walked me through every detail of the Cuban threat, Brock. After a lot of research, it finally made sense."

"What?" Brock stood up and walked over to the window. He peered out, narrowed his eyes, and thought of Sydney. What he'd give to hold her tonight.

"Are you listening to me?"

"Yes, Dad. What did Sam say?" Brock asked.

"I think you know. If you don't, you should. We couldn't gain intelligence on it because it didn't exist. We searched everywhere, spent money we could've kept in our pockets. The reason we couldn't find one was because it didn't exist. Instead, it was a Jett-threat."

* * * *

Outside, the snow accumulated and high winds kicked up another notch but it didn't matter. Inside the Kane house, the temperature rose at a steady pace. The building tension added a few degrees of spice.

Luke, as Jett expected, took the lead. He draped his arms over her back and whispered sweet nothings in her ear. The only one Jett heard was the confession everyone in the room understood anyway. "I've always wanted you, Sydney."

"You have?"

Okay, so everyone realized it but Sydney.

"Yes, a lot," he said. "You're the only woman I ever wanted."

Jett confirmed it. "Yep, he saved himself just for you."

Riley watched them curiously and Kevin lazily scratched his neck, apparently in deep thought. Jett waited for one of them to start with the running joke among them but no one bothered. Right now, it would only give Luke a clear advantage with Sydney, so why inform her about his brother's upstanding man-issues?

"We want to keep you with us from here on out, Sydney." Jett simplified everything in a matter-of-fact tone.

He glanced over at Riley and he didn't look too happy with his chosen words. "Assuming we all suit," he quickly added.

Sydney snapped her wrist and slapped the mantle. "What does that mean exactly? Suit?"

They discussed *this part* privately among brothers. Mr. Kane would have their skins if he ever suspected what they did behind closed doors. If he realized what they were looking for in a lady, then it wouldn't take much for him to connect the dots and realize what kind of plans they had for his daughter. He'd probably catch the first plane home and stop their ideas before any of them had a chance to spin little Sydney right into motion.

"Riley, you tell her," Jett growled.

Kevin grabbed a straight-back chair, twirled it around like it had the equivalent weight of a feather, and found his seat. His hands hung over the back of it and he looked down at the floor as Luke paced across it.

"Maybe this part can wait," Luke finally said. "It's not a big deal."

"Actually, it is," Riley corrected. "And," he added, "It's non-negotiable."

"It's a good thing I came prepared," Jett said. He focused on his brothers, one at a time, taking the time to drive home the point. They were smart enough to catch on and each of them smiled or winked simultaneously.

Riley stared at her breasts and smiled. Jett caught his breath when he remembered the way she felt mashed against his chest. If he had to guess, Riley thought along the same lines as he did. Jett couldn't wait to clamp her pretty nipples and allow a slow moving vibrator the same opportunity he wanted…an outright attack on her sweet little pussy.

His mouth watered at once. Good grief, he still jacked off in the shower imagining the way she arched against him that one July fourth night. Now, the time drew near. Soon, they would have her stripped down to nothing and prepared for toy play.

"You see, Sydney, we want to make you our lover, maybe even our wife."

Her jaw dropped. "Your what?"

"Close your mouth, Sydney. You might catch something more than flies with four hard cocks in the room."

She took Kevin's words under fast advisement. She snapped her mouth shut and blinked repetitively.

"Sydney, what Jett means," Riley began, "is something you've probably already heard from your girlfriends. We have a certain kind of woman we like to find in our beds."

She arched her brow. Oh yes, Jett thought, she understood precisely where this conversation headed.

"We want a submissive woman."

"I'm sure," she said. "But of course you would. Doesn't every man in the world?"

Oh hell. This wasn't going according to their plan. They wanted her to jump up and down, right before she knelt before them and asked for permission to suck their dicks. Nope, they struck out the first time. They'd have to try a better approach.

On a positive note, Jett didn't detect sarcasm in her answer but imagined it was there all the same. She stared at Luke and Jett braced for it. She found her weakest link.

"Luke, where do you stand on this? Do you want a submissive woman?"

"What do you want, Sydney?" Kevin didn't allow Luke to answer.

Thank God. Everyone in the Donovan household realized Luke would take Sydney anyway he could get her.

She turned her focus away from Luke and glared at Riley. "This is your idea of a joke, isn't it?"

"No farce here Sydney," he said. "I want you to understand from the very beginning, I will not have a woman in my bed unless she is willing to submit to me in every way. It goes beyond sex with me. If and when I put a collar around your neck, you'll wear it from now on. It won't come off because I won't stand for it."

"I feel the same way," Jett said. "And Luke and Kevin, too."

"I see," she said. "And let's say I'm willing to consider it, where does that leave us with our fathers?"

Kevin decided to answer. "That's a good question. Let me start by saying our fathers, and you should already realize this, refuse to accept outsiders. They will never let a stranger get too close because anyone can quickly become an enemy. Play dumb if you want, but you damn well know what your father does for a living. If you don't, you at least have some idea of the danger he brings on his family."

Sydney's eyes dropped but then she held her head high, tossed her hair back and defiantly responded. "Oh you mean how it's a death sentence to live in Sam Kane's house?"

"Is that what you think, Sydney?" Riley asked.

"You all knew Mom. She adored my dad. For her, the sun didn't just rise and set in him, it existed because of him. He was her strength but he became her death.

"I remember how she used to watch for him just so she could touch him, like the only thing that mattered to her was her hand on his cheek or his voice filling the house. Only he wasn't home much. When he wasn't here, she drank herself to sleep so she didn't have to face the loneliness. Soon, I don't think she felt anything for him at all. She stumbled around this world in a complete stupor. Sometimes I wonder if she ever heard the intruders who robbed our home and took her life."

Riley and Jett exchanged a knowing look and then turned to Kevin. He narrowed his eyes on them. He understood their silence.

"The whole thing was a cover-up, wasn't it?" Sydney asked, frowning.

Jett and Riley knew the truth. She was right. It was a revenge kill. Her two step-mothers met similar fates. One died in cross-fire on a mission trip as the only female operative in the Kane-Donovan organization. Sam's last marriage ended badly, too. His third wife died in her sleep from a sleeping pill overdose.

Her eyes misted over and Jett started to ramble about the business side of their arrangement, in an effort to change the subject. "We have to be very careful because a woman could blow our operations wide open."

She cleared her throat. "What sort of operations are *we* talking about here?"

"She probably doesn't know all of it," Kevin said. "Sam still thinks she's his little girl in pigtails."

"Yeah, I get that now," Jett replied. He scratched his head. He also understood the pain he saw, too. His own mother died at the hands of a monster and the fifth and oldest Donovan son might as well have. He witnessed it all and left to fight for a cause he'd never win soon after they buried their mother. Their families knew pain. They recognized heartache and he understood Sydney better than anyone else ever would.

How did he tell Sydney that her father was a professional government sniper? How did he explain what the man did for a living when there were so many aspects to his job description? Sam Kane was so intelligent and personable that he could win friends overnight and influence them to hand over guarded government documents before lunch was served the very next day. Then by nightfall, if required, he'd break bread with his enemies and slice their throats over dessert.

"As far as I'm concerned, Daddy is a farmer, just a rancher who made good deals and great business decisions. I'm assuming your father had similar luck."

Jett took a deep breath but couldn't find the heart for it so the master negotiator of the family, stood up and handled it. Kevin was the kind of guy who didn't care to put everything out there on the table.

"Your father is a leader and he leads a pack of killers, a select team of government trained assassins who for the most part, work in teams of two or often alone. He goes undetected most of the time, but his past will eventually catch up with him and even our father worries about safety concerns. Sam took too many chances and he has a weakness, his daughter. Unfortunately, some of his enemies know it."

"I see, so I'm a liability, is that what you're telling me?"

"Yes," Riley said, shooting straight.

"No," Luke tried to make the pain go away.

Riley offered more insight. "Our fathers are contractors, of sorts."

"Sure they are. I don't know what your father does in his spare time, but mine has supported us from trading cattle and horses, period."

"Ahem…Sydney, do you really believe that's how your father made his money?" Jett asked.

"Well isn't it?" She batted her eyelashes and stared back at them.

Now Jett was stumped.

* * * *

"You're proud of her aren't you?"

Brock grinned. "Very."

"I can see how important she is to you."

Brock glared at his father. "Can you?"

"Yes," he said. "Do you love her enough to die for her?"

"Without question."

"Do you love her more than you love yourself or your family?"

"Absolutely."

"Do you love her enough to kill for her?"

"Thousands."

"Would you kill her to prevent her suffering?"

Brock paused.

"Do you know the correct answer?" his father probed.

"There is no correct answer," Brock told him.

"If it was required to prohibit pain and suffering from a well orchestrated torture, would you kill her?"

Brock swallowed back the bile in this throat. They were trained to respond immediately to this question. He wasn't prepared to answer it truthfully but he wasn't a man who looked his father in the eye and told him what he wanted to hear.

"I want to know right now!" He rushed over to Brock and grabbed him by the collar. "Would you kill her to save her pain and suffering?"

Brock narrowed his gaze on his father. "If it was Mom, what would you do? Would you kill the woman you love to save her?" He spat the words back at him and watched as a flash of recognition entered his father's eyes.

"No," he said honestly. "Not now."

Chapter Seven

If the Donovan brothers thought for one minute, even a few unimportant seconds, that they could shake her down, they were mistaken. She knew more about her father's line of work than she would ever admit. She grew up in the shadows of his profession, ready to move on a moment's notice. She was the one who had more identities than a fugitive running from justice.

She waited patiently for the Donovans to explain. She understood where all of this was headed. She knew her father would never accept an outsider. She didn't need a Donovan man to tell her.

Sydney's father was controlling. He managed all aspects of her life. Now, he wanted to pick the man, or men, she was allowed to spend time with and why not? She always let him get by with it.

Naturally, her father would want her with a man, or apparently several men, who maintained enough of a tight grip around her to ensure she had a fighting chance to live her life. It didn't come as a surprise when the Donovans mentioned their expectations.

What shocked her was how they described what they expected. The fact that they planned to take her to their bed made her knees knock together. She pressed them only tighter when she thought about submitting to them, something she spent the better part of the day thinking about anyway.

When they talked about 'suiting', she played dumb. Oh, but she knew. She once heard a similar term from Master Brock. She closed her eyes and tried to remember how her Master proposed a training period but she couldn't think straight now. She fantasized.

Her fascination for the Donovans started at a young age. She played with Barbie dolls growing up and her fantasies came alive. Her mother once scolded her because she had Barbie and *Kens*. She had them numbered one through four and they were all in the same bed. They discussed *making* babies. Her mother finally took her dolls away when she changed their names to Riley, Luke, Jett, and Kevin. Maybe her mother wasn't as delirious as Sydney thought.

"Sydney," Riley began hesitantly. "Our fathers are not cattle farmers."

"Oh?" she continued the act. "Well, technically, I guess in our case, you're right. We do have Bitch and a few other horses."

"She's not this naïve," Kevin said to himself more than the others as his cheeks swelled with hot air. "Sydney, drop the act. We know. We're part of the inner circle. You can talk openly with us."

"What are implying?"

"Nothing, we're telling you exactly the way it is. It's a front, Sydney," Riley said. "All of it. Our place and yours is nothing more than a front and a retreat for our fathers to relax whenever they aren't working."

"It is?" she questioned.

"Yep, it always has been," Riley continued. "And I think you're smart enough to know it, too. Don't play the ditzy role with us. We've never been particularly fond of dumb women."

"Oh, I don't know about that, Riley. Some in this town might debate that issue." She studied her fingernails and then continued. "Besides, I wouldn't dream of it. I'm sure you're tired of those kinds of gals landing in your beds. Lord knows you've had plenty."

If they wanted to take her for a dumb broad, she'd observed enough of them to slide right into the role. Only she wasn't sure if it was worth the time they'd waste. It was time to have a serious chat with her father. Only, with him away, it wouldn't happen soon.

She missed her Master. She longed to see him, touch him, talk to him. He always advised her on these matters. Often her father relied on him to take care of explaining things to her. Where was he when she needed him most?

"You understand why you were shipped off so much, don't you Sydney?" Kevin asked, impatiently.

She felt a double edged sword whip around her gut. She didn't know what she was supposed to share with the Donovans, only that they provided an out if she ever needed one. It was the only thing she'd ever been told. If she needed a cop, call the Donovans. If she had a question, call the Donovans. Whenever she had a need and couldn't reach her father, her first call made should go to a Donovan phone.

"For the record, whenever I left, I wanted to go. I like adventure and Daddy never forced my hand."

"Sure he did, each and every time he told you to leave," Riley mused.

She set her jaw. "That's not true."

Riley yawned. "It is."

Luke steered the conversation. "Your father and ours are wanted men."

"They're often wanted by various governments due to the information they are able to buy and receive from informants," Kevin added. "Then they have other job descriptions, too. Those tasks often earn them a high placement on various undesirable lists."

She knew all about those. She never once thought her father moved her from one location to another for cultural enlightenments.

"Why would you tell me something like this if Daddy never bothered?"

"Because we've had a plan in motion for quite awhile now," Riley explained.

"You mean where I'm concerned?" she asked.

"Yes," Kevin said.

"Oh, you mean crooks only sleep with crooks?" she asked.

"I can see where you might think of us as the undesirable spawn, considering what you've been through yourself," Kevin answered. "But it's not as bad as it seems. Our dads aren't criminals. They work with an elite team of special forces within the military."

"Oh really? Then tell me this. Why am I hearing about this from you? Why don't I see medals of honor or government checks for my father's work?"

"You never will, Sydney," Riley explained. "They do not exist on any government radar."

"Your dad always wanted to protect you, and for the record, Sydney, we're willing to do the same," Kevin sounded sincere. "We will forever live in their shadows, and if we want to stay alive there's nothing we can do about it. Sometimes, we'll have to run, maybe more often than any of us would like but the thing is, we can still have some level of normalcy if we stick together."

"I see." She understood a little more than she let on. "So you four devised a plan and..." It was kind of open-ended when she just cut off her pursuit of answers.

"Actually," Jett began. "Years ago, our fathers briefly discussed it, but it wasn't something they wanted to decide for us. Love doesn't just happen and lust is even harder to find between men and women. Anyway, dad got wind of our little affair and everything just started to unravel from there. The final decision to approach you was our decision, not your father's or ours. We're big boys, in case you haven't noticed. We know what we want in a woman."

"Oh, but I'm sure they both manipulated it," she said. "And for the record, we did not have an affair. We acted like children with hormones kicking our ass in public. That's all."

"Uh-huh," Jett muttered. "Keep telling yourself whatever you want but I think you know what went on between us was far more than child's play."

"Tell me something, Sydney. Are you really against the idea of four men taking care of you?" Riley teased her.

"I want the one man, one woman kind of thing," she whispered. "I want the normal kind of life I never had."

She also decided a long time ago that if any one of the Donovan men ever approached her with endearing propositions, she'd jump at the chance. What they offered complicated things. She only imagined one or two of them making the advances. Never in her wildest dreams had she envisioned this.

"We're offering something better. By the time we're through with you, I think you'll beg for the four men, one woman kind of thing," Riley hummed with assurance. "Besides, we're not giving you a chance to choose between us. It's all of us or none of us."

She gulped. "All or nothing, huh?"

Kevin stepped closer. "Come on, Sydney, stop pretending you aren't interested. I know you're turned on by it. You've shifted those pretty little hips in just the right way to capture our attention. You caught it and you've held it. Thing is, you're attracted to all of us. Maybe you never counted on this but you won't say no."

"I uh..." She backed away from Kevin and Riley caught her by the hips.

"You're what?" Kevin asked. "You want me to make you a list of pros and cons?"

Damn, he was such the politician. If he played a role in underground operations, she knew without a doubt they used him in the capacity of negotiations. She swallowed over and over again. *Or interrogations.*

The Donovan brothers always captivated her heart and now Sydney realized why. Maybe she'd always belonged to them.

Sydney thought back to the precious hours she spent with her Master. Whatever she felt for him was intense, so strong in fact that the separation from him almost killed her, but maybe he prepared her for this. Maybe he wasn't supposed to sleep with her because down deep he knew if he did, he'd take something that didn't belong to him.

They stared back at her, waiting for her response. No doubts, this was the way it was supposed to be from the beginning.

She was a Donovan woman through and through but she'd always love the man who helped her prepare for them. No one would ever take her Master's place, not even those she first loved.

"Okay, you're right." She felt relieved the second she confirmed it. "And since you are, where do we go from here?"

* * * *

Zaxby glared at the latest text message.

Your crew is ten miles out. The storm held them. What's your location?

He'd love to tell him Sydney Kane's bed. The Donovans were lucky bastards.

Outside the home.

His boss must've wanted Kane to suffer pretty bad to send a crew of his men into a storm like this. He pulled out his night goggles and brushed the snow away from the lens. It didn't help. When he raised them to his eyes, a gust of flakes covered them.

Get out of the weather until they arrive. Intelligence provided. Donovans will stay there tonight.

No shit. Only a madman looking for a little revenge would weather this storm.

He never thought the Donovans would leave. They were going to stay and play with Sydney and he had to take cover in the barn. Life wasn't showing him much favor. The only thing he'd find in Kane's fancy stable was a little warmth and a bunch of overpriced horses probably as spoiled as Sam Kane's daughter.

Did you receive the last instructions?

Yeah, ass-hole, I did. He didn't bother with a response.

Zaxby tried to determine which way to go. He couldn't see two feet in front of him. He started walking and it that's when it hit him.

His luck, when dealing with the Donovans, sucked.

Regardless of what happened now, or the help that would soon arrive, a sudden truth threatened to suffocate him. It was all uphill from that point forward and they faced one hell of a battle, if they ever reached the top.

* * * *

Riley looked up from his homemade stew. He sipped from a wooden spoon and sampled it. "Needs some salt," he stated to an empty room.

Kevin, Luke, and Jett walked in around the same time. Luke and Kevin shook off their coats near the back door. They'd taken a final tour around the property just to check things out and didn't get very far.

"Didn't make it to the barn?" Riley asked.

"Couldn't see it," Kevin advised.

Jett had the task of leading Sydney to a hot bath and whatever he saw, and Riley could only imagine, put a little color in his face. He smirked as he watched him. "Damn devil, aren't cha?"

He snickered and slapped him on the back. "Smells good, wife."

"I got your wife," he carried on with his meaning made obvious when he pointed upstairs. "And I can't wait to do something with her."

"Sam keeps the salt and pepper above the sink," Luke said before he sat down on a bar stool. Jett hopped up on the breakfast bar and let his legs hang off to the side.

"You're in a good mood," Kevin said. "Anything happen up there we should know about?"

"Nope, but it could have," Jett informed. "I'm telling you, she's going to make training a bitch. She's so ready for a man, she'll beg for cock. I know she will."

Luke took a deep breath and then snickered. "I hope she wants to fuck twenty-four seven."

"I bet so," Kevin said. "Any man who doesn't know what it feels like to sink into a slick pussy is bound to find heaven in her. I guarantee it."

"So what happened up there? Remember, we agreed. No secrets."

"He's jealous." Jett winked at the other two and then turned back to Riley. "What's wrong big brother, are you afraid I'm sampling the honey?"

"Maybe not yet but..." he narrowed his eyes on Jett. "You undressed her didn't you?"

"Yep," he said before he rubbed his cock with an open palm. "Damn right, I did."

"Can uh..." Luke nodded toward Jett's lower half, "that kind of thing wait?"

"Nope, it can't. You didn't see what I saw upstairs, little brother."

"Ah hell." Riley swatted Kevin and Luke on the back at the same time. "I remember my first time, don't you Kev? Luke is going to shoot off before he even gets inside of her tight little snatch. Don't worry little brother, I won't laugh too hard when she figures it out."

"Figures what out?" Sydney asked from the doorway. She tiptoed across the floor in her bare feet.

Riley's jaw dropped. "You look plumb edible."

All mouths opened as they watched her in a mesmerized state of confusion.

"Something wrong with the bath water?" Kevin asked.

"No," she said before she grabbed a wine cooler out of the refrigerator and allowed the towel to drop to the floor.

"Mercy sweet baby." Luke stared in amazement. Jett grinned and winked at Kevin who in turn smirked at Riley. All four remained seated. Riley put his hand up to make sure they didn't jump no matter how fast they all wanted to shuffle.

Sydney turned around and tilted her head toward them. "I don't know exactly what you all expect from me." She lowered her eyes. "But I'm ready for it. I don't want to wait."

The hell she didn't know. This was some kind of stunt, a way to call them to the front and ask them to either come out swinging or forget it altogether.

Riley and Jett discussed this with Kevin a hundred times. Kevin swore someone, somewhere introduced her to the lifestyle. They tried to trace it and came up empty-handed. Riley was sure of it now after he had a little time alone with her.

Clearing his throat, Riley challenged her. "Are you trying to find out whether or not we'll spank you, Sydney?"

"She is," Jett replied. "You know she is."

"You like a spanking, don't you doll?" Riley asked.

"I never said." She dropped her eyes.

"You didn't have to," Kevin whispered.

"I was soaking in my great big tub all alone with nothing but large bubbles surrounding me. I started thinking about how much I'd like to have some company." She bit her lower lip and held it under her teeth. "Am I permitted to ask for it or do I wait until something is decided for me?"

Riley stepped away from his brothers and bent down. He handed her the towel. "I want you to cover up, Sydney."

The hell he did. She might as well bend over.

"No, you don't," she said. "You want me naked. That's what all of you want, isn't it?"

Jett cleared his throat. "I tried to explain this to you when I left you upstairs. We'll decide when and where to take you."

"Damn it, Jett," Luke said. "I have no problem with here and now." He motioned for her. "Come here, Sydney."

Riley swung his arm back and caught him in the gut. He stopped him before he reached her. "Jett, go get that duffle bag of goodies. I think we need to introduce our toys to Sydney and we should do it now. What do you think?"

"I'm with you. We need to get her in shape for us."

Sydney looked down at her body. "Is there something wrong with the way I look?"

Riley gave her a good up and down evaluation without laying a finger on her. She was some kind of beautiful. Her nipples were little beaded pearls, her body was a perfect showplace of slender curves and simply splendid. Something wrong? No. Something hard was more like it. He reminded himself of the training she needed. First, hello and then goodbye. Damn, what a woman.

She cupped her breasts. "You think something is wrong with these?" Mischief danced in her eyes.

"Hell, no," Luke and Kevin said simultaneously.

She ran her fingers up and down her sides. "Are you sure?"

"Trust me, baby," Jett said. "If I found one flaw on you, I'd love to tell you about it. This kind of perfection brings on a little defiance." He slapped her bottom and she yelped.

"Why did you do that?"

Riley's dick twitched as he watched her. Oh, she was good. And she was also caught.

She wanted them to step into the role of her Masters, no doubt about it. He might defy all odds and resist the urge just because she was trying to draw him out, or rather—all of them.

"What?" Jett asked all wide eyed and bushy-tailed.

"Smack me?"

"I swatted your sweet ass for getting out of the tub without permission," he said.

"Luke," Jett grinned. "I want you to take her back upstairs and sit with her until we get up there with a few toys for her.

"You want him to do what?" Kevin asked. "Are you serious? She's all but fucked if he takes care of her."

"Luke, can we trust you not to fuck her?"

"I uh…don't know."

"At least you're honest. Kevin, go with Luke and Sydney. Riley and I will be there shortly."

Kevin took the towel from Riley and started to drape it over Sydney but changed his mind. "Go on, I'll walk behind you."

"No, I want the towel back now please," she said blushing.

Kevin swatted her with it. "I bet you do but you see Sydney, I don't want you to have it."

Luke acted very uncomfortable and Riley noticed. They needed to keep an eye on him. Luke didn't know much about the lifestyle they chose a long time ago so maybe they'd put him in a few situations to test him.

"What's wrong, Luke?"

"Riley, shit. Give me a break, will ya?" Luke muttered before he followed Kevin and Sydney up the front steps.

Riley turned to Jett. "Okay, so why didn't you tell me she'd act out?"

"I never expected this. Hell, how would I know what she's going to do?"

"For starters, you almost screwed her in a public place. You know things about her none of the rest of us know. Is she passive or aggressive when a man approaches her?" Riley paused as if he expected a full evaluation right then and there. "Does she try to put her hands all over a man or does she wait for someone to lead? You know more about her than anybody here so start telling me what to expect."

"Tell you what Mr. Dom of all Doms, I'll give it some thought and get back to you. One thing I can tell you is that this towel thing was unexpected."

"She reconsidered her action though when we didn't jump right up and pay attention."

"Speak for yourself, big brother. Every dick in this room danced and if any one of us had been here with her alone, we would've taken the opportunity and you know it."

Riley rubbed his forehead with the ball of his palm. "What happened upstairs?"

"Nothing." Jett grinned.

Riley narrowed his eyes and shook his head. "Remember who you're talking to."

"Okay, nothing much."

* * * *

They had just started up the steps when Jett rounded the corner and handed a blindfold to Luke. "Put it over her eyes."

She lowered her head and then her eyes in a submissive gesture. Kevin's cock twitched under his tight fitting whitey tidies. Damn if she didn't fool them.

She was a submissive waiting for the right Doms. She bowed her head a little more and allowed Luke to tie the bandana over her eyes. She knew what to expect.

"If she's not a hot one," Kevin said before he took her hand and then led the way. "I want you to take three steps and then bend over for Luke. Show him your pretty little pussy, Sydney."

"I can't just stop and—"

"Sydney," Jett's firm voice stopped her from whining. He stood at the bottom of the steps with a smug expression. "I want you to stop right now and bend over. Kevin, help her stretch out over a few steps. Luke, shift her hips so she's spread wide. I want to see, too."

"Of course you do," Kevin teased. He gently took her arms, sat down on one of the hardwood steps and held her wrists. At the same time, Luke grabbed her roughly around the waist and quickly caressed her bottom and thighs. She parted her legs.

"Perfect," Jett said from below. "Riley, come here quick and look at this."

Her pussy lips parted and a sparkle of her body's natural heat glistened around her labia. Luke stared and his eyes went wild with lust.

Jett took a few strides up the stairs and Riley waited in the foyer with enough interest to keep him rubbernecking it.

"Good Lord, that's a pretty sight, huh?" Riley studied her closer and upon further inspection, decided she needed one of them to touch her. "Luke, little brother if I were you, I'd finger that sweet ass or pretty little pussy."

"Riley, I thought you were cooking." Her hips rose and fell. She tried to find a more comfortable position, or maybe a hand, better still, a dick.

"Silence, sugar," Jett said. When he approached her, he twirled the riding crop over her flank. "Remember, we talked about this upstairs. I told you the second you came out of the water, you were stepping into a whole new world, remember?"

"What is that?" she asked.

"Listen to me, Sydney," Jett said calmly. "Listen to my voice, I want you to kiss the end." He held the leather end to her lips.

"No," she said. "I don't kiss objects I can't see."

Riley looked up then. "So help me, you will. I have one here in my pants you'll even suck on before you see it if I decide it's something I want you to do."

Kevin smirked. "What's the matter Riley? Have you finally met a woman who can keep your interest?"

Riley paced in the small area below them. The foyer wasn't large enough for a good run and go. Jett almost felt the sexual frustration from where he stood. Riley seldom pranced. Right now, he looked like a caged animal waiting for permission to join them. He scratched his chin and glanced up at her again. "Shit howdy, if that's not one fine looking sight."

"Thank you, Riley," she said.

Jett shook his head, and raised his hand high, to devil Luke more than anything else. Luke's eyes widened and before he raised his hand to stop the blow, Jett winked, lightened the strike by lowering it halfway, and then popped her rose-colored bottom.

"Jett!"

"Luke did it," Jett told her.

"I know better," she whimpered, rolled her hips and arched in preparation.

"What was that?" she whined.

"You loved it," Kevin chuckled. "Want another spanking?"

"Tell me what it was first."

"A riding crop," Luke said before swapping a look of uncertainty with Kevin.

"It's okay," Kevin mouthed. "Give her a few swats to the flank, Jett."

"Kevin, I am not a horse for crying out loud!"

"Yes, I know that, but are you a bitch?" Jett asked and smacked her a few times. "Are you, Sydney?"

"Well, I don't know. How should I know? Are you comparing me to my horse?"

"Why, because I mentioned flank?" Kevin watched her.

"Yes. Are you comparing me to some sort of animal?"

"You know better. But since you asked, what do you do when you're not at home, Sydney? Do you run whenever you're free? When your daddy sends you away, do you play naughty games with bad girl toys or do you sit in your apartment all alone and read sexy novels and watch dirty movies?" Jett ran the leather end over her bottom and down her crack. "Do you ever get yourself off, Sydney?"

"No, of course not."

"Sydney," Kevin drawled. "Tell us the truth. You can't hide the truth from us."

Jett tossed the crop to the side and moved in behind her. Stroking her bottom with his palms, he licked up and down her spine. Gaining the reaction he wanted, he smiled when she shivered and then rose over her fast. He spanked her like an adult spanks a child. "You're fibbing to me, Sydney."

"Oh God! Riley! Kevin! Luke! Do something!"

"Tell him the truth," Riley responded. "I want to hear it, too. Do you ever get off with your own hand, Sydney? Do you use a vibrator or sex toys?"

Her body visibly shook. "Do you want me to tell you I do?"

"I want the truth, Sydney. That's what we all want. We want you to trust us enough to always tell us the way things are." Riley propped his elbow on the banister.

"I do."

"You do what? I didn't catch your meaning," Riley said with a big grin. "Damn!" He reached in his pants and maneuvered things around for a little comfort. Then, he moved to the side of the wall so he had a better view of her pussy.

"I get myself off. Do you want to watch?"

"Hell yeah," Kevin said.

"Not yet." Jett wrinkled his brow. "Sydney, do you know why subs are punished? Do you know why I have to punish you?"

"No," she replied.

"Because you were a naughty little vixen," he said. "I took you upstairs and left you in the tub for a reason."

"You did?"

"Yes, I did," he said. "I wanted you to wait for one of us to join you. Now, after seeing you like this, we can't proceed like we first planned."

"You can't?"

"No," Riley said. "We won't wait, Sydney."

"Do you know why?" Kevin asked.

"Uh-huh," she answered. "You want me. All of you want me."

"Yes, you're right." Jett patted her hip before running his fingers under her and dipping right inside her pussy. "Hell fire, you're hot."

Her back bowed and she braced herself by mashing her palms against Kevin's stomach. She moved forward and back. Jett moved his hand and she groaned. "Oh God, you can't play with me like this."

Kevin kissed her forehead. He moved his hand to her pussy and left it under her, cupped right outside of her cunt. His mouth lingered over hers. "Do you know how we're going to take you, Sydney?" He whispered against her lips.

She shook her head and didn't make a sound but her body began its search. She pressed down on Kevin's hand.

"Please, Kevin. Do you know how long it's been since I've—?"

"Tell me," Kevin demanded. "How long?"

"A long time."

"Why?" he narrowed his eyes.

She braced herself for more questions. Maybe she told them too much with the confession. Did they read between the lines? Could they tell by her hunger that there was someone else that had left her thirsty for more?

Kevin moved out of her way. "Crawl, Sydney."

"Crawl now?"

"Yes, Luke is behind you. I want you to ease your way up the steps and I want you to think about something."

"What, Kevin?"

"I want you to think about sharing every aspect of your life with us when we ask you specific questions. Can you do that, Sydney?"

"Yes," she said. The second she replied, she felt guilty. Her Master wouldn't want certain aspects of their time together shared.

Maybe they wouldn't ask. She closed her eyes tighter behind the blindfold. She knew better.

"Good," he growled. "Because I want to know more about your first Master."

She shivered all over. "My first Master?"

"Yes, do you have a problem with telling us about him, Sydney?" Luke asked, the anticipation obvious in his voice. "We want to know how you responded to him."

"You want me to—"

"Sydney." Kevin interrupted her. "You will tell us. In fact, I want to know right now. We know you had another relationship. Now, we want you to describe how you felt about him. In three words or less, tell us how you responded to your last Dom."

"With respect."

* * * *

Brock heard his father and pulled the chord. He didn't want his dad to see his woman with her pussy lips open and her juices free falling from her cunt.

He rubbed his hand over his neck and tried to play it off but he realized his attempt failed.

"I just spoke to Sam. He wants you to give him a call before you go over there." He glanced at the monitors. "Electrical problem?"

"I killed the power."

"I see," his father said. "Any particular reason?"

"Things you shouldn't see."

"Perhaps there are certain things you shouldn't watch as well."

"How do you figure that?"

"She isn't aware that you're watching her with other men. How would she feel about that?"

"Are you trying to psychoanalyze me?"

"No, I'm a father asking his son how he feels about a situation I'm sure is uncomfortable."

Brock replayed the last image he saw in his head. The way she professed her respect for him to her other handlers now, made him want to rush over there and gather her in his arms. Cradle her until morning. Instead, he sat in his miserable chair in front of his bright monitors.

His father wanted to talk about his feelings right now? Right now when Sydney was probably getting her pussy tongue-fucked all the way down her long hallway?

"What did Sam want?"

"Call him," his father said.

Brock started to hook up the computers again. While he only yanked the main chord, the other wires were criss-crossed and tangled up now. Much like his emotions.

"I don't know how he can let this kind of thing go on," Brock yelled out before his father left the room. "I mean how does this sort of ....arrangement, make a father feel?"

"Sam Kane isn't like anyone else I know. I would imagine after his tortured past and numerous attempts at a monogamous relationship, his greatest concern is only for his daughter's safety and happiness. I don't think he worries so much about modern-day expectations or how the community will view her, the locals here seldom see her. The only thing he's concerned about is her health, happiness, and overall well being."

"And you think she's happy now?" Brock wanted an outsider's opinion.

"She will be," he said before walking away. "As soon as she sees you again."

* * * *

"We want you to crawl, Sydney."

Riley smacked his lips. "Regardless of who touches you, what you want or feel, keep crawling forward."

She stretched her neck and tried to peer out from under her blindfold.

Luke pressed his hand to her hip but he didn't spank her. Kevin reached around him and took care of it. "Don't peek."

Smack! Smack! Smack!

"Oh God, yes," she whimpered.

Startled, Luke took a minute and then reached under her middle, forcing her legs apart as he leaned over her back. He twisted his fingers inside of her while his cock mashed against her ass. "Heaven help me if I get out of these jeans, I'll fuck you for days." He made the promise before he ground against her. "Do you like my fingers inside of you, Sydney?"

"Yes," she said breathlessly. "Please move them faster, Luke."

He withdrew. Good for him.

"Do you know all the ways we can please one another, Sydney?" Jett hissed at her ear.

She nodded and moaned as she struggled to find a finger, hand, cock, lips, just anything to get her going, set her off. They loved to watch this kind of show, the struggle of a submissive eager for more.

Jett popped her on the hip. "When I ask a question, I want you to answer me with a yes or no or a full answer. Do you understand?"

"Yes," she whispered.

He smacked her ass again. "And answer with Yes, Master Jett."

"Okay," she replied and he ran the crop over her crease slowly moving it under her, toward her pussy.

"I told you. Answer with yes or no, Master Jett."

"Okay, Master Jett," she reluctantly replied.

Jett sat down on the step parallel to her torso. He caressed her side and then reached under her and smoothed his palm over her mound a few times. "I can feel your heat Sydney. Are you wet, too?"

"Oh, she's wet," Kevin advised.

Luke pursed his lips and excitement danced across his face. "Answer him, Sydney. Are you wet?"

"Luke, you didn't give her time to answer," Riley said before he too moved closer so he could feel for himself.

"I'm…yes, Master Luke and Master Jett, I'm wet."

Jett looked at Luke. "I hope to hell you knew what she was talking about."

"Funny," he said setting his jaw.

Kevin chuckled. "I thought so."

"Do you want to fuck us, Sydney?" Riley asked before nudging Luke.

Her breathing changed as if it caught in the center of her lungs. "Do all of you want to fuck me?" she asked. "I mean at different times, of course."

Jett leaned over and kissed her cheek before Riley knelt beside of her and whispered a promise. "Yes, Sydney, we do. We're all going to fuck you. Sometimes, one will watch while three of us screw you and other times we're going to have you one on one. Do you like the idea of fucking all of us at one time? I bet you do."

"I'm scared," she said. "I don't know where you'll all fit."

"You'll think of something," Jett promised before slapping Riley on the head.

Kevin tugged her forward and she landed on his lap. She pressed her cheek against his thigh. He stroked her hair and then nodded when he noticed her shoulders relax. Jett smacked her three times on her bare mound.

"Ouch!"

"Thank him," Riley demanded. "Thank Jett for scolding you when you whined."

"I didn't whine," she complained. "I'm just curious, that's all."

"We'll explain everything," Riley told her. "Soon, you'll never question what we tell you to do. You'll understand how to respond. Your body will always remain responsive once our training is successful. You'll know what we expect and how to please us."

Luke looked at her bare bottom. "Do you like having a man's cock in your...ass, Sydney?"

"I uh...don't know."

A smack and a swat came down at one time. Riley smacked her rear and Jett slapped her pussy. "Now, try again. If you're going to answer any of us, make sure you do it properly."

"Okay, Masters, I'll answer you with respect." There wasn't any humor in her voice, only acceptance.

Jett stood and Riley took one of her hands and placed it over his crotch. "I want you to feel me, Sydney. Feel that?"

"Yes, Master Riley."

"Good, Sydney," Riley whispered. "Can you tell me what you want to do with my cock?"

"I don't understand, Master."

"Like hell you don't," Riley said. "Try again."

"Do you want to fuck it or suck it?" Kevin coaxed.

"Suck it," she said with a smile. "I really like to suck cock."

"Ah shit," Jett said before eyeing his brothers. "What a way to proposition your Masters."

"Tell me what you'll do with me when we're alone together." Riley probed for the sexy kind of answers. After her last one, so far, so good.

"We're not alone..." she grunted out her reply. Jett smacked her bottom over and over again and she whimpered and then made a bold request. "Please, take the blind-fold off. I want to see who is where."

"Soon," Jett said with a groan. "And I've changed my mind. Boys, get her in the tub. Riley, get downstairs and finish supper. Luke and Kev, when you're done up there, dry her off, completely, and then bring her to the table nude. Starting tonight, she's going to eat with us the way she'll always join us at our table. Sydney, you'll eat naked. In fact, you'll stay nude most of the time when I'm around."

"Who died and left you King of Kane's place?" Riley snipped.

"Nobody yet but if I don't get my cock inside of her soon, hell is going to look like one heck of an inviting place."

"You don't say?" Riley exclaimed. "How about we send a telegram and tell Satan you're on the way?"

Luke looked lost and Riley assured him. "You'll catch on soon enough. In fact, with Jett out of the way, we may let you go first."

Kevin took her hands and pulled her to him allowing her breasts to mash against him. "I'm not rushing this kind of pleasure," he looked at Jett. "Not for you or anyone else."

Kevin wrapped his arms around her back and held her close stroking her long hair. "What do you say, Sydney? Do you want us to take our time with you or are you excited to have sex with us?"

She flinched. "I want to know what it's like, Master Kevin."

"Yes," he said before he kissed the top of her head and waggled his brows at Luke. "I imagine at twenty-three years old, you can't wait to find out."

Chapter Eight

Since the Kane and Donovan properties were located in the middle of nowhere and the weather made traveling the roads impossible, Brock anticipated the drops. The guys from Caracas didn't have a lot of sense and they didn't care to endanger their men.

If the current threat was backed by the Caracas cartel, money and manpower wouldn't present a problem. Brock anticipated bodies dropping from the sky and they'd probably send their guys in groups. It made his job easier because the assassins would cluster together.

He walked over to the window and stared into the darkness. Whatever they had going on over there, most of their foreplay was taking place on the staircase. He could hear comments, approval, and then see someone move forward or back. Once they encouraged her beyond the first landing, he couldn't see much. He didn't think anyone had fucked her yet but they would. Soon, all of them would know what it felt like to hold his Sydney.

He gritted his teeth and held his breath. Damn it! How many times had he passed up his opportunities? How many times did he withhold sex for fear she wouldn't be able to move on with her life when he moved on with his? How many times did he deny her, himself?

He wasn't sure if he could stand someone else touching her when his hands were made for touching her, his arms burned and throbbed. He longed for her, for the chance to hold her again.

The phone rang and he snatched it from the bedside table.

"Brock?"

"Hi, Sam."

"How you doing, son?"

"Not too great. How about you, sir?"

"Probably better than you are about right now."

Brock detected a hint of rare compassion in his voice. Men in their business rarely showed it.

"What can I help you with tonight, sir?"

"You can start by getting your ass over to my house."

* * * *

Riley and Jett were seated at the table when Kevin and Luke joined them.

"I thought Jett told you guys not to leave her alone."

"Yeah and so what?" Kevin turned to Jett. "This stops before it starts, Jett. You're not going to take the lead with her, understand?"

"She's comfortable with him," Riley said. "She'll listen to him."

"I don't think so," Kevin rubbed his chin. "She makes eyes at Luke like he's the only man on the place. That is of course, when she's not looking hard at me."

"I'm sure that's true." Riley laughed and passed them long enough to grab a few bowls from the cupboard. "So she's soaking now?"

"Yep and she's lucky Luke here didn't join her. Man, she has one hell of a body."

After a few chuckles, Riley pointed to Jett. "Alright, talk fast."

Jett shifted his stance, almost immediately. He looked combative and his mood changed, evident first in his expression, and then in his tone. "Mr. Kane had good reason to worry. Kevin, after you left with her this afternoon, Dad came over here to give us a full report. It was right after we searched the property and between the news delivered and what we found, we may be in for a long night. It looks like someone *was* here. A soft pile of cigarette butts were fifty yards away from the family room. By the looks of it, whoever stood there last night or early this morning, stayed awhile."

"No way, we would've spotted someone," Luke tried to digest the new information. "What time did we leave here this morning?"

"Around five," Jett said. "Someone could've scoped out the place, waited until we left, and then kept a sharp eye on Sydney."

"Do we know who we're looking for?" Luke asked.

"Not exactly, there are several threats we're checking out, but I gotta tell you—"

"It's inside then?" Kevin interrupted before Jett said anything more.

"Yeah, it's starting to look that way," Riley replied. "Maybe someone on Sam's team, possibly even Dad's."

Luke slammed his hand against the table. "Sam knew there was a threat and he left her?"

"Damn it, Luke, he left her *with us*," Kevin pointed out. "I guess he thought she had a better chance with the four of us than him right now."

Luke's brows gathered. "He's not well?"

"No, he's not," Kevin said. "He's at Vanderbilt University undergoing some tests but it's not good."

"After talking to her earlier," Luke stated with some hesitancy, "I'm afraid she's going to run when she finds out how we're involved."

"You mean you think she'll have a hard time when she realizes what we do for a living, too?" Jett crossed his arms. "It could happen, you know. Luke, we're not going to lie to her. She'll know from the very beginning who and what we are. We were born into this, but all four of us entered the training period by choice. No one forced us."

"Maybe not," Luke pointed out, "But Sydney didn't get to choose."

"No, she didn't, but I don't think she's had such a bad life," Riley added thoughtfully. "Do you?"

Kevin shook his head. "Right, I'm sure every teenage girl in the country would've loved to have been her. Sam yanked her from school, sent her to a desolate location and told her home school beat the hell out of homecoming parades and proms."

"She always adjusted," Riley informed.

Kevin winced. "And you and I have talked about this." He turned to Luke. "I think someone on Sam's team trained her for the lifestyle. No doubt she had a Master, she's admitted that now, but I think his main goal was to prepare her for right now, this moment."

"Another Dom trained her for us?" Luke asked.

"Not exactly," Jett interjected. "What Kevin believes is that Sam allowed another man to…get pretty close to her."

"Uh-huh," Luke said, watching Kevin. "Don't you have anything better to do during the day than to think about who may or may not have touched Sydney and why?"

"Actually no, I don't." Kevin shifted his weight, braced himself against the middle kitchen island, and crossed his ankles.

Jett and Riley exchanged a glance proving the occasional secret existed, even between brothers. Riley gave Jett a quick nod and he retrieved a duffle bag from under the sink. Dragging a manila envelope from the front pocket, he pushed the tiny brass tab to the side and opened it.

"What's that?" Kevin narrowed his eyes on the glossies as Jett passed them around.

"Various photographs of Sydney. They arrived at the post office this morning."

Riley handed off the pictures without looking at them. He'd seen them before. "These pictures were taken from the last five places where Sydney spent her time away from the ranch. Someone, perhaps whoever placed each individual threat, spent time trailing right behind Sydney wherever she went."

Luke shifted through the prints, crooked his head, studied each one and then passed them off to Kevin. "Okay, so they prove several things—"

"What they prove," Riley interrupted, "is that someone placed threats on Sydney, lured her away from her over-protective father, allowed her to get comfortable in her surroundings, perhaps even find some happiness—"

"And then the threat ended and she was returned home," Jett finished. "The photographs were numbered. Dad picked up on the pattern. Every stack came in the same way.

"The photographs began with the bodyguards showing up here to pick her up, moved through her adjustment period, the choosing of new apartments or safe houses, and her day to day activities. Then you'll find the photographs with Sydney by herself, the captured looks of loneliness, then those of contentment, and finally acceptance, maybe even a bit of happiness found in her new life."

"Then the bastard pulls the rug out, the threat ends, she can leave her new life, and return home," Riley added.

"What a sorry SOB," Kevin said. "Do you think we're dealing with someone who is obsessed with her or are we dealing with a psychotic Dom? In many ways it sounds like someone is controlling her environment, and I think it's very possible it's a means of control practiced by wannabes, what do you think Riley?"

"I think it's messed up, is what I think."

Jett stared at the photograph on top when they handed back the pictures. Sydney sat by a window in a rocking chair. Her hands were folded neatly across her lap and she looked lonely. Her brown hair drifted over her shoulders and her eyes were set with an intent focus.

"This is one of my favorite photographs. She looks somewhat complacent. I studied all of these in the order in which they were sent. Her expression in many of the pictures, tells a story. She was waiting for the order to return home. The photo following this one showed her leaving the very next day."

"You think she expected her departure, then?"

"I think she's smart and I believe she knows someone is watching her. She may even know she's in danger, but has decided to defy it by living her life the best way she knows how."

"Which is?"

"Through acceptance? Obedience?" Kevin questioned.

"It's possible," Riley shrugged. "She may be playing along with someone she trusts."

"You think someone is pulling her strings like this and she trusts him?" Luke looked like a thought like this could send him to an early grave.

"Yeah I do," Riley said.

"Hell, anything is possible." Kevin snapped.

The room fell silent while Jett shoved the photographs back in the red bag. He left it on the floor.

"Riley, you might as well tell them what happened in the laundry room," Jett said.

Luke's brow arched. "Don't tell me you fucked her. Please God, tell me you don't get those bragging rights."

"It's worse," Jett stated without an ounce of enthusiasm.

"What could be worse?" Luke asked.

Kevin's skin took on an ashen tone. "What did she do exactly?"

"It's not what she did," Jett informed. "It's what she said."

Kevin and Luke waited. "Well?" Kevin finally asked.

"She referred to me as her Master during a pretty intense moment."

"She did what?" Luke asked for clarification.

"She called me Master without my instructions or permission to do it in the first place. She's trained as someone else's submissive and lived in the lifestyle for a number of years. It was a slip when she said it." He lazily rubbed his cheek with the back of his hand. "Now, we have to find a way to get through to her and find out more about this Dom."

Jett leaned over his bag and shoved a few guns out of the way. He tucked them deep inside the pockets. When he straightened his back, Luke was in front of him.

"I wanna know what kind of deals you'll cut with me. I want her....alone."

Riley was amused. "You're asking him?"

"Not a chance," Jett said. "I've been fantasizing my way through far too many sleepless nights."

Riley finished placing everything at the table. "Jett and I don't think it's wise for you to move in too close first."

Luke slapped his hand on the table. "What do you mean?"

"It's not normal for a woman to step right into the role of a submissive and accept four Doms so easily with her strong personality." Riley pointed at Jett. "Remember that woman we kept around for a few weeks when we were in Phoenix?"

"The woman had a name," Jett reminded him. "Carla."

"Yeah her," Riley said. "Remember how feisty she was and how she claimed she wanted to submit but then questioned everything we did?"

"Sure but this is different, Riley," Jett said.

"How?"

"We've known Sydney for as long as she's been in this world, for starters. She grew up right under our noses. Luke graduated with her for crying out loud! She's not some broad we've picked up in a nightclub interested in submission for games."

Riley rubbed his chin. "I think she's been interested in the lifestyle for far longer than any of us realized. She's *practiced*."

"Oh, I don't know," Kevin said ready to debate. "It's possible she just wanted to get our attention. It's not like the whole world doesn't know about our preferences. Do you think she's read up on submission and—"

"No, she's gone to someone for training," Riley said. "Or like I said, she's practiced it, lived it. These pictures make me believe it all the more. Considering the fact she's been on the run a lot, her experience definitely came from the inside."

"Hell no," Kevin said. "No way."

"If she knew what we wanted in our women, but didn't know much about domination and submission, it's a strong possibility that she'd let someone teach her. It's even possible that the one who trained her knew about us, too," Jett suggested.

"Damn," Luke said.

"That's not to say she's already been heavily involved in the lifestyle or even practiced it for any period of time, only that she may have sought training and advice from a Dom. What I fear is that she was played from the beginning. She may have requested and received the information she needed from a man just waiting in the shadows for the right opportunity."

"Let's say you're right," Jett said thoughtfully, "Do you think she's trained as a submissive or a slave?"

"There's a difference?" Luke asked.

"Sure," Jett looked at Riley. "Let him explain. He seems to have all the answers."

"Jett, when it comes to pussy, I am your go-to man," Riley exclaimed, trying to lighten the mood. "Listen, here's what I fear. I think she's going to have some misconceptions about what we expect. It's possible she's been with a wannabe and been introduced to Domination and submission under slavery practices, and if so she may not have a good idea of what she wants. I'm pretty sure she wouldn't know the difference between submission and slavery because depending on who trained her, she probably didn't have the option of choosing one over the other."

"It would make sense, I guess," Kevin said.

"Look at her father," Riley said wearily. "She's used to doing what she's told. When she's asked to do something, she's ready to give up everything and move on a moment's notice because her father expects her to mind him. She may not like it but she knows he has her best interest at heart."

Kevin stared at Riley. "So you think Sydney is ready to give us all rights to her freedom of choice and she'll want us to make all of her decisions?"

"Yeah, I do," Riley replied. "And Luke, there's your biggest difference. She doesn't want to make her own decisions or reserve the right of choice. She needs to feel like she's someone's slave, or maybe it gets her going, who knows."

Jett ran his hand through his hair. "If you're right and she was someone's slave, he could've told her to keep her training private."

"Possibly, I've heard of a lot of wannabe trainers enslaving their subs and part of their training includes their ongoing devotion even if they later find another Master. Many of them won't talk about their past training or previous relationships. If this is the case and the guy was on Mr. Kane's payroll, she could be in a lot of danger and we may have a tough time protecting her."

Riley only hesitated for a second to stir his soup and then he turned around again to voice his concerns. "We could have a psycho out there practicing some kind of mind control under the pretenses of Domination and submission. We could be looking for someone who is planning for a kill when the time is right. Our enemies are real. They want to punch where it hurts the most. If there are pictures of her day to day life, I shudder to think of the others out there. Those are the pictures that could break a father and destroy a man."

Silence swept over the room and the men buried their conversation. Riley broke it off after some time to reflect on what he wanted to believe and what was right in front of him. "She's spirited, still has a lot of spunk but there are things that get my attention. She lowers her eyes and bows her head. That's just for starts. If I'm right, there's only one place where she would've had an ongoing opportunity to live as a submissive."

"Inside," Jett said. "Someone her father trusted to guard her."

"Right," Riley took a deep breath and slowly let it out. "And God help the man who used his position to take advantage of her."

"And if she's familiar with submission, we'll never know it if what you're saying is true," Luke said, careful to keep his voice low. "She's a strong woman. She'll resist anything she feels might signify betrayal."

"I don't think she's demonstrated a lot of strength," Kevin said. "I mean she does mind her father and look at her. She's in her early twenties waiting for his next request. Her father tells her to leave and she's packed up and out of here within a few hours. He allows her to come back and she leaves whatever life she's made for herself and comes running home, knowing the whole time, the vicious circle continues and she'll soon leave again."

"Um," Riley said. "Sounds more and more like someone taught her to obey."

Jett sat down and ran his hands over his face. "I don't know. Mr. Kane is a stubborn man. He rules his men with an iron wrist, just in case he doesn't have a fist available. My guess is she's willing to let a man guide her because she's always depended on her father so much. If she trusts the men in her life, I imagine she's going to do what they tell her to do. Sydney trusts us because she was taught to trust us. But we have to remember something, we're not first in line to earn her confidence. Her father handed her over to men who raised her when he couldn't and she was expected to conform immediately."

Riley rubbed his chin with his thumb and forefinger working over the bone. "I didn't count on her compliance this quick." He slammed his fist against the counter. "Damn it all! I know someone else has…" the words stopped spilling. He didn't have the right. She was legal, an adult woman with many desires. Any man with eyes would want to see her, any man alive would want to touch her, hold her, and perhaps even own her.

"What do you think, Kevin?" Luke asked with obvious disappointment in the question.

"Maybe," Kevin shrugged. "I think she's a virgin though and I'm not sure why another Dom would leave her untouched. Jett, you said you thought so, too."

"Yeah, I do but someone else may have introduced her to certain forms of submission. She's been involved with other men before. Dad said she had a pretty hot relationship with a Senator's son. Maybe we need to find out just how warm things got between them."

"A Senator's son?" Luke asked.

"Yeah but the Senator wasn't happy about it once he ran a background check on Sydney and her family," Jett continued, "There were enough green flags to warn off anyone with political connections."

"You mean the good Senator couldn't trace her?" Kevin asked.

"Exactly," Riley replied.

"Do you think this guy has anything to do with the way she's responding to us?" Luke asked.

"I don't know. Maybe." After some thought, he changed his mind. "No. I don't think he's our man. We'll find out soon enough. Dad has someone checking him out," Riley stated. "Without a doubt, Sydney knows what is expected here. She might tell us if she's been through any kind of trial period with another Dom. It's not going to matter much either way in the end *unless* he's on the inside and working her over for a grander plan. There's a lot of evidence to suggest it."

Jett frowned. "I don't like it. I don't want to think about her with another Dom and I damn sure don't want used merchandise."

Sydney walked into the kitchen with her white terrycloth robe clutched in her balled fists. Her chestnut hair looked a little darker, more chocolate now, with her wet strands clinging to her cheek. She took a deep breath and they all held theirs. No one said a word until she did.

"Define *used*, Jett."

Jett refused to dance around any subject. He met it head-on. "Are you a virgin or aren't you?"

"Why does it matter?"

"It matters to Luke," Kevin said with a chuckle.

"Why just Luke?"

"It matters to all of us, actually Sydney," Jett admitted.

"I am a virgin," she said. "At least in the way that counts."

"What does that mean?" Luke asked.

"She's never been penetrated by a man's dick," Riley answered. "Is that what you mean?"

"Yes," she said.

"I'm going to let the formalities slide right now, Sydney," Jett told her. "But you need to understand something. We want your respect all the time and we'll earn it. Once it is earned, a Dom expects his sub to show him the respect he deserves. Do you understand, Sydney?"

"Yes," she answered. "Master," she quickly added.

"Very good," Jett grinned. "Now then, Sydney, what can I do about your punishment tonight?"

She looked around the room and then glanced down at her robe.

"Yes, you know what I'm talking about, don't you?" Jett walked over to her and lifted her hair off of her shoulders, holding it up for her so he could watch it fall against her back when she discarded the housecoat.

"Yes," she said. "I wore a robe and you wanted me to come downstairs without one, but Kevin and Luke were supposed to bring me downstairs. I assumed plans changed when they didn't come back."

"You did?" Riley asked.

"Yes, Master Riley, I did."

"I see," Kevin jumped in right away. "So it's our fault because we weren't there to guide you, right?"

"Pretty much," she said before hurriedly adding, "Master Kevin."

"Not quite," he scolded her. "You have to understand something, Sydney. You are expected to do everything we ask you to do. After we make a request, we want you to follow our guidelines without reminders or the need for attention or company, do you understand?"

"Yes, Master Kevin." She didn't like it and her raised brow showed a little confusion. "So you expected me to wait?"

Kevin laughed. "Got a problem with patience, don't you?"

"Yes, I do, Master Kevin."

"Oh boy, Riley will have fun with you, subbie," Kevin said, biting back a wide grin. "He loves training those who are impatient."

"Screw you, Kevin," Riley said. "I personally have a problem with impatience all the way around."

"I don't. Not in the least. I've waited for this one for three years and as long as she's with us, I can wait another three more. I don't have to fuck her but I do have to see her, touch her and watch her find pleasure," Jett said, opening her robe.

Her nipples were ripe for pulling. They were pointed and hard. Riley even gasped when he saw them.

"Sweet woman," he muttered, impressed.

"Take it off," Jett instructed, cupping her breast with one hand while rubbing his thumb over her nipple in a clockwise fashion.

"Do it, Sydney." He made the demand with a louder voice when she didn't slide it off of her shoulders all at once.

The material fell to the floor. Luke stood up with his hard erection threatening to make the zipper on his jeans look seriously flawed. He walked over to her and Jett moved so Luke stood behind her cradling her against his erection and his chest.

Riley watched. "Sydney, if you're still a virgin, why do you act like you're familiar with Domination and submission?"

"I don't know," she said. "I mean I don't feel comfortable talking about it right now."

"Too bad," Luke whispered in her ear. "We asked a question and when we ask you something, we want you to respond with the appropriate answer."

"Okay, Master Luke, I'll tell you."

"You will?"

She grinned sweetly at the others. "Yes, but just you, Master Luke, when we're alone."

Riley was on to her game. She wanted Luke first and he couldn't blame her if she'd saved herself for one man. She had to have some insecurities and he wasn't all that opposed to letting his brother go first. The problem was found in Jett. He didn't want to discuss it.

"No way," Jett spoke up with opposition right off the bat. Luke and Sydney spending time together alone soured his mood. "It's a bad idea."

"I don't know," Kevin said, turning his head to check out the raw form of one luscious woman. "We sort of owe him the first night with her when you think about it."

"You think so?" Jett asked.

"Yeah, I do," Kevin replied. "What do you think Riley?"

"I don't care who gets her in bed later," Riley stated, straightening out the placemats. "But she is going to face her punishment first."

"Do you want me to kneel or stand in a corner or—"

"That's it," Jett snatched her wrist and drew her tight against his chest. "You are far too familiar with the life of a submissive. Why?"

"I…I don't want to tell you right now," she said, defiantly.

"Do you want your punishment before, after, or during dinner, Sydney?" Jett asked before handing her over to Kevin.

"Give it to her during dinner," Kevin suggested. "I want her pussy filled while we eat."

"Raise your hand, Luke," she said, amused.

"Cute, Sydney," Kevin remarked.

"I like the way you think," Riley exclaimed, before Jett pulled a thick vibrator he retrieved from a small bag near the kitchen door.

"You come prepared," she chirped. "Do you always carry the tools of your trade?"

"Yeah baby, I have the one you want most on me all the time," Jett said, adding a wink and wicked laugh. He then tossed the small toy at Luke.

"If that's not the smallest vibrator I've ever seen," Luke stated, eyeing it.

He found the small switch on the side and quickly asked, "Can women come with one this small?"

"It's wide, even if it's not long," Kevin pointed out. "It'll do the trick."

She shuddered while they discussed her ability to orgasm. "Really, is this necessary? I mean do we have to talk about cocks and dildos like it's common to discuss over a good meal?"

"I didn't ask you for input, little submissive one," Luke replied with a gentle smile. He added a playful smack to her bottom. "I should spank you for coming down here in a robe. You'll let us use the vibrator and if not, I'll turn you over my knee."

"Later, Luke," Jett tossed a lube tube toward him. "Dip it in this first and then shove it in her ass. Make it sting, too. I want her to know it's there."

Yep, Jett was pissed. She played the wrong game with him when she hand-picked Luke over him. Jett had waited on her for three years, but he forgot something, Luke had waited a lifetime.

* * * *

"What are you doing?" Jett snapped a few seconds later.

Riley's jaw dropped. "Oh, fuck me. She's presenting."

"I know what she's *doing* but I mean…I…damn it!" Jett replied before he started pacing. It took a lot to rattle him but she managed to do it.

"You asked her a dumb question. I don't expect her to answer. If you can't see for yourself, then I see little reason in making her reply to stupidity," Riley said, before he walked around her. "Sydney, why did you kneel?"

"I wanted to wait for Master Luke to give me the vibrator," she said without hesitation.

"I see," Riley deadpanned.

She lowered her eyes and stood up then with her hands behind her back showing her consent the best way she knew how since the kneeling thing didn't go as planned. She parted her legs. Luke dropped to the floor and the others sat down at the table and watched.

He slid the toy over her mound a few times. She immediately flinched when he touched her labia with his fingertips.

"Like that, don't you?" he asked.

"Are you a virgin too, Luke?" She already knew he was because of the subtle hints his brothers left here or there in casual conversation.

His cheeks turned red. "You think I don't know what I'm doing?"

"You know exactly what you're doing, but you want to do more than touch me and that's the problem, isn't it?"

Luke smacked her pussy. "I didn't ask you to argue with me, Sydney."

"Again, please Master," she said softly, but her eyes watered from the sting.

He slapped her again and she cried out in pleasure. His touch was hot. The heat pooled in between her legs. He touched her with the end of the vibrator and she almost came. He backed away from her, shrugged and then his nostrils flared. The smell of sex filling the room.

"Do it, Luke," she whispered. "Please, do it."

"What do you want him to do?" Jett asked. He picked up his spoon and started playing in his soup bowl. "Do you want him to finger you or lick you? There are certain things you have to ask for specifically and right now, it's a requirement. We can't read your mind, Sydney."

Luke blew a steady stream of warm air over her mound. She flinched.

"You heard them. Ask for it, Sydney. I'll give you what you want."

"I'd love it if you'd fuck me, Master Luke," she purred, before she dropped to her knees.

Once she was eye to eye with him, he bit down on his lower lip and she watched as he fought the temptation to kiss her. She wanted to devil him some, so she moved close enough to kiss him but then rather than ask for it, she licked her bottom lip and waited for him to take her gesture as an invitation.

"Do you want me to kiss you, Sydney?"

"Yes, Master Luke, I do."

"Do you want me to finger you while I kiss you, Sydney?"

Oh hell, did she ever.

Luke pressed his mouth to hers. He kissed her softly before he nuzzled her cheek. "Tell me Sydney, come on sweet thing. Talk to me."

"I...yes, please I want your fingers inside of me." *And your tongue and dick. Anything, everything, you.*

Luke tilted her chin up and watched her as he ran the thick toy across her pussy. "Turn around, Sydney," he whispered.

"Luke?"

"Do it, please," he said before adding a gruff, "Now," for his macho image more than any other reason.

When she turned around, he helped her secure a position on all fours. After she did, he squirted the lubricant down her ass. With little warning, he tapped her outer ring and pushed the toy into her anus.

"Luke?" she exclaimed.

"Does it hurt? Or do you love it?"

"The vibrations are...too much."

"Resist it," Luke ordered, before he turned her and helped position her flat against her side.

With her ear pressed to the floor, he caressed her back and kissed her flesh with an open mouth. Her body responded to the vibrator and he knew before he fingered her, the moisture poured from her cunt.

"Now, you're ready to come, aren't you Sydney?"

"Can I?" she asked.

He glanced at the others and then shook his head rapidly. "Not yet, Sydney."

"Somebody taught our little brother too much, too soon," Riley said proudly.

Luke spread her legs and watched as the small vibrator worked as a secure butt plug. The vibration prepared her, ensured her pliable bottom adjusted to the impalement. The outer ring milked the toy. He had to hold himself with a flat palm in order to keep from shooting off like a bullet without a target.

She pulled at her nipples and moaned, closing her eyes and rolling her head to the side. "Yes, oh yes."

"Shit, look at that," Kevin said. "This is better than dinner and a movie."

He tossed his napkin on the table, walked over to the refrigerator and grabbed another beer. "Fuck her or eat her, but do it before I get through here or you can stand in line. You two are making me horny and I don't plan to play games tonight. I'm going to know what it's like to stroke that pretty little pussy in a matter of a few hours."

Jett took a bite of stew. "This is pretty good, Riley."

Jett liked to call the shots, and he pouted because Luke had the best of it right then. Jett wanted Sydney's complete trust before any of them penetrated her. Too bad. The globe didn't revolve around Jett when the axis in question was Sydney's pussy.

"Yes, little brother, it's mighty good, and the stewing around here is better than what I have in the pot. It provides hearty entertainment, let me tell you," Riley said cleverly.

"What's that supposed to mean?" Jett dropped his spoon.

"He's just enjoying the show," Kevin replied. "Pay attention, Jett. You might learn something."

Jett narrowed his gaze on Luke and shook his head. "I doubt it."

Riley moved his jaw around, swallowed the food in his mouth, and then pointed his spoon toward Luke and Sydney. "You're right, Kev. This is better than anything I ever imagined."

Chapter Nine

Zaxby pulled out his cell phone and glared at the screen.

Location?

The vibrations of communications hummed throughout the area. Several men were with him now and they planned to camp out in the barn until they received the order to move. Two or three men were in place on the Donovan property—somewhere around the fence line— in case anyone tried to leave the Kane house.

Another person stated an *inside* position. Whether inside meant the Kane house or Donovan's place, he didn't know, or care. He was there to kill, not provide strategic planning for the others.

Sam Kane had a state-of-the-art barn complete with a waiting area and heated office. Fortunately Zaxby knew it when he sought cover. He made the best of the situation, all things considered.

What a shame they had to torch the place when their job was finished. Too bad everything Sam Kane and Mark Donovan had worked for in a lifetime was going to go up in scattered flames followed by a loud boom.

This crew meant to leave them with nothing to show for their efforts. All the killings, the manipulations, the records destroyed, the brutal torturing, the money exchanged, all of it was for nothing.

Donovan and Kane were going to lose everything important to them. By the time Zaxby's boss finished with them, they'd feel like broken men and know what it was like to have their lives destroyed by the very business they worked like crazy hell to protect.

Zaxby leaned his head back against a stack of lumber. His pager was buzzing wild now. He read the number. Damn it. He picked up the phone and dialed.

"Yeah?"

"Zaxby, man, I'm so cold my dick is frozen in a permanent erection."

"That's what you get for jacking off to too many porn movies."

"Porn? Hell no. What I have is a front row seat to one of the hottest shows in the south."

Shit. He missed more of the Sydney does Donovan program. "What are you talking about?"

"I'll trade points with you and let you see for yourself. I'm telling you, man. You'll thank me for this later. Sydney Kane is in the kitchen with the Donovans and so help me, I swear they're going to fuck her. All of them."

"Then why don't you stay and watch?" he snapped.

"It's kind of hard, if you know what I mean."

He did. He knew all about it.

Zaxby shut the phone and stared down the barn. They were divided into teams of two and Zaxby had never worked with Paul Rines before, but he remembered what it felt like to stand in Paul's shoes a few hours earlier.

Zaxby took a deep breath and slowly exhaled. He pulled a cigarette from his pocket and lit it. Instead of watching Sydney, he'd smoke.

It pissed him off that things came down to this. He basically liked Sydney. He'd been on a few trips with her, guarded her for several months at a time, and he allowed himself the rare indulgence and thought about her as a woman, rather than Sam Kane's daughter.

For days he questioned whether or not he had the balls to team up with the others for this mission. He questioned himself for one reason only.

He knew the real Sydney without the Kane name and the story behind her father's legacy. Zaxby was hired, at one time, to guard her with his life. Now, he'd take it. Maybe it was for the best. Brock ruined her for better men. The crazy son-of-a-bitch trained her as a submissive right before their eyes.

And now the Donovan guys were going to enjoy her. He took a long drag off of his cigarette. He wished Brock was around to see this now.

On second thought, he shuddered, it was a good thing Brock wasn't there. With fewer men sent in for the job than originally expected, the last thing he needed was a Brock-sighting.

Then again, sometimes death appeared and claimed the victims in many forms. Those left behind often suffered the worst. Sydney Kane, whatever she was doing with the Donovans, would destroy a man like Brock.

Zaxby stared at the ceiling. He wondered if his boss would let him keep Sydney alive. He pulled out his phone and dialed. There were some women worth fighting for. Sydney was one of them. Only because, she had a greater purpose than anyone realized, she was the only woman who could help with the demise of one man.

* * * *

Sydney wanted Luke to touch her. With designer lips like Luke Donovan's, she yearned for the feel of them and the sooner she felt them more intimately, the better. She thought of another man's lips, similar in shape, and revisited the past briefly. She focused on the image and Luke's lips at the same time.

It was a long time ago, she reminded herself. Her heart hurt, if for only a minute. *He's not coming back. Get on with life.*

Luke pressed her body against the cold floor and kissed her as he straddled her chest. The pre-cum glistened from his tip and Luke's brothers observed them with a tight upper lip. She doubted he'd fuck her but, he wanted her mouth on him.

Kevin rubbernecked it and peered under the table. "What 'cha doing there, Luke?"

"Eat your soup," he snapped. He fisted his cock and ran it back and forth over her bottom lip.

"With what he's dripping, Sydney, you're going to get a throat-load the second you suck. Just go ahead and start swallowing now," Riley advised, then continued to shove one spoon after in the next between his lips.

She sensed the turn of events in every nerve ending and saw a new tenderness when Luke pulled away and slid back down her belly. He tapped the end of the toy a few times until she moaned out loud. Then, he braced himself against his palms placed on either side of her head. He leaned down and kissed her, made love to her mouth in a way no one ever attempted before.

His lips possessed hers in a right of ownership, one she willing gave to him right away. The way his tongue slid inside her mouth to greet her kiss proved his hunger led him, fed him, tugged him forward. He sipped on the tip of her tongue and let his cock hang at her chest.

In that instant, she surrendered herself to him completely. She'd never try to explain it to anyone because she didn't know how or why it happened exactly or so perfectly. Only that it did. The way he looked at her when he kissed her had a lot to do with it.

Luke cared for her deeply. She saw it in his eyes. He wasn't going to let a little teasing force him to take her, to do so now ruined years of established trust and they had a history.

They'd attended the same schools, when she was permitted to attend the public classrooms. They often rode on the same buses, played on the same soccer teams, and there was trust there that went beyond what any of the Donovans knew.

They were listed as her first-call. She always knew her father trusted the Donovans so she trusted them because he trusted them. With Luke it was more than her father's approval. It was first-hand knowledge and the understanding that he truly saved himself for her.

"Now what, sweet thing?" he asked as his lips parted hers. "Tell me where you want my lips," he mumbled against their broken kiss.

"I want you to…" she knew the others would punish her the moment all three spoons clanked against their bowls. Riley peered across the table.

"Go on, ask for it, Sydney. Do you want him to eat your pussy?"

"Yes, I want you to, Luke…Master Luke."

"I can't wait," he said before he moved across her belly and held onto her nipples with his forefingers and thumbs rolling them simultaneously. He moved his mouth to her mound and inhaled her scent. "One thing about it, you smell better than Riley's stew," he said and then nipped his way closer to her pussy lips.

Holding her breath, she closed her eyes. Luke dipped his head and dragged his lips across hers claiming her as his with ever stroke of tongue, each whisper and whimper.

"Oh Luke," she muttered. "Master Luke, please."

He sucked at each flap and played with the skin, running his tongue up and down her flesh. He mumbled against her opening before he tapped the butt plug and she trembled in sheer delight.

Riley scooted away from the table and pulled her hand away from her body the second he saw her reach for her clit.

"No, Sydney."

"Riley, please. Oh God, you have to…" She tried to pull away from him defiantly.

"You're spanked if you do that again, Sydney." Riley said, caressing her arm. "With a paddle."

A losing battle behind her, she focused on Luke. "Please Luke, go deeper."

Riley grinned. "Hell, if you want a tongue to ride, Kevin is the brother you want."

Kevin stuck his tongue out and wiggled it up and down. Sure enough, she saw the advantage. It looked like it belonged to some kind of foreign animal. Long, meaty, and ready to give her as much pleasure as any man's dick.

Luke pressed his finger to her clit and her body jerked. Riley pinned her shoulders to the floor. "Do it again, Luke," he instructed.

Rotating it this time, he applied pressure and then moved his tongue forward. He swiped from left to right and then quickly reached between his legs and held his cock.

Jett wiped his mouth off, stood and then knelt beside them. He reached behind him and grabbed the bowl from the table. He offered it to her.

"Do you want to eat, Sydney?"

"No, God no. I need to come. Please Jett."

"You will, later tonight. If you're good, you'll come."

Luke kissed her inner thighs and then backed away from her rather than complete the project he started between her legs.

"Damn it! This isn't fair."

Riley smirked. "You deal with her. She needs punishment for such an outburst. Jett has everything set up in the garage."

Her heart thudded rapidly against her breastbone. She had visited several slave chambers when she was on the move with Master Brock. He kept her in an orchestrated state of arousal but he always refused to give her what she needed most.

She obediently played his games until she'd desired him more than anything in the world. Later, she grew tired of them when she realized all she'd ever have with him were games without a declared winner.

Her Master finally offered her an ultimatum, one she'd waited to hear since meeting him. He promised to make love to her if she agreed to become his slave for life and never return home to her father. She didn't make the deal and he didn't touch her. Instead, they parted ways, but she knew from the second she waved goodbye, they'd meet again. They always did. Only this time, three years slowly passed without one word from him. Often, she worried she'd never see him again.

Jett placed the bowl back on the table. He rested his long arms against his knees, leaned over and pinched her nipples. He stared lovingly, longingly at her pussy, and then he stood up.

"I want you shaved all the time," he said before clearing the table. "Luke, the swing is set up. I want her punished now."

"But...Jett," she started to protest.

"Do you want more punishment than what you've already earned?" he asked, then walked over to the kitchen door leading out to the garage. He held it open. Luke led her through, and she gasped at what she discovered. At some point, they transformed her father's garage into a sex dungeon of sorts.

"You are so dead when my father comes home."

"This stuff won't be here," Riley promised.

She wasn't sure if she should act excited or hit the garage opener and run like mad into the freshly fallen snow. Would they torture her with sex and continually deny her? Surely not. Oh hell, she couldn't think about it. She knew it was a viable option. The only other Dom she'd known in her life, held sex over her head like an unearned reward.

"When did you do this?" she asked.

"We worked on it while you were in town," Riley said, sounding proud of what they accomplished without her knowledge. "Don't worry. It's easy to take down."

"Good," she said.

Luke stalked around her. He instantly made her his prey when his brothers shut the door to separate themselves. He touched her nipples. "You have large areoles."

"I do?"

"You don't know?"

"And you do?" she questioned. "I mean, I guess they're large in comparison to what you've seen somewhere else but are they—"

"I'm a tit guy, Sydney. I've looked at enough of them on the internet and I watch movies. A guy has to do something. Trust me when I tell you, I've seen plenty of boobs. I've messed around, I've just never let things go too far."

"Then how do you know what you want? I mean, are you just following what Riley and the others want or do you make your own choices?"

He laughed. "I'm not like them in all ways," he said, moving a few of the dildos around on the rotating contraption tapping the one in her bottom when he passed by her. She jerked with recognition.

The sex machine with the dildos rotated on a mechanical apparatus like it was created it to fuck several women at one time. Luke gave it a spin and made sure all of the dildos were attached to their metal rods. Ten wands were capped at the end with the generic dicks and a black pad, something resembling a half-cot was underneath the machine.

"I'm scared now," she said with her eyes wide open. "And excited at the same time, Luke."

She watched the sudden change in his expression when his mind was made up one way and then conveniently, changed to suit his own needs the next. In that instant, Sydney realized she didn't want to just submit to Luke Donovan, she wanted to become his slave.

Understanding the difference between submissive and slave, she knelt at his feet and waited for him to reach for her or make a command. Maybe he wanted her to stand or maybe he'd lift her up and carry her to the machine, but whatever he did to her, she trusted he would choose to do it for her own good.

When she was with Luke, she wanted him to have all powers over her. She once gave Master Brock everything she had, she willingly gave the man complete control over her mind, body, and spirit. She still missed him, maybe now more than ever before.

Luke patted her on the head. "I've waited a long time for you, Sydney, and there's no way I'm going to let a machine do something I'm more than man enough to do myself."

"You're supposed to punish me," she said quietly.

He took her hands in his and held them to his lips. They both kissed their clasped hands simultaneously and their gaze met, held, and burned.

"Are you nervous?"

"Yes," she responded truthfully. "Are you?"

"Do you want to stop before—?"

"No, Luke, I don't," she whispered. "But can I ask you something?"

He nibbled at her ear. "You can ask me anything."

"Are they going to be upset?"

"Disappointed maybe, but no, I don't think so."

"Are you sure?" she asked before eyeing the toys.

His hot tongue darted in and out of her ear while the vibrator jiggled in her bottom. Set to a low twitch designed to spontaneously send shocks through her anus every few seconds, she never lost the awareness of what they placed in her rear.

"Pretty sure," he said. "Not positive. You never know what will set off Jett, or Riley for that matter."

"Precisely what I thought."

He took a deep breath and sucked on her fingers, nibbled her knuckles. He pulled one finger after another inside his mouth, and then swirled his tongue over the tips again and again.

She dropped her hands to her sides. "Why *did* you wait?"

Parting her stance, she bowed her head and crossed her hands behind her back. Her breasts pushed forward like her previous trainer instructed her to do when presenting herself to her Master.

"For you."

"Yes, for me," she said, misunderstanding the way he responded.

He lowered his forehead to hers and gripped her shoulders tightly. "No, I mean I waited *for you*."

"You could've had any woman you wanted."

"I *want* you, Sydney. There's never been anyone else for me and there will never be anyone else in the future. Only you."

No way. Every woman in Abingdon would place her on a hate-list now. Luke Donovan loved her. There wasn't a doubt in her mind.

"Do they feel the same?" she felt comfortable asking.

"Riley is a tough one to figure out, so don't try. I imagine Kevin feels something but it won't happen for him overnight and Jett is so crazy in lo..." he stopped. "We care for you in our own different ways."

"Why me?"

"Why not you? Look at you, Sydney. You're sexy, sweet, and gorgeous in every way. I don't think I've ever known a woman more beautiful and if I ever meet one on the streets who even comes close in comparison, I'll smile, tilt my head and run home to you. It's more than skin deep for me and I think it is for the others."

"When did you know?" she asked, in an attempt to understand. Sure, she'd had her Barbie and Ken fantasies but those ended when her new adventures began. It was like her father allowed her to play Bonnie with three or four Clydes. Sometimes, she even had more men guarding her than the average government official. She was forced to leave her Donovan-fantasies behind and she trained herself at a young age to accept it.

Then she met one of her father's young guns, a trainee who found his first job with her. Brock kept his distance from her for a long time, but when he decided he couldn't stay away any longer, he introduced her to a world she never knew existed. Brock helped her get past her insecurities and taught her what it meant to be submissive and obedient.

He wanted her to call him Master Brock and demanded it from the beginning. He preferred slaves to submissives. He never made her think otherwise. He wanted a slave for life and his commitment to training her went beyond anything she'd ever seen in her life. She shuddered as she thought of him. The way they transformed her garage made her remember him now vividly and she truly missed him.

Master Brock kept her in a constant state of arousal and often when her father called for her return, she reluctantly returned home fearing the separation but at the same time, grateful for the time away from Brock. Her body became dependent on his desires and her whole purpose was to concentrate on how to feed them.

Luke winked. "Some fantasy, huh?"

She must've zoned out. "I'm sorry," she said with a saucy grin. "You were getting ready to tell me when you decided to flip over me."

He was touching her, pulling her closer. "I overheard your friends making fun of you once. It was all in good fun and right after you left The Tavern. I ducked behind some trees when I heard someone ask you if you were still a virgin. I wanted to hear your reply and I did. I must've jacked off every day for a year after that," he admitted. "With your name on my lips each and every time."

Her mouth dropped. "I remember what I said, Luke. If you were there, why didn't you come out and say something?"

"I heard you say that you were saving yourself for a Donovan but I didn't hear my name specifically. If I had, then maybe things might have been different but I couldn't be sure. Back then, the idea of us all together was nothing more than a bizarre fantasy."

"How about now? Is it still just a fantasy?"

"The more I watch you with them, I see it's where we all belong. I'm anxious for you, and I want you more than I can tell you. I also want you first," he stated with plenty of confidence.

He took his cock to hand and rubbed it over her hip. She looked down and watched. It was erotic. The way his shape formed as he touched her, the interesting way the color changed with the size.

"I'm so horny. I swear, I might die if you deny me."

"I'm not going anywhere," she whispered in his ear. "You own me." The way she said it alarmed her. The raspy voice she used to tell him she belonged to him frightened her.

He pulled back and looked at her with lust in his eyes. "Do you want someone to own you, Sydney?"

"I want you to take control, Luke. Make me yours."

He framed her face with his large palms and stared into her eyes. "You are mine."

She gripped the back of his neck and then kissed him hard on the lips. The kiss had a name, it wasn't just one the French could claim. It was a cowboy's kiss, a mercenary's tongue—defiant and controlled— and it was special, because of who delivered it.

A few breaths were needed and he backed away to let her have them. They looked at one another like lust drove them and love guided them, or at least encouraged them to take things slow.

"Do you want me to kneel in front of you now?" she asked.

"No, I want this first time to be special for you. I'll do whatever I can to make it memorable."

"I can submit to you, Luke and it's going to be just as special."

"Not for me. This first time, let's not place unnecessary demands or pressures on one another."

She wasn't quite relieved but she acted like it. He was nervous about making love to her, and she understood. Since it was their first time together or with anyone, they needed time to explore their intimacy without lifestyle complications. Even if it was something they wanted to willingly embrace.

As virgins, if they tried too hard to incorporate everything they planned to experience in a Dom and sub relationship, they might lose their moment. She couldn't risk it. The way he responded to her was perfect, better than anything she imagined.

"Let's go over there," she suggested, pointing to a dimly lit corner in the garage.

If anyone opened the door, they'd have to skip the steps and take a few strides to the right to see them. Her father's old '57 Chevy remained covered in the far corner. It provided a barrier. Onlookers wouldn't spot them right away unless they decided to go outside in the bitter cold and watch from the small window.

His moist tip pressed harder against her flesh and she reached down to stroke him. She moved him through her hand again and again and he moaned when she knelt in front of him and licked his slit. Before she could suck him into her mouth, he yanked her up and then swept her into his arms. Carrying her to the corner she suggested, he picked up the lighter and lit the candles on a nearby shelf, right next to the planted sex props. Jett made the place into a cool cavern of delight. They'd have to thank him for his attention to detail.

"Their edible," she told him. "The candles are flavored. They're sold at a lot of the sex shops."

"How do you know?" he asked.

"I'm a seasoned virgin. They're chocolate, too," she smacked her lips.

Luke pressed her body against the floor rug. "I... I don't know if I can touch you without coming."

"If you can't, Luke, it's all right. It's just me and you. No one has to know what goes on here, right now, except us." She stroked his cock and then pressed her mouth to his tip, she merely kissed it and the pre-cum dampened her lips. When she sat back up, she swiped at the taste.

"Sydney," he said in a husky voice. "Come here."

Her lips parted, and he moved with the shift. He dared her to use her tiny little teeth as he licked around their shape and she wanted to nip, bite at him and draw blood. Not because she liked the taste so much, just because she liked all forms of pleasure, and often found it in small doses of pain.

He held his cock at the base and dragged it across her opening. She spread her legs more, grabbed onto his shoulders and urged him forward.

"I want you to have my virginity. Show me what it feels like to be everything to one another, even if it's for a little while."

The vibrator continued to buzz in her rear. He flipped it twice and watched her response. "Do you want me to take it out?"

She shook her head. "I want you inside me, now," she whispered.

Luke kissed her lips and stroked them with a nice caress as he eased his cock beyond the folds of her pussy. "Oh sweet heaven," he said, swallowing tightly. "So this is why sex is such a big deal."

He started to move all at once. Then, he thrust into her with uneven strokes.

God love his heart, he tried to take it slow as he wiggled his way into her space. She was wet, stretched, and ready. Brock told her a long time ago, sex wouldn't hurt her so much after the training he put her through and he was right. Oh thank God, he was right.

Sydney wrapped her legs around Luke and he shifted inside of her, going deep and pounding hard. She rolled her head to the side and stared out into the darkness. This was good, really good. Perfect.

"Oh God, Sydney, come."

He moved quicker than she bargained for. "Oh Sydney, let me have you."

She closed her eyes, capturing the dream and holding fast to it. She was where she wanted to be. She had a man who wanted to hold her, love her...fuck her.

He hammered into her faster and faster punching at her walls, stroking her forward, taking his first ride of a lifetime. "That's it sweet thing, ah yeah! Coming...Damn it."

He shoved her knees forward, under his arm pits and pounded away, working for achievement, reaching his climax and shooting off inside her vagina like he wanted to leave a permanent piece of him buried deep inside of her. His grunts were filled with so much pleasure, ecstasy exploded all around them as he pumped his seed deeper and deeper.

"Harder," she muttered. "Luke!"

"Holy shit!" He kept coming. Beads of sweat poured off his brow and he dipped his head, licked at her nipples and finally crashed against her lips in a committed seal of satisfaction.

"Oh God, Sydney, I'm sorry. Give me a minute. Just a minute."

"Shh…" she whimpered, and then assured him, "I loved it, Luke. You have no idea."

The way the Donovans had toyed with her, touched her, spanked her, and fingered her, she was glad Luke came right away because she matched him stroke for stroke. She arched her back and rolled her hips forward over and over again until they were breathless and drenched in the aftermath of pleasure, a true bath of their spent lust.

When he pulled out, he kissed her with a smile so wide, he had more lips than teeth involved.

"Thank you," he said.

"Anytime," she said smoothly.

"Are you okay?" he asked, before he moved his hand across her forehead and brow. "Tell me I didn't hurt you," he said, releasing her legs and sliding away from her.

"I'm super," she replied. "I'm really good, Luke."

"Oh, I know how good you are," he growled. "I'm so horny around you that I'm all ready to go again."

He fisted his cock and stroked himself hard, striking at his cock like he might beat a drum. "Give me a hand here," he said, motioning for her and then lifting his arm. He wiped the dripping sweat from his cheek as he watched her. "Please, Sydney. I need more than once. One time will never be enough."

She smacked her lips and then inched her way back into his steamy kiss. She touched him everywhere and he returned the favor, tweaking her nipples, patting her ass and tapping the end of her new favorite toy. They had to touch one another, caress and stroke. In a matter of seconds, Luke was begging for another opportunity to thrust inside of her. This time, he took things slower.

Locking her arms high above her head, he moved into her on a schedule. He took one stroke, then two or three more, withdrew all the way, and allowed her to feel his tip at her opening. She bowed her back and arched for him.

"More, Luke!" Please more, she thought. *Don't make me wait.* Brock kept her hungry for sex. Luke fed her.

Many times, she had begged for cock, asked for special exceptions, Brock never gave in. He kept her insatiable and never offered her anything close to this.

Luke was different.

Sydney felt him all the way to her belly as he drove into her time and time again with a slow pace and a determination across his face. He wanted her pleased. He wanted to come *with her,* not *at her* with only her eyes to guide him. He wasn't a calculated lover afraid of touching her. Luke knew he wouldn't break her and so what if he did, they could shatter together with the orgasms they found in each other's arms.

"Damn it! Luke, harder," she cried.

"Fuck me, Sydney. Wrap your legs around me again. Come and get it, lover," he said with commitment in his cause.

She laughed out loud when he waggled his eyebrows. She thought of Kevin and how fiercely he looked at her. Oh yeah, she had a whole lot of loving to do and a whole lot of man in each of the Donovans.

What woman turned away something like this? *Not this woman.* Her Master trained her for this. She wished he could be there to see her, to witness what he helped her so willingly become.

* * * *

"So you want to try it out?" Luke asked.

He reached over and gave the rotating dicks a quick spin in passing. They laughed. It was something to watch.

"No, not really," she said. "I'm sore now."

"With what we have planned for you, I think you're right to take a pass."

"I know I am. If it's a choice, I don't want the artificial. I prefer the real thing now."

He eyed the swing. "Don't guess you'd consider just dressing the part for the swing, would you?"

"No," she said about the time Jett opened the door.

"Shit, Luke. She is *unable* to deny you anything. She's in training and you haven't even had her on one of these…machines." He stopped talking and stared at her belly. "What the hell is that?"

She gasped and quickly looked down fearing the remains of their pleasure stuck to her skin and gave them away. Instead, he pointed at the passionate hickeys Riley left behind earlier.

She shrugged. "You'll have to blame Riley for those."

"Riley!" he exclaimed, and then turned toward the steps leading back to the kitchen.

"It takes two," she purred.

"Something seems different about you. Did you enjoy your punishment?" Jett asked tentatively.

She resisted a smile but gave everything away. "I did, very much, Master Jett."

Luke shook his head. "I'll tell you what's different. Sam is going to take a look in this garage and go the hell off. You all should've considered keeping this shit over at the house."

"What does this have to do with the way she looks right now?" Jett questioned.

Riley appeared in the doorway along with Kevin. "Ah shit," they said in unison.

"She's been fucked hard," Kevin announced enthusiastically.

"And too many times, too, if I had to guess. He was a virgin, remember," Riley said with a smirk. "Damn," he said it again. "Damn," and again.

"Jealous?" Luke asked.

Jett studied him and then slapped him on the back. "I would be if I believed you tapped that sweet little pussy first. I don't think you did." He paused, circled her and then stopped to watch Luke. "Did you undress?"

"No, of course not, I just whipped it out and told her to get on for the ride."

"You didn't. I know you didn't." Denial. He wasn't going to believe it.

Jett had the ability to think fast on his feet and see a lie before it was spoken. In his personal life, he couldn't see the clear evidence in front of him. Sometimes Luke wondered about him.

"Jett," she started to explain but before she had the opportunity, they heard a knock at the back door.

Riley and Kevin grabbed something from inside the door and tossed it at Jett. Kevin handed her the robe she'd left in the kitchen earlier.

"Stay here," he said.

Jett put his fingertips to his lips and moved along the wall toward the one window in the basement and peered out. He nodded, pointed and mouthed the word.

"No one we know," he confirmed their fears.

A few moments passed and then Jett twirled his index finger above his head and pointed to Luke waggling his fingers between him and Sydney. He was careful to press a fingertip to his lips. He glanced around the garage like he thought someone was there with them.

Jett grabbed something from the tool bench and flew up the steps, shutting the door and leaving Luke to defend Sydney. She heard their footsteps as Riley, Kevin, and Jett raced across her kitchen floor.

"Hurry, Sydney," Luke said, helping her put her robe on. He continued to look around the garage.

He pointed. "Get those boots on over there. If something happens, go for our place and get there fast. Go to the back of the house and crawl through the dog opening. It leads to a tunnel under the property and everyone that is shot through the chute is scanned, Dad had you programmed a long time ago. When you slide through, you'll empty into a room that looks like a control room, stay there and wait for us."

He swallowed hard and then grabbed her hand. Shoving her under the metal table, he brushed her lips with his. Before he backed away, the door swung open and Jett stepped back into the garage.

Shaking his head, he motioned for them. "Come on out. It's nobody."

"Nobody?" Luke asked. "In this weather?"

"Nope, a friend of Dad's just had the wrong place."

"Oh," Luke said instantly catching on. "What happened to the upfront business from the get-go?" He snapped at his brother in passing.

Jett snarled. "You tell me."

Riley and Kevin stood next to the fireplace peeling off their clothes. They took off into the deep snow and didn't make it far so they turned back.

"Snowshoes?" Luke asked.

"Shoes, hell," Riley complained. "The bastard had a snowmobile."

"Shit," Kevin said. He held his hands close to the flame. "This guy is playing with us."

"What guy?" Sydney questioned before going to the window and taking a quick look for herself. She didn't have to ask. She felt him there watching her from the shadows. She knew precisely who stepped up and knocked on her backdoor and she didn't have to guess why he chose the particular moment to do it.

Master Brock watched her love another, give her body to someone completely, and he didn't like what he saw. Brock was out there, watching over her, protecting her, craving her.

And he was mad as hell.

Chapter Ten

The Donovans acted like men on a secret mission. They ushered her upstairs, blindfolded her and then left her there. No one explained anything to her. No one offered to give her an estimate of how long she'd wait by herself and frankly, it was nice.

She welcomed the opportunity to reflect on her time alone with Luke. It was time to think about how she felt about their unexpected and uninvited guest.

Her father's trusted soldier was out there somewhere. Cold, maybe hungry, but forever indebted to her father, Brock served his country but he followed Sam Kane.

She realized now, Brock wanted to keep her safe while her father was away, but why was he there lurking outside? Had her dad sent for him? She wondered. Why did he knock and run? Brock didn't run from anything, nothing at all, except maybe intimacy.

He was fooling himself even now. They were as close as two individuals could be and they established their bond without sex. Oh, but how they'd fooled around.

Brock mastered the art of arousal and kept her in tune with her body and her desires while fulfilling his, no matter how perverse they were. Sydney decided a long time ago, Brock had a few issues when it came to women, but she accepted them because they were *his* issues.

She often wondered where their relationship would have ended if she'd chosen him over her father. Would he have remained in contact with her dad or would he have told him that he gave her the choice to choose him or the only life she'd ever known.

Brock controlled her. She never resented it until she realized he trained her for slavery and yet fudged on his end. She only realized it after she read up on Domination and submission versus slaves.

The sound of heavy footsteps warned her she soon faced another challenge. Adrenaline was high and the Donovans were horny.

"Did you find him?" she asked. "Whoever he is?" she added.

"No, Sydney, we didn't." Jett answered, irritated. "What the hell are you doing here, Sydney?"

"I'm...waiting...for you."

Jett grabbed her wrists and pulled her up. "Are you? Are you waiting for me, for Riley, Kevin, and Luke or do you have someone else?" He bit at her lower lip and then led her into a crumbling kiss. One that left her reaching for him with her tongue.

"I...I know what you're thinking..."

She knew what they were thinking because she knew the truth. They had to suspect it, too.

"There is something out there, Sydney!" Riley raised his voice and she bowed her head. "Someone you know parading around your property in the dead of winter. Who is it?" He yanked her by the arm and she twisted her head trying to follow his voice.

She heard zippers fall. What the hell? Were they going to try and fuck the truth out of her? Screw her for answers? She gulped for air.

Riley held her close. "Damn you for hiding secrets that could get you killed."

"He won't hurt me," she said in a barely understandable voice. "I know who it is and he will not hurt me."

"Who. Is. Out. There." Kevin making demands or asking questions she didn't want to answer highly irritated her. It was out of character for him to raise his voice in a woman's presence. Then again, her emotions and her feelings were completely out of sequence, too.

"I can't tell you right now. I will, but not yet. One thing I know for sure is that he's here for Dad."

"Or maybe he's only here for you." Riley replied, then released her. "Kneel," he told her.

She did it immediately.

"Count to twenty, release the bandana, and then you can look at us."

When she opened her eyes, she couldn't believe what she saw. Seated around her, Jett, Luke, Riley, and Kevin were stripped down to their birthday suits. They stroked their cocks and each Donovan looked like he had pleasure on his mind, but stress in his eyes. She took her time staring from one brother to the next and she observed each of their physical features.

She saw why Riley kept sex on the brain. With a ten or eleven inch cock, what man didn't have sex in mind every morning when he woke up? She wondered if the others felt intimidated. He looked at her with marked amusement, stout hunger and stroked harder every time she glanced back at his dick.

Kevin's dark eyes pierced through hers. He licked his chops to remind her of another special man-feature. His divine tongue offered a woman countless hours of unmatched gratification. She didn't have to guess, she saw the devilment dance in his eyes and his hand quickened when his tongue swiped out with a friendly reminder.

Jett and Luke looked like sex undressed, raw and rough, most definitely the kind of men a woman never tired of finding in her bed. The six pack abs, hard arms, and fit legs promised they were *manufactured* for sex, but their broad shoulders proved a woman had a place for her hands when she held on for the ride. These men packed the punch with tight visible balls, a long and wide shaft and good looks to match.

"This is a dream," she said before the euphoric feeling she felt earlier washed over her again.

"No, honey, this isn't a dream," Riley assured her. "This is your life now. The one you are going to live as our woman, Sydney. Do you understand?"

"Yes, I do."

She also realized why they were in a rush to dominate her now. They believed whoever waited outside was a man she completely trusted. They didn't share her sentiments on any level. They probably feared for her safety all the more and assumed whoever was out there not only watched, but waited.

If so, she thought, let him watch this.

"Are you sure you're ready?" Riley asked. "While you're here with us, right now, this is all about us. When this is over, you know what you have to do, don't you?"

She nodded. They wanted a name. Maybe by then, she'd give them one.

Jett spoke up with his first request. "Sydney, I want you to crawl over to us one at a time. You'll take one of our cocks in between your lips until you are told to stop and then you'll move on to the next one."

"You want her to what?" Luke's eyes glimmered with new hope.

"Don't worry little brother, we already know this leaves you in a vulnerable position," Riley said without hiding his amusement. "Hell, with her mouth, if she sucks cock like she kisses a man, we're all in trouble."

They were all in a lot of trouble.

Luke already understood just how much.

Sydney smacked her lips and stared at his cock. Then, she began her crawl. Luke's cock was wide and long, maybe not the largest of the lot, but the best proportioned. Just thinking about it made her damp. The more she stared at it, the more she wanted it hanging between her legs again, tempting her with a slow screw.

Sydney wanted to fuck Luke while the others watched. With the bubble of pre-cum already glistening at his tip, she wondered what they would do if she climbed on top of him and told him to fuck her, *again.*

They'd make her punishment hurt. Angry Doms with hard dicks scared her, or at least, Master Brock once frightened her. His punishment wasn't brutal but he ruled over her with a tight hold.

She crawled over to Jett and winked. "Not on your life," she said before she bypassed him and headed straight for Riley. She debated on whether or not to wrap Riley tight in between her lips. Instead, she narrowed her gaze on Kevin. He whipped his cock in between his fingers and heaven help her, she knew he wanted to come just by the way he watched her from under his eyelashes. He beat at his stick with a fast hand and her mouth watered.

"That's right, little subbie, come on over here and taste my cock," Kevin coaxed.

Oh God, was this the same Kevin who drove her to town just hours earlier? She gasped, slithering across the floor where she discovered for herself how much he needed her.

His labored breathing surprised her, but the way his hand and fingers stayed involved in an articulate pattern enticed her. She wondered if the way he threaded himself heightened his arousal or if he even realized he worked his cock in the same fashion again and again.

She focused on his eyes. She always loved Kevin's eyes. They were deeply set under natural lashes that curled to his lids.

The whole act he staged was far too erotic and it made it near impossible to remain locked in his gaze.

Sydney wanted to suck his cock first and if she lowered her head, she wasn't going to look at him while she did it. If she watched him watching her, she'd orgasm. She knew her limitations. Her Master taught her to stay in tune with her body. She already wanted to come now and no one offered to touch her.

Using his knees to steady her approach, she pushed his legs open, dropped her jaw and caught the purplish engorged tip between her lips. Now what? She stalled for time, uncertain if she should suck only the head or if they expected her to take the whole thing between her lips with all of them looking on.

Sure, she thought. *Suck it up. All good subs know how it's done. Do it right.*

She recalled an explicit movie she watched once where the man asked his lady to deep throat him. Brock liked her going all the way down on him. Didn't most men? Uncertainty lingered because she only knew one man's deepest desires. The man who kept her bound to him mentally even in his absence.

Kevin raised his legs and braced himself against his palms. "Suck it all the way, darlin'. Don't just take the tip. I want you to take the whole thing a few times. Make me come."

He stared at Jett and his brother shook his finger at him. "I thought we agreed to wait."

"Maybe you can but I can't....Oh God, that's good, Sydney, take it deep, baby," he said, before he arched his back. His hips moved forward, rolling toward her faster and faster.

She sucked his dick all the way in, as far as she could take it. His thick shaft felt smooth even with the veins bulging against his skin. He slid across her tongue and she consumed every inch. He moved with her and his strokes came in a precise rhythm as he pounded between her hollow jaws.

In a matter of seconds, she concentrated on the salty texture. It covered the head and she tasted it more when she licked around the tiny slit. She sipped it when she felt a little more leak onto her lips. Maybe sucking cock was an acquired taste. If so, she quickly decided four dicks to devour guaranteed she'd stay well fed.

Kevin moaned, but he didn't offer to touch her. She felt the heat rising between them, the sudden change in size when his shaft swelled against her cheeks.

Then, he jerked. Right before he grabbed her head, he shook all over and the tremor alone provided enough warning. Suddenly Kevin watched her with a wilder, more intense, focus. He saw her, he really saw and appreciated her as he fucked her mouth. He bumped against her throat until his balls slapped hard against her chin.

"Don't stop now, Sydney. Let me come in your mouth. I'm going deep, babe. Real deep. Ah yeah, swallow it, subbie. Swallow. Oh yeah, that's it…so good, little subbie. Ah yes, you're so sweet."

Sydney caressed his balls while she sucked him. The second she pressed against his sack with two fingers, he shot off in the back of her throat like an extra spray of his excitement remained trapped until she touched him.

He hammered into her mouth now and shouted her name as he came. Startled by his reaction, and the outpouring of verbal satisfaction, Sydney tried harder. She puckered more with each suck and she swallowed fast, making sure every drop he spilled, she drank.

When he finished, Kevin collapsed against the floor with her lips still fastened to his shaft. He stared at the ceiling. "Damn…she's got that part down pat," he said. "Holy shit," he exclaimed. His legs trembled and he wiggled against her mouth, seemingly unaware that his size diminished by the second.

Jett gave himself one tug after another and she saw him in her peripheral vision. "You've sucked him long enough, baby. Come on over here and give me what I want."

She started to stand and walk but Riley snapped his fingers and pointed to the floor. "Oh no, you don't. Crawl to Jett."

"I can't," she whined. "My knees are shaking."

Jett reached for her and brought her to him. He spread her across his lap and rubbed her rear. "Are you refusing your Masters, Sydney?"

"No, I just…I wanted you to know I'm numb from the…the experience."

Riley moved closer to Jett and Sydney. He touched her hip with his index finger. "Sydney, have you ever given a man head before?"

She stared at him blankly. The room resounded with four wallops against her bottom.

"Oh Jett, stop," she cried. Her hand instinctively lingered around her mound when he turned her to face him.

"Don't touch what belongs to me," he said slapping her pussy.

"Jett!" She moaned before he moved his hand under her cunt. Oh how she needed to come!

"You're so wet and hot, Sydney. I want nothing more than to suck on your sweet little clit. Would you like me to sip on your juices, Sydney?"

"Yes, Master, very much."

"Good. We're going to keep you wet and ready most of the time. Do you understand why?" He bit at the side of her breast and she felt a trickle of her moisture slip down the inside of her leg.

"Yes, Master," she whispered and then returned to all fours. She tried to nip at his lips and Riley smacked her a few times on her hip.

She knew she shouldn't ask, but she couldn't help herself. "Please...will one of you fuck me?"

"Baby, I've been waiting on you for over three years. I can wait a few more hours to get inside of you. Right now, there's something you need to do for me."

Luke chuckled and she turned around to look at him because his laughter was so completely perverse, it startled her. He held his cock forward. "Yeah, I have a similar need over here too, Sydney."

"Do you?" she asked with a puckered and lopsided smile. She started to slide over to him when Riley stopped her.

"Riley? I want to go to Lu...Master Luke," she corrected.

"First I want you to suck my cock and while you're giving me a blowjob, Jett is going to eat your pussy."

"Are you serious?" she asked enthusiastically. She should've just squealed out her excitement.

"Jett?" he waited for his brother's confirmation.

"I'm going to take you right to the edge, baby. Just to the cliff and then let you hang there until you're begging me to fuck you," he spoke the words of warning and it sounded familiar.

Brock, she thought. *You should be here, too.*

"Good," Riley said as he slid his cock over her lips in a clockwise fashion. "Are you ready for Jett to lick your pretty little pussy, Sydney?"

"Yes, Master Riley," she said.

Was she ready? Oh yes. Most definitely.

Riley looked at Luke, Kevin, and then Jett. "First, I gotta tell you all something," he tilted Sydney's chin, released his cock and she sucked him in on her own accord while he talked to the others. "This Master stuff is weighing on my nerves because it's...Oh God yeah...it's....holy shit....since it's Sydney and all...I..." He pressed down on her head and she ran her tongue over the crest before taking him to her throat.

"What I mean is...we can make an exception. Shit! Oh yeah baby, that's it. Suck deep, hard and deep. Don't go easy. I'm coming."

Jett fingered Sydney with one hand and pushed her head down on Riley's dick over and over again. She even saw Kevin prop up on his elbows to observe.

Riley grabbed her by the ears and held her firmly. He parted his legs and just fucked her like a man out of control. She sucked and swallowed, licked the tip and flicked his balls with a sudden tap. With two or three more light caresses, he sprayed the back of her throat with his salty spill. He backed away from her quickly and shook his head.

"Sweet damn, that was hot," he said staring at her breasts in genuine approval. "Where'd you learn how to suck cock, Sydney? That's something you practice. Where'd you get the experience?"

"Kevin," she said wiping away his juices from her chin.

Jett grabbed her legs and pulled her under him, tucking his hands under her ass. He narrowed his gaze on his brother. "When?" he asked.

"Today," she replied. "Just now."

Jett nibbled at her thighs, parting them by working his mouth up and down her legs until she had no other choice but to let her legs fall to the wayside. He blew his way straight into her pussy and licked at her clit until she tried to grasp the carpet. She only pulled tiny threads of it but it was enough to warn Jett.

He reared back and pushed her legs up. "What's wrong, baby? Do you love it or hate it."

"I need to come, Jett," she purred. She should've said she hated it.

He flipped her over on her stomach and spanked her bottom over and over again. "You don't ask me to come, Sydney." He popped his wrist and spanked her. "I'll tell you when you need to come, okay lover?"

"Yes," she said. "Anything you say."

After Jett spanked her, he gave her a sensual massage.

She trembled with gratitude. The spanking made her wet, the massage soothed away the sting. "Thank you."

"You're welcome, Sydney. I enjoy spanking you…a lot."

She reached her arms out in front of her. Riley's fingertips touched hers and he looked at her much differently than before.

"Riley, you don't want me to call you Master?" She felt a surge of relief when she asked the question. So far it was the only part she had a problem with and she had a feeling they knew why. She grew up in the heart of a religious community and she'd feel uncomfortable referring to any of them in public as her Master.

She knew enough about Doms to know many practices behind closed doors often followed the submissives and slaves into public places. She wanted to submit to them but wasn't interested in drawing attention to their private lives.

"Do you want to call me Master?" Riley asked.

Kevin studied her. "We're willing to negotiate some things and this is one of them. Luke said he thought it was silly and Riley thought he detected some resentment there when we asked you to refer to us properly."

She straightened her shoulders and looked at Kevin. "I'll refer to each of you in the way you feel is best for me and for you."

"Good answer, my sweet Sydney," Jett said appreciatively.

He disappeared in between her hips and dipped his head again, sucking her folds into his mouth. He lapped at one and then the other and then rose over her. He kissed her then and watched as she tasted her own tangy juices from his tongue.

He added his thoughts then. "I don't have a problem with dropping the Master reference but only on one condition."

"Yes?"

"In our relationship, we must have trust and open communication. We want you to understand that none of us will penetrate you until you give us your complete trust and this means we want it in all areas. Do you understand what I'm expecting, Sydney?"

She glanced at Luke and then back at the floor. What had she missed? How did they deny what was right in front of them only hours before, "Yes, I do."

"Good, then you can continue to call us by our first names only, unless we ask you to address us properly. But Sydney?" he walked over to her and held his dick out to her.

"Yes?" she said, swiping the slit and savoring the musky flavor.

"I want you to understand that we don't *dabble* in BDSM. Do you know what I'm saying?"

"Yes."

She lowered her head and nipped at his cock with her lips, careful to keep her teeth away from his flesh. She lapped at the end and then raised her eyes to meet his.

"I'll do whatever you tell me to do and I'll trust you to make the best decisions for me always. I do trust you, Jett."

Her statement gained attention from all of the Donovans and they quickly asked for clarification.

"What do you mean, you trust Jett?" Riley asked. He quickly regained a second wind and held his cock in his hand and twisted it gently, clockwise.

"I trust all of you," she sweetly admitted. "Since I was a little girl, I've trusted you." She batted her eyelashes and supped on her meaty straw, drawing out Jett's full taste.

Riley turned to question Jett. "This sort of changes plans for tonight, doesn't it?"

"Yeah, it does," Jett agreed. He ran his hand through his hair and then pointed at Luke. "You heard the lady. You have her trust. Now, you get to decide what to do with it."

With a crooked smile, Jett patted her on the head and then brushed her cheek with his left hand. His thick fingers moved across her bone structure and everywhere he touched her, his caress lingered until he stroked the next stretch of flesh.

Bending down in front of her, he pressed his palm against her belly. "I want you to lay down, Sydney."

His body covered hers and for a few seconds, she thought he planned on taking things as far as she wanted him to go. Instead, he slid up her body and stopped himself at her chest. His knees locked under her armpits. Holding his cock to her lips with one hand, he reached behind his back and patted her mound with the other.

"I want you to suck me until I pat your pussy. When I slap it, stop. Give me a few seconds and then start again."

She didn't respond with words. Instead, she took him all the way to the back of her throat and he pinched her nipples and manipulated them until they felt like hard little pebbles.

After a few minutes of torture and pain, she moaned against his cock. She thought she might die if someone didn't relieve her of the wanting, of the pleasure waiting to find her and yet she didn't know how to ask for it with such a heavy cock driving past her tongue.

He slapped her pussy all at once and she released him. He pulled out and waited a few seconds watching her for a reaction, perhaps hoping to find one. She had one. Oh God, did she have one.

Before she let him leave her altogether, she grabbed his ass and jerked him against her mouth again. He pumped his cock into her throat all at once and groaned as his cum filled her mouth with the heat found in a hard man's release. Oh, how she'd craved this experience, this very second of knowing.

"Damn it to hell!" He moved into her hard and quick. "Oh God, Sydney. Don't stop sucking. Take my cock, baby. That's it, suck harder, ah yeah. Good God, that's sweet."

She sipped from his tip and held him against the roof of her mouth for as long as wanted to stay there. When he withdrew, he quickly yanked her hard against his chest, unable to catch his breath.

"I should punish you," he said firmly but instead of showing anger, he gave her approval. His mouth crashed against hers and he fed his hungry lips by drowning them in hers. He let down his guard and finger-fucked her right to the brink of an orgasm.

Luke jumped up quickly and demanded answers once he released her. "What did she do wrong?"

"Tell him, little submissive one. It's your place to know. Tell him where you disobeyed."

She swallowed again and again still marveling at the taste of Jett while faintly catching the tangy remains from Riley and Kevin. She cleared her throat and squeezed her legs tightly together. "He told me if he slapped my pussy, to wait. He wanted me to wait until he regained control." She looked down at her bare feet and then returned her focus to Jett, "Right?"

"Very good, Sydney, now you have to choose your punishment. Do you want to stand in a corner with a vibrator?"

Not really. She didn't want a dildo with four cocks around. Were they crazy?

"Can I stand in the corner with Luke, instead?" She asked biting back a smile.

He brushed her cheek with a simple kiss. "I like the idea of standing anywhere with you."

"Luke," Riley muttered in warning.

"Punishment, think punishment Sydney, okay? You went against what I told you. I should've pulled out and maintained in control but—"

"Don't blame her because you got excited." Luke said pointedly.

When he mashed her nude form against his, the tip of his cock lingered at her opening. "All I have to do is hold you up a little bit, bend my knees, and I'll sink right into that tight little snatch," he said with a tempting smile. "Let me fuck you, Sydney," he mumbled against her ear. "Right now," he said before whispering, "Again."

She bit her lip. A cry formed at the back of her throat. Did she release it? Did she whimper? She hoped not. She wanted this. God help her, after what she'd shared with Luke, she wanted him now more than the first time. What was wrong with her? Did she only care about sex? Was her truest purpose in life to provide and receive pleasure?

Before she answered by responding to her lust, the doorbell rang and interrupted everything.

* * * *

"What the fuck?" Riley exclaimed.

Holding his clothes in front of him, Riley rushed to the window and Jett yanked up his pants. Luke released a jagged breath and Kevin cursed out loud.

"Mother fucker," Kevin said, stepping into his faded jeans. "It's one of her father's guys." He took off down the front stairs.

Sydney felt like slumping down against the wall and fingering herself regardless of the idiot on their porch. She knew who deserved to wear the title. Down deep, regardless of how she fought against her better judgment, she realized who they'd find there.

The only man who turned her on just to send her away was mere steps from her now. Her bodyguard, the one who made her more aware of her sexuality than any other man in the world, only to let her go home and practice what he taught with her neighbors.

Oh yeah, she knew precisely who stood on her porch and she understood why he finally decided to knock. It was cold outside and hot as hell behind her four walls.

"Who the hell is out there in this storm?" Luke asked as he dressed.

"Kevin said it looks like one of Sam's men," Riley replied before backing away from the window. "Sydney, take a peek and see if he looks familiar." He held the curtains back for her.

In a matter of seconds, she confirmed it with a gasp. "He was on the last assignment." She tried to play it off and realized instantly, it didn't work.

"Are you sure?" Jett asked narrowing his brow. "How well do you know him?"

"I know him."

"Uh-huh," Riley remarked. "Know him well do you?"

"I know him," she said again. "Get him to take off his sunglasses and you'll see. He has lime green eyes with a tint of yellow streaming across his pupils."

Jett glared at her. His upper cheek flinched with recognition and she caught it. Still, he demanded more. What he wanted to hear, he wanted to know from Sydney. "Who the hell is he, Sydney?"

"I just told you," she said calmly.

"Now, tell me what he means to you!"

"Leave her alone," Riley demanded loudly. "I told you whoever it was would come back, didn't I? I don't think it's a social call. Somebody alert Dad. I'm going down to greet our guest. Maybe he'll tell me what he wants with our Sydney."

She grabbed her robe from a nearby chair before she started for her bedroom. "I'll get dressed and meet you downstairs."

This should be interesting.

No, this was going to be pure hell.

Chapter Eleven

Jett was waiting for her in the hallway. She'd rather face a firing squad than deal with what waited downstairs.

"Jett," she mumbled as she walked passed him, "I'll see what he wants."

"I know what he wants," he said sharply. "Kevin and Riley are talking to him now. I want to find out what he is to you."

Her gut roared with sharp pains all at one time. *What is he to me?* At one time, he was her everything, her only reason for getting up in the morning, or maybe even drawing air. Master Brock was her purpose.

"I spent some time with him on the last assignment. He's going to take one look at me and know someone here has me pretty worked up. It may not go over well."

"Is that a warning?" Jett growled before he slammed her against the wall forming a human enclosure and shielding her with his large body.

"If you weren't intimate with him, how would he know?" Jett inquired.

She swallowed hard and fought back tears. *Why now, Brock? Why now!* "I...I never had sex with him but he...he just observed me and he went everywhere with me for nearly a year."

"Uh-huh, I see. So what's the guy's name?" Jett asked gripping her shoulders.

"Everyone calls him Brock. I think it's his last name."

Jett released her. "Brock?"

He looked like he took a punch to the gut.

"Yes," she said rubbing her arms. "He was assigned to my detail."

"One assignment?" Jett's face tensed. "Answer me, Sydney! One detail?"

"Yes." Damn it to hell. "No, no…no. I'm sorry, Jett. I don't want to talk about it. There were several assignments. I'm not sure how many. He's trusted, uh…one of the higher ups, I think. He's in charge of the assignments now when I'm sent out of town and he's thorough."

Was he ever, with one exception… where a woman needs a man to follow through most.

"I'll bet he is," Jett growled.

"He's one of Dad's men," she informed.

Luke shook his head when he joined them. "No, he's not one of *your dad's men*," he told her. "He's one of *ours*."

"No, I'm telling you. He's been assigned to my relocation and guarded me before. He works for Dad and Dad probably called him in at the last minute."

"Why?" Luke asked. "Why would he? Think about it. He trusts us too, Sydney. Our dad is on leave. He's right next door."

Jett took a deep breath. "We didn't move fast enough for Daddy Kane, so he sent in reinforcements to let us know he was still in charge of all situations." He started to walk away and then changed his mind. "And for the record, this is the kind of stunt your father and mine are known for, Sydney."

"This isn't a stunt, Jett," she said confidently. "Dad sent him, why else would he come out here in this weather?"

"Huh," Jett deadpanned. "That's what I'm wondering, Sydney and I'm pretty sure you can figure it out. If not, I have a funny feeling Brock will tell us everything we want to know."

* * * *

Kevin opened the door wide and kept an open palm on his lower back right next to his gun. He focused on the man in front of him, but his eyes didn't stop moving around the yard. If someone else was out there, he wanted to see them before any shots were fired.

"Can I help you?"

Riley was behind him with a pistol lowered to his side out of the visitor's view.

"Sure," he said in a slow drawl. He turned around and studied Kevin before he acknowledged Riley with a tilt of his head. "Mighty cold out here. Do you fellows always run around without a shirt in the dead of winter?"

Kevin started to say something.

Riley beat him to it.

"What can we help you with?" Riley asked. This time he stepped away from the door enough to let their visitor see his weapon.

Amused, he glanced down and then said, "I'm here to see Sydney."

"Sydney is busy," Riley snapped. "*Real*, busy."

"She is?" he asked in a deep baritone voice before adding a chuckle. "I imagine you're right. I bet little Sydney has her hands full here."

"Yes, she does," Riley said defensively. "Can I relay a message to her?"

Kevin studied the man in front of them. Something was strangely familiar about him. He didn't like the fact that he couldn't spot a vehicle anywhere. Then again, the guy may have walked in from the gates. He might have the access codes if he worked for Sam, but why the hell would he bother in this weather?

"Are you from around here?" Kevin asked before the guy had the time to answer Riley.

"Yeah, I am. Just tell her Brock stopped by. She knows me and she knows I'll be around."

"Brock, you gotta a last name?" Riley stuck his hand out in an attempt to shake it and knowing Riley, tug him inside and start a good ole southern brawl.

"Yeah, I do." He said when he reached for Riley's hand, took it and shook it. "It's Brock Donovan," he let the dark glasses fall to the bridge of his nose. "I'm your brother," he nodded at Sydney as she nearly tumbled down the stairs when she heard the news. "And she's my girl."

* * * *

Sydney paced across her bedroom floor. Back and forth she marched from one wall to the next. Brock was Brock Donovan, once called Marcus, named after his father.

Great. Super. Disastrous. Hell.

Why didn't her father tell her the Donovan four was the Donovan five and why didn't the other Donovans ever mention their older brother? Oh, this was bad. She fell on the bed and looked at the ceiling. She kicked her legs out and had a good unladylike temper tantrum, but she didn't feel any better.

What the hell was her father doing sending her on road trips with a Donovan? Why didn't he tell her before this turned into the royal mess it became in less than the time it took for Luke to get off from his first fuck?

"Damn. Damn. Damn."

A knock on her bedroom door only fueled her anger. When she saw him, her knees buckled under her and she didn't even say hello to him. She just turned her back and flew up the stairs. The only thing she heard was Jett's voice behind her. He told him that he knew from the moment Sydney said his name, who he'd find at the bottom of the steps.

"Why the hell now?" she screamed out at the empty room.

After the sleepless nights, the wet dreams, the decision to move on and the urges to turn back, Brock Donovan almost ruined her. He took away her fight and her desire to have any other man.

Right. He did that, huh? No, he took away her desire to have anyone else except those like him...them...the Donovans.

"I hate men!" she screamed aloud.

"The hell you do," Jett said when he picked the lock and made his way right on into her room.

"What do you want, Jett?"

"I want you to kneel," he said, approaching the bed. He tapped a crop at his side and waited for her to follow his request.

"I'm not in the mood," she told him wringing her hands in the process.

"Right now, Sydney, I don't give a shit about your frame of mind. On your knees, baby. You were warned when we started this. We're for real and we don't play games. I want your respect and I expect it now."

She glanced up at him and noticed how firm his expressions were, how stiff his high cheeks looked right then. His moist eyes were darker, colder, much more intense than she'd ever remembered seeing them.

"Jett, can we talk about this?" she asked before she squirmed to the other side of the bed and hopped up. By the time she made her way to the end of the mattress, he was there, waiting and wanting.

He grabbed her around the waist and stared at her lips. He yanked her to him, her chest pressed against his and he shook his head to the left and then the right like he tried to battle some sort of inner debate.

"Damn it, Sydney! Why didn't you tell us?"

"I ...I...didn't know..." she stuttered. "He doesn't really look like the rest of you."

The hell he didn't. Now that she thought more about it. He acted like them and he resembled Riley and Jett. Then there was his loaded attitude. Oh yeah, he was most definitely one of them.

"You knew. You had to know. Your father would've told you."

"He didn't and Brock never told me—"

Jett's lips crashed against hers. He kissed her like he'd waited for the right time to kiss her like a man kisses a woman he only wants to love. He caressed her cheek with one hand while he kept her hair pulled tight against her head with the other.

Her mind shut down. Every nerve ending in her body reminded her of how much she wanted Jett that hot summer night. She pressed her lower half against him and nudged his cock with her center.

The kiss turned hotter. He held her cheeks with both hands and dragged his teeth along her teeth nipping at her lower lip.

He sucked her tongue and brought about one sigh after another, a need so profoundly obvious that it scared her. She reached for his zipper and then froze when a loud thud rammed against the door. She gulped and immediately stopped.

He tried to catch her, most likely prepared for her next move. She flew across the room, ran into the bathroom and slammed the door.

* * * *

"Why you arrogant ass," Jett shouted, realizing as he opened the door which brother stood on the other side.

"I want to talk to Sydney," Brock said. "Alone."

"It's not a good time. In fact, your timing has been a little off all day, man," Jett said defiantly.

"Listen, I can understand your anger. I can even relate to the way you want to keep me away from Sydney, but it's not going to happen."

He walked across the room. "Sydney, get out here now and assume your presenting position!"

Jett was angry as all hell. "Who do you think you are?"

Brock paced the floor. "She's still mine, Jett. I don't care if you used her as your submissive, but little brother she already has a

Master, a man who cares deeply for her and one who will not, under any circumstance, give her up."

"You care for her?" Riley asked from the doorway. "That's real interesting, Brock. Why don't you tell us where you've been for the last ten years then, huh? See, I don't buy the fact that you have feelings for Sydney when you weren't able to care enough about your brothers to stay in touch."

"The last ten years?" he began with stark sarcasm. "Let's see, for the most part, I've been assigned to Sydney," he admitted before shooting Luke a peculiar look with a lot of meaning behind it.

"You knew about him?" Jett asked his youngest brother.

"Hell no," Luke said before he locked eyes with Brock.

"Oh no," Brock chuckled. "But he sure benefited from what I've taught her, haven't you baby boy?"

Luke narrowed his eyes on Brock. "What the fuck are you talking about?"

"I saw you two in the garage. I watched the whole thing, listened too. I'd say she gave you one hell of a first ride."

Riley set his jaw. Kevin threw his arm back and made the first move stopping Luke from leaping through the door.

"That's not your wisest move," Brock said with thick arrogance. It must've worsened with the years, Jett decided.

He took a few steps and sat down in the rocking chair. "Sydney, I'm not going anywhere, doll. You might as well come on out here."

"If she's so interested in her Master, then why the hell is she hiding in the bathroom?" Kevin asked before looking at Luke. "So you fucked her?"

"Damn straight he did," Brock supplied the answer before he glared at Jett. "And she looked like she wanted even more than he gave her. Damn, we all missed out."

Riley ran his hand through his hair. "Did it ever occur to you to call us? I mean, since you came here I'm assuming, you knew how to find us. We've been here since you left, since birth you know. What the fuck is that, man? Dad lost mom and then turned around and lost you—"

"Shit, Riley, are you that dumb?" Jett asked. "Dad knew, didn't he Brock?"

"Count your blessings," Brock answered, throwing out familiar words. "Not the trips you missed."

"Dad knew," Kevin stated flatly.

Brock grinned. "Of course he knew. After all, we're all walking in Dad's heavy footsteps." He pursed his lips and then looked over at the door. "Sydney! Get your sweet ass out here!"

Kevin glared at him. "You're unbelievable."

"How long have you been with Sydney?" Jett inquired.

"Long enough," he responded.

"Care to put a timeframe on it?" Riley asked. He moved inside the door, folded his arms over his chest, and kept his back against the wall.

"What you want to know, Riley is how often I've fucked her, when it all started, and as many details as I'm willing to give, right?"

"I don't care about that," he said.

Brock chuckled. "Like hell you don't."

"We don't," Kevin said. "Because I don't think you fucked her."

"I know he didn't," Luke said. "I was her first."

Brock acted amused. "And what makes you the expert, virgin dick?"

He set his jaw and Kevin gave him a look of warning. Riley and Jett added one, too.

Dismissing his anger, Luke said, "I don't think she lied to me."

Thank God, he let it go.

Jett didn't want to stand between Luke and Brock. Luke always had a concealed temper and Brock never took a punch without returning a few, unless he'd changed a lot in ten years. Jett didn't think they were that lucky.

"Why wouldn't she, Luke?" Brock inquired. "She's not been exactly honest with you fellows from what I can tell."

"How the hell would you know?" Jett asked.

At the same time, Brock withdrew a tiny device from his pocket. He pressed play and they immediately heard several intimate exchanges between Luke and Sydney. "Wait, that's the wrong channel. Here's the one I want." He looked down at the device, hit a button and smiled. "You'll like this selection."

They want to punch where it hurts the most and if there are pictures of her day to day life, I shudder to think of the others out there. Those are the pictures that could break a father and destroy a man.

Riley's private conversation with his brothers blared through the handheld equipment.

"What the hell does that prove?" Riley asked restlessly.

"That she lied to you. I have pictures and she let me take them. You can ask her. She'll tell you. I sent you the photographs."

"Why did you send those if you knew you were coming back here?" Riley asked.

"I'm an unusual species. I wanted you to see the Sydney I know."

"You're twisted is what you are, Brock," Jett said. "He sent them so we would think exactly what we thought—that she had a Dom on the inside."

"If you wanted to share," Riley said recklessly, "why not send the nudes?"

"Because he didn't have them. She wouldn't dare. She'd dread the day something like that would show up on Sam Kane's desk," Jett said.

"Not if she trusted her Master and she does."

"We're back to this, I see?" Jett asked.

Luke rubbed his jaw. "I don't believe it either, but I don't care if you have pictures. As far as her virginity goes, your loss buddy, what can I say?"

After an uncomfortable silence, Luke cleared his throat and then said, "I may have waited a while for sex, but I waited for Sydney and evidently, she waited for me. That's gotta be tough for you to swallow. Big bad Dom, like yourself."

Luke was pushing. Jett studied Brock's face and saw a flash of anger and a splash of hurt, lingering in his eyes. Luke might get that left hook if he kept it up.

"So I guess pampered penis here thinks she's the one, do you Luke?" Brock asked. "She saved herself just for you, huh?"

He gritted his teeth again. This time, he took a step in the wrong direction with clenched fists.

"Don't Luke, he's not worth it," Riley warned.

"I have a lot of reasons for believing she was a virgin," he said quietly.

"Like what?"

"Don't answer him," Riley said, staring at the bathroom door. Sydney was hiding and it was Brock's fault. If he could take him, he'd lay his sorry ass out. Then, he might let Luke have at him.

Kevin moved forward. "You've trained her, but you must have some kind of weird fetish or something."

"Fetish?" Brock asked. "Not the right word here. Control works better."

"Something," Kevin said, shaking his head. "Why the hell wouldn't you fuck her? Big guy like yourself afraid of falling for her or what"

"Trust," Jett said. "She never trusted you, did she?"

Brock refused him an answer. Instead, he started rambling about her training. "Let me tell you what I know about her and then you can decide for yourself if she trusts me or not."

Jett couldn't wait to hear this. He knew enough about Brock to know the reason behind it. The way Sydney reacted when she saw him told enough. She loved him. No doubt about it.

She had feelings for him, but for some reason, Brock didn't believe he had her complete trust. Without it, he wouldn't take advantage of her. She was Sam Kane's daughter and Brock still remembered her like Jett and the rest of them did on occasion, as their neighbor girl with pigtails and big eyes. How did anyone abuse the power of trust from a woman who instilled it in someone so willingly and did so blindly? She didn't know who Brock really was and for once he did the decent thing. He left her alone where it counted most.

And if he didn't, God help him.

Brock locked eyes with Riley. He must've assumed Riley would have the most interest in a training report. He probably guessed about right by the way Riley immediately changed his stance and paid closer attention.

"Sydney is trained and controlled more than any other submissive any of you have tried to pull into the lifestyle—and don't ask me how I know—I know.

"She craves it. She wants it so much that she doesn't know how to live without it. She fears her limitations in some sexual situations, but accepts that she will forfeit control whenever she's with me.

"Sydney fears failure, and on occasion she has a hard time with punishment, especially canes and whippings with a crop. She does have a high pain threshold and will push herself if she's with the right Dom, me, and she is very sensitive to her G-spot. She orgasms easily and damn it all, she loves sucking cock and that's why I was able to resist fucking her. I kept my dick in her mouth and she loved what I gave her in return."

He wiggled his tongue in a perverse move, but Jett didn't buy it. Brock didn't tongue-fuck her. Why would he bother if he knew he wasn't going to get his dick inside of her? It didn't make sense. He was far too selfish, wasn't he? Besides, no man on earth had that much control.

"She's hands on, too. If she's giving head, she wants to touch, feel, caress." With his legs splayed open, Jett saw Brock's chosen words quickly provided him with too much excitement.

"Did you come here to protect her, watch her with us, or because you've finally decided to screw her?" Riley asked, leaving nothing for speculation when he did.

"All of the above," he said, skimming over the answer by continuing with his odd report of her apparent training. "Sydney is tight, I'm assuming you agree since you've fucked her, Luke," he hesitated and the amusement danced again, his eyes flicking with satisfaction. "She likes to be hand-spanked and keeps her pussy shaved. She enjoys having it slapped, by the way."

"You're one piece of work," Luke said, leaping for him. This time, Jett stopped him.

"Don't you see?" Luke asked, grabbing for his collar. "He's here to control her."

"Damn straight, rookie prick. I do control her."

He swallowed hard. Jett saw his Adam's apple move over and over again. "Why now?"

"Because I love her," he said. "Do any of you?"

The room fell quiet. After awhile, it hummed with the stillness. Brock had clenched his fist on his knees when he asked the question. Jett noticed how cold his eyes were all at one time. This was a trick question, the kind Brock generally pulled out of thin air right before he knocked the last breath out of someone when the answer he wanted wasn't supplied.

Then again, maybe he'd changed, he reminded himself once more. A lot of time passed. He really didn't know his brother at all.

Jett felt his eye twitch.

"There's one love-sick pup," he said gaping at Jett and then glancing over at Kevin when he moved for the door. "And another," he added before turning to Luke. "You got inside of her tight little snatch first, I imagine you feel something."

"Fuck you, man."

"Yep, there's three. How about you Riley, do you love her?"

"I don't know, Brock. I haven't had time to discuss it with her."

He laughed. "And I just bet you'd do that if you had the chance right now, huh?"

Riley stared at his brother. "Cut the bullshit. What do you want? Are you here to toy with her or what?"

"That's what I thought, Riley. Yep, we gotta a full house here. You're all crazy about her."

"What. Do. You. Want." Riley repeated himself.

"I want what you four already thought you had."

"He's here for Sydney and the selfish bastard won't share," Jett informed the others, they might as well prepare for it.

"Ah," he moaned, scratching his chin. "Still upset over the dirt bike thing from, what was it, fifteen years ago?"

Before Jett revisited the past and Brock's notorious selfish ways, everyone moved closer and Kevin spoke up. Jett saw his eyes mist over and knew his brother wanted answers only because he wanted to make excuses for him. Kevin was a family man and he loved his brothers.

"How did you do it?" Kevin inquired. "I mean how does a man walk away from his family and just disappear?"

"You ought to know. Dad tells me all four of you have gone through the training. That's part of the reason you want Sydney, isn't it? You want a woman you can share, so she's not left alone in your absence or left unprotected in your death? Someone who is content with what she has, enjoys the ranch, will worship the ground you walk on and leave the second you tell her to disappear. You want the trained, the accustomed and Sam Kane's daughter is both, not to mention sexy, beautiful, and willing to submit."

Jett stared at the bathroom door.

"Oh, I get it," Brock said. "She didn't know you were going to lead the same life her daddy chose. I bet the five of you are harboring all sorts of secrets, aren't you?"

"Damn you, Brock. You decide to come on back in here and stir up all sorts of problems. Is she that important to you?"

"Yeah, Riley she is," he replied, moving his hand over his cock. "Damn straight, she is."

"Then why haven't you made her yours then?" Luke blurted out, still curious about the sex, no doubt.

Hell, Jett wanted to know about the sex, too, since his little brother really did fuck her, when he should've been punishing her.

"I didn't claim her…yet," Brock reminded. "There's more to love than screwing and there's more between us than sexual relations, I promise you."

"Mind control?" Riley suggested because he'd thought it since the beginning.

"Mental bondage, mind control, how about just plain old love? She's bound to obey me whenever she's around me. You'll see. She made the decision a long time before any of you made a play for her, even you Jett."

"So, you want to stick around now?" Jett asked. He didn't want to share her with someone who had such a history with Sydney, but he didn't think he'd have a choice.

"I'm going to stick around now," he said on a promise. "It's time to settle down. Maybe even start a family soon."

"Uh-huh, I'm sure Sydney will love the idea of little ones," Riley said.

"She does what I tell her to do," Brock assured them.

"Oh really?" Kevin laughed out loud. "I see how well she minds you. In fact, it looks like we've all lost control now, no thanks to you."

"Don't worry about me. I can quickly reestablish trust with her, it won't take long. She knows she can trust me." Brock's confidence was supreme. It wasn't an act. He thought Sydney belonged to him.

Riley paced back and forth. "So this whole time, you've been on various jobs then, right?"

Jett narrowed his eyes on Riley. He knew what to expect from Riley and Kevin. Brock had been their hero. At one time, he'd been his too, but after their mother died, he ran and he couldn't forgive him that easy. Could he?

"I've lived as I was trained to live. I served my country and those serving it to the best of my ability. You'd do the same in my shoes so don't expect me to apologize. The Underground Unit will pull you in and then spit you out when they're done with you. I know what I'm talking about. I've been on deadly assignments and fought my way out all alone. Even Dad and Sam couldn't help me."

Jett felt his lips curl and he fought back the bile in his throat. Any Donovan fighting like he'd fought on his last mission made him sick to his stomach. Jett knew all about those operations. They were the trips where no one made it out alive and those who did only survived to come home to a hefty lump of cash and often a shorter lifespan with a new death threat looming.

Riley could relate, too. He pissed off all the women and their drug lord husbands on most missions. He made a sport out of fucking the women who had husbands who deserved infidelity. The last trip cost him. He might look over his shoulder for the rest of his life, or at least until his enemies in Caracas were taken care of properly.

"You're right, I would've done the same thing," Riley admitted before he offered his brother his hand.

Brock stood, took it, brought him in for a tight embrace and was too easily welcomed right back into the family by Riley and then Kevin. Luke didn't rush right into his arms for a big brotherly hug. Instead, he crossed his limbs and demanded answers.

"So where does that leave us with Sydney?"

"You'll have to ask her pretty boy," Brock said in amusement.

"The hell we will," Jett said defiantly.

"Dad told me you were the worst. He was right. You have it bad for her, huh?" he asked over his back before he made his way to the bathroom door.

"Shit, I don't have the patience for this," he said, pulling out a thin wire from a slick silver compact case. He slid it down the side and gave it a hard tug. The door popped right open and he grabbed her around the wrist.

"Hey baby," he said with a thick drawl and a wide grin.

"Brock," she barely greeted him.

"I've missed you," his tone suddenly changed. He lowered his lips to hers and waited for her to kiss him. She did. She did it in a way that told a thousand tales in just one simple story.

Her hands locked at his neck and her tears came in droves as she kissed him like it would kill her if she didn't. He immediately gripped her hips and thrust against her. He growled into their kiss and licked at her like he knew what he was doing.

"Now, Brock," she whispered, nipping at his lips one more time before she backed away from him. "Why don't you go find a nice dark corner somewhere and fuck yourself?" Sarcasm oozed through every syllable and she swiped hard and fast at the tears still drifting down her face.

Jett and Riley exchange glances and they all resisted the urge to smile, proud of the way she stood up for herself. Brock looked surprised and far from amused.

"Don't look at one another like your shocked," she said waving her finger at Jett and Riley. "You both thought I had someone else and you were right."

She threw her head back and tried to resist more tears before she choked out a small confession. "I can only imagine your surprise. Yes, your brother trained me as his slave, not his submissive—in case he forgot to mention it—isn't that right Brock?"

His lips twitched and he shoved his sunglasses high on his nose.

"The sun isn't shining in here, Brock," she said watching him as he unhooked his belt.

"Sydney," he took a few steps closer. "I want you to kneel, right now."

"You don't own me!" she shouted. "You never owned me!" Her outburst was expected, then again the anger wasn't. Sydney typically didn't act out this much. Jett knew why in an instant. Brock had the ability to hurt her, to rip her heart in half and apparently he succeeded.

To his surprise, Brock relinquished his control. "The hell I didn't! I own every piece of you from the inside out. Now, on your knees!"

"Screw you, Brock," she spat her words and then stormed out of the room. Then, she turned back around and landed straight into Luke's waiting arms. He immediately cradled her against his body.

"Please, get me out of here," she cried.

"I wish I could," he told her. "But this time, I don't think I can."

Chapter Twelve

"What the fuck are you talking about?"

The voice on the other end of the phone made Zaxby wince. He felt the hairs stand up on the back of his neck when he heard the shouting in the background. Evidently, Zaxby wasn't the only one worried.

"Brock is a Donovan?" the boss asked again for confirmation. "How do you know?"

The question asked was one he answered with regret.

"I just saw him at the Kane place and I've been watching a lot of history unfold. Brock is not who you originally thought. He's Mark Donovan's oldest son."

Zaxby paced the sawdust floor and peered through the cracks at the snow whipping around outside.

"Then this complicates things."

"Yes it does," Zaxby said.

"Are you afraid of him?"

Hell yes. "No," he lied to the boss. "It's just something you needed to know. Let me hear from you in a few hours. Make a decision and I'll honor it."

He shut the phone and lit a cigarette. God help them all if they'd underestimated the Donovans. If Brock was one of them and Jett and Brock were brothers, they'd overlooked a few facts. Kevin, Riley, and Luke were as deadly as their brothers.

Zaxby wanted out and he wanted out now.

* * * *

"This isn't what I had in mind!" she shouted at the top of her lungs as the machine moved over her. The revolving dildos would soon penetrate her one at a time but first, the Donovans would force her to listen and that might be tough since the excitement already fueled her body. Oh God, why did she have to stay ready for sex? Why did she ever agree to this when Luke told her to trust him?

"You knew about Brock," she accused Kevin, Riley, Jett, and Luke as they watched.

"Are you going to use your safe word?" Brock asked from a corner somewhere. She couldn't see him. She stretched her neck and rolled her head from side to side and couldn't find him.

She wanted to use the word, their word... ice cream. Only, she didn't want to use it right now. Even as she lay bound to the thick padding, the rotating device called to her. She wanted to feel it move over her, watch as the toys lowered and then played with her. Oh, but what she would do right now for some nipple clamps.

Since she'd spotted the equipment in her garage, she'd wanted to use it. Brock kept her tied and bound to a lot of gadgets and toys, sex equipment like this one kept her aroused for days, even after she enjoyed them. She gasped as he stepped out of the darkness. He looked at her hard, the lust bulging in his veins, the evidence thick in his pants. Had he ever desired her as much as he did now?

"Ice cream," she muttered.

She mumbled the word because she wasn't sure she wanted to use it but at the same time, regardless of the machine, the toys, the arousal waiting for her, she wanted to know if he came back for her. Would Brock Donovan finally claim her or did he only want to play more games?

"They didn't know about me, Sydney," he told her, acting as if he never heard the safe word and maybe he didn't. The buzz of the machine was loud, piercing enough to make all of them shout as they spoke.

"No one could know, Sydney. I worked for your father on a team that doesn't even exist. We are trained for silence. They couldn't know."

"You could've told me!" she screamed. "I told you all about them! Everything I ever felt for your brothers, I've told you and you acted like you didn't even know them! You had me describe the way I'd....oh God, I can't even think about it now! Just get out! Go back to the hell you've created with your father and mine. Leave me out of it."

If he left then, she'd die there.

"I can't do that, sweet slave and you know it. I've tried," he said as he caressed her mound.

His touch set her on fire. Her heart raced, pound after pound, it thumped harder and harder against her chest.

"Don't," she warned.

She remembered how aroused he kept her. She loathed the way he turned her on and then left her reaching for him, aching for him, believing he only kept her hot and ready for her own good. It wasn't for her own good. It was for his.

"I don't play your games anymore," she said before he twisted his fingers into her vagina.

Oh, but she would, she was already dripping with excitement. He was her love drug, the most potent narcotic known to womankind.

"Riley! Jett! Please do something," she begged and then swallowed again and again. *More. Please, God, don't leave me wanting for you this time.*

"This isn't a game, Sydney," he said, slamming the machine to off-position. "I sat outside there," he pointed to the small window and then watched her for a reaction. She realized what a true view he had of her romp with Luke. He added more after a short pause. "And I saw how you responded for my brother. Do you have any idea how hungry I am, Sydney?"

He pushed the machine back and leaned over her. "Do you want me and my brothers or just me?"

A wicked grin formed on her mouth and she didn't fight it. "What if I just want your brothers?"

"I know better, slave," he replied, hurt lingering in his eyes.

He slapped the red button. She spun around and around until the largest dildo slid into place. She squealed with the first penetration. The rubber cock impaled her pussy with a deep thrust and she called out his name as she came, defiant in her refusal to wait for permission. Her thighs crushed together and her arms jerked as she made a show out of her climax.

"Damn," Riley said, rubbing his jaw and studying Luke. "Did she give you anything like that?"

"Shut up and watch," he growled.

She turned her head from side to side and locked eyes with Jett. His hand fell to his belt and he reached under the material. She saw his stance change. He moved his hand in and out of his pants, his body slowly moved with each tug.

The machine jerked and the wand left her. Another dildo moved toward her. She wanted men, not mechanical dongs.

"Ice cream!" She shouted out her safe word. This time she meant it. Her nipples throbbed, her pussy ached. She wanted, no she needed, a man's dick, not a toy, not a machine, a real live man to satisfy her longing. She needed Brock, but she wanted all of them.

"Fuck!" he exclaimed, his hunger apparent when he hit the controls and stopped her punishment, and her pleasure.

"It's her safe word, no doubt." Riley said with a lot of satisfaction. He started to loosen the binds around her hands and Kevin released her ankles.

Riley addressed Brock, "This has gone far enough."

Riley lifted her from the black pad and she hooked her arms around his shoulders. "Jett, get the bag over there in the corner. I put it next to the door."

He handed her over to Kevin. "Take her upstairs. We'll be right there."

Kissing her hard on the mouth, Riley caressed her head. "And for today, you're no one's submissive, no one's slave, Sydney. We'll earn your trust and then we'll start at the beginning. Do you understand?"

She nodded, gratitude surged through her body. She didn't trust herself with Brock now and she didn't trust the new lust lingering in his eyes. She wanted to step out of the lifestyle for a few days, revisit her goals and her own desires before she lost herself in Brock Donovan again.

"Get her out of here," Riley snapped at Luke and Kevin. "You stay," he ordered, pointing at Jett. "We have a lot to work out between us."

* * * *

They waited until Kevin and Luke carried her away. They couldn't sever the tension no matter how hard they tried now. Jett wasn't accepting Brock and Riley had witnessed a new Sydney in Brock's presence. He resented it.

"What's wrong, Riley?" Brock asked. "You act like someone busted up your party."

"Someone did," Jett accused. "You."

"You're corrupt," Riley began. "You always have been. Even as a kid, you had perversion running through your veins."

"You don't know what you're talking about," Brock said, shaking off the insult like he never heard it.

"Oh yes I do, big brother," Riley said. "And I know Jett here probably agrees."

Jett didn't say either way.

"I saw something in Sydney just now that I've never seen before," Riley said sadly. "And I don't want to see it again...ever. Are we clear?"

"What do you think you saw exactly?" Brock asked.

"I said, are we clear?"

"Hell, Riley. I can't agree to something when I don't know what you think you saw."

"She's afraid. I fucking stared down at her and saw fear, damn you!"

"Did you see fear or lust? Do you even know her well enough to know the difference because I do! What you saw was a woman who wants so much that she is afraid of what will happen if she doesn't get what she wants from the man or men she craves. That is what you saw!"

"Bullshit," Riley said recklessly. "I think you've played too many games with her."

"I've loved her," he confessed.

"You've loved her?" Riley questioned.

"The best way I know how," he admitted.

"Well, it wasn't good enough," Jett said.

"Then you show me how you two think a man should love a woman."

"Is that a challenge of some sort?"

"No, not at all. I took care of Sydney but believe me when I tell you, I know where I let her down. I expected her to turn over her entire life to me and yet I wasn't willing to give her the same consideration in the ways I should have.

"Dad warned me when he saw me getting too close. I should've backed away. I should've talked to Sam and told him how I felt about her. Instead, I sent her home. I gave her an ultimatum and I used sex to get my way."

"You withheld it, you mean?" Riley asked.

"Yep, I did."

"You're a wannabe is what you are, Brock. You should've given her security and a sense of your acceptance. Instead, you used it against her by placing conditions on the relationship. The very thing she needed from you is what you withheld from her. Damn it all, we can't expect her to submit to us right now," Jett said, looking over at Riley.

"You're right," Brock said bitterly. "I fucked up."

The brothers stared at one another in shock. Brock admitted defeat? Maybe there was some hope for him after all.

"Well, it's not the first time a Dom hasn't gotten it right. I could tell you plenty of stories about Riley," Jett said with a wide smile.

"Save them for a few hours," Brock suggested. "I want to see Sydney first. Then you can both tell me what I've missed over the past few years. Personally, I can't wait to hear your version of what happened at the fair three years ago. From what Sydney told me, she's never wanted to fuck so bad in her life."

Jett grinned. "She told you that?"

"Oh shit," Riley groaned. "You should've kept it to yourself."

"Yeah, but now he's going to go upstairs and act like a stud for hire and since I'm sharing my girl—"

"She's not your girl anymore," Jett quickly reminded him. "She's always been *our girl.* That's not going to change just because you're home. We share in this family. We always have. Maybe not the dirt bikes and horses or the secrets of our assignments, but when it comes to the important things, we share."

"Beautifully spoken," Riley said as he slapped his brothers on the back. "Now, you two can stand here all day trying to figure out one another but I have a pretty young thing waiting on me upstairs."

"Just you, huh?" Brock asked. "I don't think so. After watching her with Luke, I'm here to tell you, she may not care where we are right now."

"They were that good together, huh?" Jett asked, digesting the information.

"Oh yeah, she's hot, boys."

They all started for the door. They had wide grins on their face and hard cocks in their pants. And yeah, Sydney had three more joining her so she might as well expect it. Something told Riley she was more than ready for them.

Jett shook his head in disbelief. "So you spied on them? You go low, man. Real low."

"Maybe, but as soon as I get out of these clothes, I'm going deep. Real deep."

Chapter Thirteen

She was in his favorite position and she wondered how he'd respond when he saw her. Maybe since so much time had lapsed, he wouldn't be able to resist her or perhaps there really was something wrong with him.

They once played games, had fun while it lasted but this was something different. She felt it in every nerve ending. This was it. He was going to give into temptation. This was real. This time, they were playing under different circumstances and it forever changed them, all of them.

"Are you comfortable, Sydney?" Luke asked, moving closer and slipped the bandana over her head.

They had hesitated earlier when she requested the binds and blindfold. She asked for them because she didn't know how to be with Brock without restraints in place.

Kevin sat next to her stroking her belly from one side to the next. "You're sure you're okay with this?" he asked with devastating lust exploding around his pupils.

"Yes," she whispered.

Slowly, his fingertips caressed her nipples. "You trust us this much after everything we've put you through?"

"You didn't put me through anything Kevin." She paused and then lifted her lips to his. Rather than kiss him, she whispered beyond them, licking her words right into his soul. "I want to tell you something, Kevin." She nipped at his lips. "Can I trust you to tell you a secret?"

"Anything. You know you can."

But of course I can, she thought. She wasn't the dumb gal next door and she realized right away that the brothers, at least initially, would look for leverage with her. A secret qualified.

"Kevin, I…can't explain it but…I crave this. Submission gets me going. When I give a man control over me, he earns the right to take it and use it to empower the experience. Does that make sense to you?"

"Remember who you're talking to little subbie," he said with a satisfying smile.

"Kevin?"

"Yeah?"

"I'm so wet right now, I could die. It's the excitement. It brings an adrenaline rush. I'm a complete wreck when it comes to this sort of thing."

He didn't speak right away and Sydney didn't expect a response. She just wanted him to understand that she longed for this kind of established connection, unbreakable bond. She thrived in a Dom-sub relationship, or at least, imagined she would. What she had with Brock hardly qualified as a healthy affair.

"I never want to hurt you, Sydney," Kevin finally whispered against her lips licking his way into a hot and sensual kiss. His palm stayed flat against her belly. "We were afraid you'd run the other way if you knew what you were getting yourself into with us."

"I'm not going anywhere," she said in a small voice. "Besides, I already put everything together. Before I heard Brock today, I already gathered you were all involved deeper in our fathers' businesses than you wanted me to know. Otherwise, Dad wouldn't have willingly accepted you anymore than any other outsider."

Kevin's mouth lingered over hers again and she stretched her neck with her mouth puckered. She could feel him smiling at her as someone stood in between her legs.

"Shit," he said and then backed away from her.

"Holy hell," Luke said.

She froze. She didn't have to ask. She felt the same way the first time she saw *it,* too.

Brock pressed his knee on the bed. She was always so in tune with him that it didn't matter if she was blindfolded or not. It didn't even matter if the vocal expression of surprise from his brothers allowed her to know he was in the room. The second he was on the mattress with her, she was centered, focused on him and his needs, even more than her own. He grounded her. He was the only foundation she needed, even now.

"We agreed to take things slow," Riley stated. "What's with the blindfold and ties?"

"She wanted them," Kevin replied excitedly.

"Of course she did," Brock added. "She's a good girl, aren't you baby?"

"Yes," she purred.

"And you always do what pleases me, don't you?" Brock asked.

"Yes, I do, Master."

"Sydney," he said. "How are you feeling right now, doll?" The raspy voice she loved from the moment she first heard it intoxicated her.

She felt dizzy with need the second he touched her calf. He was staring at her pussy. Her womb clenched in repetition, pulsing with the excitement waiting.

"I…I like it when you look at me," she whispered knowingly.

"Yes, little slave, you do but what I want to know, is how are *you?*" He slapped her mound and placed his thumb at her clit. "Right now, tell me about the sensations, your feelings."

Oh God, how could he come back into her life and instantly make her need him? How did that happen? Why did she let him have such control over her? Why not give it to one of the others? She trusted them, too.

"I'm wet, Master," she acknowledged.

She dismissed the earlier discussion she had with the Donovans about the way she should address them. She always showed Brock respect. He earned it, in spite of everything, and made it known on more than one occasion, he expected it.

"Sydney."

She tried to raise her neck off the pillow when she heard Jett's voice.

"We've discussed rebuilding your trust and we're all willing to earn it again. How does that sound?" Jett asked.

"I trust you, Jett," she admitted.

Brock ran a lone, thick finger over her pussy lips. "Do you trust me, sugar?"

"You know I..." She stopped suddenly. "I know what we are to one another," she replied. "And it will never change, Master Brock."

The room fell silent again and she felt a smooth vibration scraping over her hip. Oh sweet mercenary. It was her favorite toy. The one with the perfect shape. He remembered to bring it!

"Do you know what I have in my hand?"

"Yes," she said. She fought against her restraints.

He rubbed it over her mound and kissed her knee. At the same time, someone clamped her nipples.

"Oh...oh that's so good." Finally, the attention to detail. "I've waited for those."

Her body arched and she braced herself against the balls of her feet. Fortunately, Luke and Kevin weren't pros at binding a woman. She had a lot of leeway and if she fought against the restraints, freeing herself wouldn't present a problem.

Her body reacted without the wicked wand. Her juices poured free and his mouth was there, not the vibrator, his mouth and tongue covered her.

He licked into her space and she recognized his soft, thick tongue, and the long length of it as he stroked inside her walls. She was ready to come, she needed to come until he yanked the blindfold off and Luke loosened the cuffs freeing her at one time.

She looked into Brock's eyes and down the length of her body. The wand, her favorite toy, vibrated softly against the bed and Brock pointed at it. "We don't need this today, do we Sydney?"

Quickly, she shook her head and then stared at Kevin. His contentment obvious, he looked all starry eyed dipping his tongue into her pussy. She swallowed, stared, and watched him linger there with a long stroke from side to side. She blinked unable to believe what she felt and now saw.

No one ate her pussy like Brock. No one until Kevin!

It only took her a minute to grasp the games they wanted to play now. "Oh God, Kevin. I thought you were…oh please…don't stop."

Brock rubbed his cock over the back of her hand. "I know what you thought, doll."

He stuck his tongue out and reminded her. Oh dear, what she'd give to have him between her legs now. Even with Kevin there, licking and sipping, she still wanted Brock's tongue. She glanced around the room.

Truth. This was it, a moment of truth.

She quickly did it again. Stared in each of their faces, studied everything about them. Lost herself in the idea of them as men, as lovers, as her family.

Heaven help her.

Her hips rolled forward. Kevin sucked on her clit. "Feels good, doesn't it baby?"

He made a scissor shape with his middle and index finger and spread her pussy lips for his tongue. He dipped again, slurped as he swiped and the quality of his loving wasn't anything to hold against comparison.

Kevin pulled the excitement from her, the wet puddle of satisfaction only seconds from his dip. He held her lips wider and puckered before revisiting the same spot.

"Kevin!" She wanted to touch him. Needed to hold him in place. "Please, oh please, let me come!"

Brock pinched the clamps and they gripped her nipples tighter than before. He gave them a tug and with a quick snap, they disappeared. He didn't take his time removing them from her body but instead, he pulled them off and quickly covered one nipple with his mouth just as quickly as Luke lowered his head, too.

She looked around for Jett and Riley.

"Over here," Riley said from the dark corner of the room. She saw how hard he looked and the way he touched himself was different from the way he'd tugged at himself before, when they were all waiting for their blowjobs. This was something else. He was going to get off watching them. His hand, not hers, would pull him through the pleasure.

Kevin kissed his way down her inner thigh and rolled his tongue over her kneecap. "You thought I was Brock, huh?"

She nodded, "It's the tongue."

"I'll show you a good tongue," he promised, uncurling it inside of her pussy once more.

With her palms on either side of her body, she prepared for what he gave. Once, she tried to touch him but Brock pinned her arm to her side and prevented her from it. She only wanted to pull him closer and hold him to her, make him take her to orgasm, help him give her pleasure.

"We want to see you come, Sydney," Brock said.

"Then *you* make me come," she told him but her body was ready. She wanted more and needed it right then. She snapped her legs together and tightly held Kevin's face to her vagina. He lapped at her juices and moved his head from side to side as he devoured her taste and mumbled sweet nothings against her opening.

Jett moved to the bed. "You want him to come inside of you, Sydney?"

"Yes," she said. "Oh yes, please yes."

"Good," Jett said. "We've discussed a few things, Sydney. You will never have protected sex with us. We want to know what it feels like to fuck you without barriers. Does that bother you?"

"Oh!" Her body captured and then closed around Kevin's tongue. Please shut up about this, she thought. Let me feel. Let me come. She didn't care about condoms right now, only pleasure. "Faster, Kevin."

He swiped forward, fucked her with skill and nibbled at her clit before fingering her right into orgasm.

"More!" She gripped the covers with her balled fist and fucked his face, his lips staying on her lips. His intimate kiss worked her from one orgasm straight past the next.

She growled in pleasure, the sound leaving her lungs more animalistic than anything she'd ever heard before. More lust-filled and need driven than any woman had a right to release, even in her pleasure.

She swallowed hard and watched the Donovans. They waited for her response. Oh yes, they wanted some kind of answer. She swallowed over and over again. What was the question? She tried to focus.

Doms weren't always patient.

"Sydney," Jett began. "Did you give me an answer yet?"

Oh, that's right. He was the one who brought up the unprotected sex factor. They didn't wear condoms.

She gasped. She knew better. They were anal about protected sex. She'd heard that too at the beauty shop.

The reasons behind their aversions to it, *with her*, slammed into her chest with undeniable recognition. They each had their own mindset for not wanting to wear protection and those ideas shook her harder than Kevin's complimentary oral excursion.

Did they want to get her pregnant? She blinked away the thought. Did she want children later? Like this? With them? Her pulse raced. It was bad enough that her body still shook as Kevin retrieved, closed her legs and moved away. Now this, reality and life unfolding, with the Donovans.

Did they know she was on the pill? Sure, they did. Brock knew everything about her. He would've told them he once insisted on birth control. She objected at first, for obvious reasons—Brock didn't fuck her—but he encouraged it at the time and said she might thank him later.

"It's fine," she said watching Brock. "I'm not crazy about barriers either."

Brock appreciated her compliance. "Good girl. Thank you for minding us."

He didn't give up her secret, but he most likely understood she was still protected against pregnancy. He probably suspected whatever he ordered for her before, she followed to the letter. She always did in the past. She wanted to make him happy. When he handed down requests, she eagerly acted out on them.

Exposed there in front of them, she wasn't uncomfortable because of it. She had Brock. He was back and watching her every move. He surrounded her always, just like now. Even with the other Donovans, Brock watched her through his eyes and theirs. In her world, he existed everywhere.

"Kiss me, Sydney," Brock demanded.

Luke stopped touching her and it was only when he backed away altogether that she missed his calming caresses. She felt bad because of it but so many scrambled feelings existed now and as one rolled in another drifted away. With Riley and Jett closer, Kevin put some distance between them. His departure too, didn't go unnoticed.

"Sydney, listen to me. I want you to kiss me and don't stop kissing me until I'm buried deep inside of you," Brock mumbled against her lips.

He slapped her pussy and she yelped like she expected to cry out for more. Hot heat flooded her canal and he rotated his middle finger around her opening. "Oh sweet sugar, I waited longer than I should have."

She gulped when she realized he wasn't going to tease. He shifted his weight, looked at his youngest brother and then held her hips, bracing himself over her. "I always thought you'd wait for me. I wanted you first."

Suddenly, she saw something in him that frightened her. It hurt him because she fucked Luke first. It pained him to watch another man, even his brother, take her virginity.

A flash of guilt and a stab of pain, but nothing more than that after she sank into Luke's soft and beautiful eyes. Things happened for a reason. Luke waited for her and they deserved their time together. They were meant to share the experience, alone. Brock had countless opportunities. He didn't take them and she didn't believe in regrets.

Brock set his jaw and sank in between her thighs. His alarming expression shattered her control but as he locked his hips in place, she understood why he looked uneasy.

"That's it, Sydney. Hang on, doll." He pressed again, this time with a solid thrust.

She screamed as he crossed the point of no return. Her walls closed around him and she milked him as soon as he entered her, greedy with need, she didn't care about the pain a man his size brought. The only thing she cared about was the orgasm they'd share together, the one he should've brought her the first time he touched her.

He lowered his head and bathed her nipples with a flat tongue before he rose up, arched his back and hammered into her. "Good girl, that's my Sydney." He released one growl and a carnal grunt. "Take me all the way, doll. Fuck me hard, sugar. Take it."

He reached behind his back and fastened her calves around his waist. The tip of his tongue flattened on his upper lip and he thrust into her again, a look of pure pleasure settling in his eyes.

"I trained you for this, sweet sugar. Now fuck me nice and slow."

The pain his cock brought was so thick, the pleasure incomparable, and the orgasm surreal. She came, closed her eyes and enjoyed him stroke after stroke. The whole time, he pounded deeper.

"Oh yeah, that's it doll. I feel you. Now, scream!"

Her inhibitions shattered, her body took his and claimed ownership, too. They fucked out their need, and they had a lot of it.

His thighs bunched and he gripped the back of the bed. If she thought he went deep when he first entered her, he pressed all the way to her spine now. Good Lord, she felt him at her tailbone and she didn't just scream, she cried. And then she begged for a whole lot more.

* * * *

If Jett wanted to pick a fight, he had an axe to grind. It was obvious Brock planned to stay right where he could see Sydney at all times. He wanted hands-on involvement and he made sure he remained in control.

After he fucked her, he rolled her on her side and invited Riley to slip in behind. Riley slid his finger down her crack with a well aimed tip and gently squeezed the lube into her hole.

Brock kissed her while Riley prepared her. She found strength in his lips, and hope. She could plan for tomorrow with him now. He loved her. He made love to her because he planned to stay.

Within a few minutes, Riley penetrated her slipping deep between her cheeks and Jett moved closer to watch. He rubbernecked it enough to view from the side.

He almost came in his hand watching Riley thrust in and out, rearing back like he had some place he needed to get in a hurry. Jett understood the frustration, the pent-up desire they all needed unleashed.

Riley stroked her globes and watched the movement of his hand with deep interest. "Good girl, Sydney. Relax, sweets."

The fucking stretched her to where it was easy to see her hole flare in acceptance, the expanded ring ready for anything.

"That's it," Jett said threading his erection while he watched. "Let him have you, Sydney."

Luke's eyes misted over with more lust than a man should have to suffer through but somehow they all managed. All of them, except Brock and Jett understood what he must be going through—hell—but couldn't care less.

He knew about that hell because he realized long before now, he loved Sydney, too. If his brothers moved aside long enough, he planned to marry her.

Then again, he wasn't stupid. Brock wasn't going anywhere and Luke, poor guy, might fuck her daily after having sex for the first time.

"Riley," her broken voice cracked. "Slower?" she whined. The second she whimpered her request, he withdrew.

"Sydney?" Brock brushed the fallen locks away from her brow. "I want you to do this for us, okay?"

She glanced at Jett and he nodded. He would've preferred to tell Riley and Brock to move the hell over. Instead, he granted the permission she sought.

With a wild buck of hips, she pressed her bottom against Riley's shaft and he turned up the heat by thrusting between her cheeks. Brock fisted his cock and moved his tip back and forth over her slit.

Damn him, Jett thought. He was going to fuck her again. The second Riley's eyes dropped and his pace changed, Brock gritted his teeth, and slid beyond her folds.

In a matter of minutes, he pounded the hell out of her pussy. "Good Sydney. Ah yes, so sweet and tight."

Riley screamed out and slapped her bottom. "Don't leave us, Sydney. Work those hips this way, doll."

"Holy shit," Kevin said from across the room. "Luke, look at that."

"I'm looking," Luke muttered.

Sure he was. Dying was more appropriate.

Jett wiped his chin just to make sure he wasn't drooling. The whole act, how she moved back and forth with both of them tore at his gut. He yearned for his turn.

Riley fell against her back and Brock locked his mouth over her breast. Sweat beads poured from his brow.

"Damn it!" he exclaimed finding his release. He cursed like a man who lost his load long before he wanted to lose it since it was his second rodeo of the day.

And then it was Jett's turn. He expected to share, too.

"Jett?" she said his name in a sultry voice. "I've waited a long time.

His heart skipped a beat. "Are you okay?"

"Perfect," she purred.

"Good," he said, her words warming his heart. He lightly brushed her lips with his and then followed her eyes.

Brock took a second to clean up but he reappeared before she could miss him and Jett feared his thoughts were true. She noticed when Brock vacated the room and sure enough, the little vixen searched everywhere for him until he reappeared.

Brock's air of confidence proved he knew who owned her. He didn't have to worry about sharing her with his brothers because if he told Sydney she didn't submit to them, she wouldn't. Jett saw it then and there. It was black and white, no faded areas to consider, none to be had. His brother, the one who left them years ago to guard Sydney more than anything else, had her devotion and earned her love.

"Are you ready for me?" Jett asked quietly.

"Always," she assured him before glancing at Luke. "And you too, Luke."

"You want us both?"

Brock narrowed his eyes on them and then pointed at Luke. "Be easy with her pretty boy. Riley doesn't know the words slow and gentle."

Riley chuckled, but before he disappeared into the bathroom, he said, "Her sweet bottom isn't one any of us will stamp and go, you'll see Luke. You'll know what it is to find pleasure there."

Jett pulled her over him and Luke took her ass as a gift. He slid in the second Jett moved inside of her.

"Oh God, you're slick, baby," Jett muttered against her mouth before he kissed her. Her tongue empowered him and he pressed his lips hard against hers before he started the long strokes inside her sweet channel.

Brock waited until their kiss broke and then raised her jaw upward, toward his shaft. "Mine," he said with a twinkle in his eyes.

Jett sneered. "I'll show you mine." He thrust into her twice watching for a reaction.

"Jett," she purred. "Behave."

He hammered into her with a more deliberate goal. "I always had a behavioral problem, Sydney and you know it."

He was wild about her and savagely fucked her which only made it worse. This kind of passion didn't go away. This kind of lust never eased.

Now that he was inside her cave, grinding away at the wantonness and taking a piece of her to claim as his own, she belonged to him. Heaven and earth couldn't keep him away now.

"Sydney." God help him. He almost said the three little words guaranteed to change the mood. Instead, he kissed her and her mouth opened to him like the gates of earthly pleasure welcomed him and him alone.

"Damn she's wet," Jett stated traveling down her neck. He closed his eyes and let her take him as far inside as she wanted.

"She stays wet and hot, don't you sugar? Open up, baby." Brock announced, turning her head toward him and tucking his cock between her lips.

She touched his scrotum and sucked him. He covered her fingers with his and together they held fast to a secured grip.

Brock gave quick demands. "That's it, not too much, take me to your throat. Ah yeah, good girl, my sweet little slave."

Luke's hands fastened to her hips and he moved faster and faster. "Oh Sydney, this is it. Right like this. Ah yeah, that's it. Squeeze baby."

Jett bet on her tight ass. With such a compact cunt, he dared to think about what she had on the other side.

Luke's moans and shattered cries forced Jett to find a slower pace. He wanted to match him stroke for stroke, but heaven help him, if he did, they'd tear her apart.

Withdrawing a little, he focused on something else. The truth was he wanted to love her. Sure, he needed to take her the way he watched Brock and Riley, sex her up before letting her fall in a cloud of desire but later. He'd do it when he had her all alone.

He hated sharing her with Brock because it meant her face tilted toward the side and away from his own. He wanted her locked in his gaze when things heated up and sweet hell things were hot between them.

Her pussy showed him favor and took advantage of his cock. He felt her walls closing around him and the pulsing sensation of the pending gratification.

"That's it, Sydney. Come for us, sweet girl. Show us all some of your love." Brock patted her head and her eyelashes fluttered.

Jett's position allowed him a great view of Sydney's perfect nipples. He sucked in one and then left her chest to stare into her haunting eyes, rolling her tight nipples into designer nubbins, hard and pointed, perfect for any man's tongue.

She moaned against Brock's cock and her hips jerked forward faster and faster. Just perfect. She was coming and he immediately shot off like a rocket when Luke pulled her back, threatening to break the pace and hold her prisoner to his personal needs.

Harder and harder, both men fucked her and then Brock pulled out and fell against the bed holding back and resisting his personal pleasure. She cried out after the loss but it was the gain that drew her. Her pussy milked him. Creamy and rich, her release seeped over his shaft.

"More Jett," she whispered as she lowered her lips to his and tongued her way into one heated erotic kiss. He touched her breasts with a slight tap to the side.

Luke drove home with a slap to her ass. He set the pace guaranteeing everyone that he had what he wanted and he got what he came for all at one time. He drove into her small hole and screamed out his release. "Good hell and mercy!"

"Don't go too fast, baby." Brock issued the warning when she moved with them too much. In an instant, Jett noticed how her eyes hazed over and everything changed right then.

She went to some kind of special place with Brock, somewhere none of them could go. For a few seconds, it bothered him until she redirected her focus. Together they found their own haven, a special refuge designed for two bodies, not five.

Luke slid out of her and Jett's beat changed. They fucked one another like frequent lovers and he kept his cock locked in place, her intimate space. Her body arched with his and they made easy love until she gripped at his shoulders and scraped her nails down his arms. His lips snatched hers and he kissed her until their orgasms subsided.

"That's my sweet woman," Jett said, leaving her with his kiss and his words stained upon her lips.

She flipped over unexpectedly and immediately reached for Kevin. He brushed past Jett and waited for her to move toward him.

He stood behind her and ran his fingers over the shape of her ass. Then, he cupped his hand under her.

"I want this pussy," he admitted, dipping his fingers inside.

She moaned out with every lazy stroke. Brock moved in front of her, his long, lean legs provided columns for her grip. He held her head to his cock.

"I want this mouth," he said caressing her cheek. Then, he waited for her to comply once more.

* * * *

Kevin bypassed the first hole and sank into her second. Damn it all, Brock still wanted her lips on him. She closed her mouth tight and made him want for it.

"Open," he ordered, holding her jawbone.

Kevin slapped her bottom. "Do it."

She opened her mouth and sucked the head. He tasted like homespun heaven and she liked everything about his salty existence. He swelled into her mouth with each and every inch somehow disappearing between her cheeks. His masculine smell filled her senses. His weight shifted without mercy and he stroked after a pleasurable release she needed him to find between her jaws.

Brock slid down her throat and her gag reflex never bothered with a true response. She focused on Kevin instead.

He hammered into her center filling her with his size and leaving her astonished in many ways. She never expected him to fuck like this. He gave her one stiff dose of himself and then withdrew long enough to play with her ass, fingering her ring with a simple touch.

"You like this, babe?"

She mumbled but didn't provide a true answer. His fingers destroyed her ability to respond.

He slapped her bottom hard. "Answer little subbie."

"Kevin," she whimpered releasing Brock with a pop. "Please! I can't...I can't..."

"Oh, I think you can." He twirled his fingers into her ass and she screamed out when he penetrated her pussy again. "That's right. You can." He stroked her with ripe thrusts, his mouth at her ear nipping at the lobe, breathing heavy at her nape and then licking her wherever he kissed.

"Kevin..." She breathed his name helplessly. "You're...you're killing me."

"Ah yeah?" He withdrew. "How's that, Syd?"

She swallowed hard. Kevin had a dirty mind. Who would've thought? He was as naughty and perverse as the rest of them, maybe even worse.

Brock flashed a wicked, knowing smile. He yanked her with him as he laid flat against the bed.

"She's ready, now," Brock advised, and Kevin lost his position with the newfound information.

Brock finger-fucked her with a measured pace before he moved his cock right into place. "Good Lord, Sydney. You're staying wet for us, aren't you baby?"

He surely didn't expect an answer. She was barely coherent and lost her ability to speak.

Kevin's strokes came fast the second Brock found his spot. They rocked back and forth, shifting her along their shafts. She cried out with pleasure, screaming this time, all of their names as both men rammed to the finish. Kevin slid out after his climax, and Brock continued to thrust.

She watched Kevin clean himself and missed him immensely, his departure one she couldn't fathom after the brutal way he loved her. Yes, he gave her a piece of his heart and she realized it. She believed that she saw a side to him no other woman knew existed. No one would imagine Kevin Donovan like that, no one.

Sydney wanted to love him all over again. This time, make love to him and him alone. Instead, those rambling thoughts and ideas came and went when Brock rolled over her and held her hands clasped above her head.

"Feel me, Sydney."

She wrapped her legs around his back and took each of his loving strokes, always longing for just one more. "Brock...please, let me have all of you, Master."

They shared a smile, a rare expression found in him, then he dropped her hands, framed her face and made love to her mouth. Stroke after stroke, his tongue and penis worked in time. "Yes, my darling subbie, I am yours, always yours, only yours...forever."

Sydney clawed at him one last time and he smacked her hip, in indication of their strong finish. Driving into her now, his lips crashed over hers. He remained inside of her long after their orgasms subsided.

Brock owned her body, heart, and soul. With him locked between her walls, buried deep inside of her, she felt beautiful, empowered, and finally loved.

Chapter Fourteen

Her feet touched the floor, sort of, or did they make contact at all? She wasn't sure. The air around her held a different texture than what she remembered before she fell asleep. She couldn't see anything but shadows, or were those imagined, too?

Maybe she was dreaming.

Guns fired and a few blasts went off around her.

No, she didn't have audible dreams. Not like this.

Someone held her tight, close enough to form a second skin. He guarded her with his own large frame and whispered something in her ear. Reassurance maybe, or was it a warning?

She tried to focus, but it wasn't easy. When her personal bodyguard released her, her hand was quickly cupped in a much larger one.

Riley was the one who dragged her. They hurried down the hallway like it opened up in front of them only to allow their passage. Then the area sealed off behind them. She heard a swooshing sound and a breeze assured her of a lot of movement. Bodies formed a wall and shielded them. Guns fired with repetition.

It was indeed like a dream, at first. Riley helped her through the darkness, like a man determined to haul his woman out of danger. He tucked her at his side and carried her away.

Sydney glanced over her shoulder. She saw men, too many of them rushing at them. Oh God, this *is* a nightmare. She reminded herself of those she used to have as a teenager. This wasn't any different, she told herself. Over and over again, she tried to make a believer out of herself. Only, it didn't work. She wasn't able to convince herself. *Reality is hard to deny.*

"Riley!" She heard Brock's voice, the anger and pent-up rage filling the area. "Riley! Tell me something, now!"

Horror. That's what she heard. Brock's rage and his uncertainty.

"Ice cream, baby! Count on it!" Riley used her safe word and gave it a whole new meaning. In the midst of all this, he used it to inform the others. She was safe.

"Riley," she mumbled. Her throat, even though dry, finally allowed her to mutter his name. She tried to keep up, hold on, survive…and above all else, live.

Her home was black. The rooms were never this dark. She felt around for a switch and Riley smacked her hand away. "Leave it off, doll," he said. "Only do what I tell you to do."

"What's happening?" she asked, ignoring the fact that he pulled her into the freshly fallen snow and lifted her into his arms. They were waist deep. There wasn't a way out.

Gunfire and loud kabooms surrounded them.

"Riley! This is crazy! You can't possibly carry me through this much snow!"

He pushed forward. Determination etched in his jaw, he seemed to swim through the drifts. A tight line of concentration drawn in his brow, he tried to hold her above him but even as he cradled her body to his, must have recognized his failure.

She was freezing and her teeth chattered to prove it.

"Shh." He pressed on, inching closer and closer to the largest tree in their yard.

"Riley! We can't make it out here. We're going to freeze to death."

"Just a little more," he said, offering her assurance. "Hold on tight, baby. We're almost there."

He stopped short of reaching the tree. His hips jerked and he jiggled his lower leg back and forth.

Panic shook her. They weren't getting out of this alive. The only positive she found in any of this was that she wouldn't live to see or hear about her father's disappointment. He wouldn't be too pleased with the Donovans either, if any of them survived.

Riley pressed forward, his body a rock of tremendous strength, he grunted aloud as he tore through nature's defiance with more power than a workhorse, more determination than those fighting wars. He wasn't ready to admit or accept a failure.

She silently prayed for them. They had to make it. Brock and Luke, Kevin and Jett, if she couldn't make it out of this, they had to survive. She didn't want to die in vain and oh heaven help her, she couldn't stand to think of Riley losing his life to save hers.

Choking back tears, she screamed out at once. "Riley! Take me back!"

He wiggled his leg again. "Shit, Sydney. Just be quiet for one second."

She looked back at the house. She saw a large form in one of the front windows. The person seemed to lurk over them, right above them, and he stood in one place, watching them. She felt his eyes on her and then she saw a gun.

Duck! Riley! Duck!

She froze and she never uttered the first word. Her senses kicked her ass and when she needed it the most, her voice failed her.

A loud click sounded out below them. Before she realized what happened, Riley grabbed her tight around the waist and they slid through some sort of underground tunnel.

"Ril......ley!" She gripped his neck as they slid down the chute.

When they landed in the open, sterile-type room, she was without the blanket he'd wrapped around her earlier and even in the midst of danger, he found amusement.

"Damn baby, give me a minute here before you strip." He laughed at his own wit. "Man, it's cold." He stared at her nipples and quickly ran his hands over her arms before moving by her.

She didn't find him particularly funny. With her teeth clattering away, she glared at him and waited for him to explain. She was chilled to the bone and certain even her blood cells had tiny icicles hanging from them.

He moved around her again and provided a little friction rubbing her skin. He tried, unsuccessfully, to work the cold out of her bones. It didn't help. "All right then. Remind me to talk to the others. You're going to have to sleep in your clothes from now on."

She folded her arms over her chest. He crawled back into the hole that just spit them out and tried to see if he could find anything they left behind there. Why he bothered, she wasn't sure. It probably held more water than his overcoat.

"Shit!" he complained wiggling out of his jacket and then stripping his hoodie off in order to hand it to her. "Put this on," he said, looking at her with a man's lust even in the wake of danger. "We have blankets and supplies in the back but you have to give me a minute."

He pulled down some sort of projector and quickly walked over to the wall where there were a lot of buttons, levers and panels. He started hitting a few of them, and then pulled out a released tray and pounded away at the keyboard found there. Then, he grabbed her and held her head tight against his chest.

A loud boom sounded out around them. He never flinched.

"What the hell was that?" she screamed, her body shaking with fright. "Riley?"

"I had to collapse the tunnels," he said, rushing to a closet and gathering socks, shirts, and blankets. He handed them to her before returning to the monitors now alive with blinking lights and a humming sound, irritating enough to draw her palms to her ears.

"You did what?" she shouted.

"There was only one way in here and one way out." He hit a button and with the maneuver, the loud noise stopped at once.

"And you demolished both at one time? Are you insane?" Her heart pounded a little harder than before, if that was possible.

"No, but you might as well know, I am a little nuts."

No shit.

She stared at him blankly and without thinking looked down.

"Ah now, baby. Look at you with your dirty mind," he said, grinning. "I've already rubbed off on you, eh?"

"Riley Donovan, let me assure you that sex is not on my mind, right at the moment."

"That's okay, sweets. It's always on mine so I can think about it enough for both of us. For now, I can cope with it, but we're going to have plenty of time in here so make sure it's only temporary. I like my subs ready when I am."

"You're not funny and right now, you're not even sexy."

"Liar," he said with a grin. "I'm cake frosting and I know it."

Good grief. Why argue with an ego? There was no way to win.

He took a quick leap forward, grabbed her around the waist and kissed her lightly on the lips. "Give me a few hours and I'm the only thing you'll think about. I swear it. There's not much to do when you're fifty feet underground and no one knows where you are or how to get to you."

* * * *

"Are they clear?" Kevin's head mashed against the master bedroom wall. "Riley? Jett? Luke?" He took a deep breath and then shoved a clip in his gun. "Brock? Damn it to hell somebody answer me!"

A large form shifted behind him, Kevin wheeled around and pointed his gun, then lowered it. "Shit, don't sneak up on me like that."

Brock grabbed his forearm and pushed him toward the large recreation room. "Would you rather I announce it so everyone can find us. Move your ass. That cry for Momma outburst, or whatever the hell you call it, just compromised your position."

Once there, Brock gave Kevin a push inside. Jett slumped over Luke's body.

"Luke?" Kevin rushed to his brother's side.

"He's all right," Brock said in passing. He moved his hand to the curtains and looked out over the yard before pointing to the door. "Keep your gun aimed over there."

"What the hell have you brought up on us?" Kevin knelt beside of Luke and ignored Brock's order. He stared at his oldest brother before he swiped Jett's hand away to take a peek at Luke's shoulder. "You gonna make it?"

Luke pressed his head against the wall. "Yeah, bullet only grazed the skin.

"Did Riley and Sydney make it out?" Kevin questioned Jett.

"They're out," Brock answered, watching the snowmobiles leave the property.

"How about everyone else? Did they all leave?" Jett asked.

"How would I know? I have no idea what the count was from the beginning. They all came out of nowhere and at once," Brock replied.

"I asked you a question," Kevin reminded Brock. "Who are you running from?"

Brock narrowed his gaze on Jett and he continued to work at bandaging Luke's shoulder. Apparently, the effort required his undivided attention.

Kevin tossed aside his weapon and rushed him. "Damn it! Answer me!" He held him pinned to the wall, his clothing bunched up in his hands. "Who followed you here?"

Through gritted teeth, Brock hissed. "I think you got the wrong brother."

With steady hands, Jett tucked in the white cloth at both corners and gave Luke a good once over. "Are you sure you're okay?"

"Good as new," he said patting the wound but wincing the second he touched it.

From a squatted position, Jett slowly stood again and walked over to the window with a pointed question for Brock. "I take it you remembered about all the tunnels?"

He confirmed it when he said, "Dad went over everything with me a dozen times before I met up with you." He pointed to the large Oak. "Leave it to Riley to make his way to the best hideout on the place."

Luke raised his eyebrow. "I doubt he sees it that way. I don't know about you guys but buried alive isn't something I find all that appealing."

"He's never been in the bunkers," Jett informed. "Dad kept him away from the business for as long as possible."

Brock stroked his rough growth of yesterday's stubble. "Well pretty boy, let me tell you all about that particular bunker. Riley chose it specifically since he's in good company down there."

"Tell him later," Kevin growled. "Tell me what you meant by 'wrong brother' and don't point at Luke because I'm not buying it." He narrowed his gaze on Jett all at once.

Brock chuckled. "Yeah, you got one of 'em in your sights. The other one is buried under that drift out there with one beautiful snow angel."

Jett's clenched fists hung at his side. Brock backed away from him and took another position near one of the other windows. Kevin moved closer to Jett searching for answers.

"Tell me about Venezuela," he demanded.

"Kevin, right now we have a few other things to—"

"Tell me about South America." Each word barely squeezed beyond Kevin's tight lips. "Now."

Luke searched for a better understanding, too. "Kevin and I know that last operation had its problems, something went terribly wrong when you and Riley were in Caracas."

"Jett, when you two came back here, Riley wasn't the same. He was a loose cannon ready to fight—or knowing Riley, fuck—anyone or anything just to work out his anger. He covers it up with humor, but he *ain't right*, and you know it!"

"Great," Brock groaned. "The one with the loosest screw has my woman underground."

"She's not your woman!" Jett shouted, and he probably believed his outburst.

"I beg to differ," Brock said, turning to check out the youngest. "Ever been shot before?"

"No, and this doesn't count. It missed."

"Barely," Brock advised.

"Jett!" Kevin screamed. "I want some answers."

"Can you wait for them, sweetheart?" Brock snarled. "I mean, considering we don't know who is still here with us, can you reschedule this walk down memory lane for another more appropriate time? I'll try to arrange tea and crumpets."

"Tell me something," Kevin began, his eyes darting between Jett and Brock. "If you two knew there was immediate danger, how in the hell could you…" He purposefully let his voice trail.

"Fuck?" Brock raised an eyebrow.

"Yeah, for starters," Kevin said.

Brock laughed, rubbed his hand over the front of his pants and then glanced outside before looking at his brother again. "You have to ask?"

"He's waited awhile," Jett informed them with his condescending tone in tact.

"Yeah, Jett, I've been waiting a lot longer than you have. For the record, I'm not real happy that I don't get to eat Sydney's pussy for breakfast."

* * * *

Sydney looked around the tidy room. The first thing that came to mind was a military compound. There were four bunks. Even though the room was small, it could accommodate eight people comfortably.

There was a built-in closet in the far wall and a door leading to God only knew where. She spotted a bathroom behind a partition when she first slid into the compound. She stood there helplessly trying to get her bearings while she clung to the blankets and resisted the urge to cry.

For over an hour, she watched Riley work. When he finally shut down the main system, he gave her his undivided attention.

"Riley, what is all this?" She pointed to the wall of electronics, the artificial intelligence dominating the room.

"The accommodations aren't five star but they ain't bad for a honeymoon hideaway, are they?"

"Riley, I want straight answers. I don't want the beating around the bush. Give me plain talk or none at all. If there isn't a way out of here, I imagine you're in for a lot of long nights straight ahead if you don't make me happy."

He swiveled in his chair, hit another button and turned around once more. The wall parted and displayed all sorts of weaponry and gadgets as well as tools and handheld equipment.

She stared at the display before she looked up at Riley again who appeared more amused than before. "Oh I get it, you'll find something better to do?"

"Trust me. I've spent a lot of time alone, sweets. I know how to entertain myself. I can help them out on the other side by digging us out from this end or I can play right here. It doesn't matter to me either way, Sydney."

"I guess not," she exclaimed, walking into the bedroom.

He chuckled as his fingers sped across the keyboard like he never paused in conversation at all. "*You* might get bored though!"

She stomped right back. "I want some answers from you! I want to know what happened out there. I demand to know where my father is and if he's okay. He's not is he? Those people up there have him don't they?"

He rubbed his forehead a few times before he gave his slow reply. "I don't know where you came up with that idea. In fact, you have no reason to doubt your dad's safety. He's okay. I can check with the others to make sure. As for demands," he paused, running his finger over her collarbone and then he said, "I don't know what kind of arrangement you and Brock had but I plan to find out everything I can. Then, maybe I'll listen to your rants."

"My rants—as you call them—have nothing to do with Brock and what I had with him, for the record, was private, between two people."

"Suit yourself," he said, a lopsided smile shaping his mouth. "There are two people locked down here, Sydney. We're both going to have a few needs. Count on it. The chemistry between us is strong enough to send out alarms to the main base but just to keep things interesting, I'll swap you for information."

"You can't be serious," she said in a low voice.

He let out a sigh and then turned his back. "Actually, you're right. I was sleeping like a bear when my dreams were interrupted. I think I'll take a nap. All of this will be here when I wake up. Besides, there's nothing I can do from down here."

He pointed to the bathroom. "It's state-of-the-art and good to go if the need arrives. Leave the door open when you use it."

Her jaw dropped. "Like hell."

"I'm serious, Syd. I want to see you wherever you are now that we're underground. I don't care if your bottom is on the throne or you're taking a shower. Don't shut that damn door."

Sydney swallowed back the rise of bile in her throat. No one ever talked to her like this before, not Brock, or even her father.

While she tried to process it, Riley continued to point out everything she might need. "There's a walk-in pantry with canned and dried foods. Instructions for the dried foods are on the envelopes.

Bottled water is behind the last row of shelves. Cases of it and more than you can drink. Any questions?"

"Yeah," she glared at him. "When do we make out and screw around so I can get some answers?"

"I thought you'd never ask."

* * * *

The men slumped against the wall with their guns in hand. They wanted to wait until there was enough light outside before they spread out and made sure everything was secure.

Brock pulled a piece of gum from his pocket and offered the others a stick of it. All three declined. "Fine, it was poison anyway."

He closed his eyes and decided a ten minute power nap wouldn't hurt and he discarded the gum. He only wanted it for flavor in the first place. It cured a dry mouth.

Jett interrupted his pending nap plans. "Riley somehow made off pretty good in this situation, didn't he?"

Brock kept his eyes shut. "I bet that's eating at you pretty hard about right now. It should."

He worked his palm around his jaw. He was having a real tough time with it too, as a matter of fact. He opened his eyes and stared at Kevin. "What about it, Kev? You think Riley is making out okay down under?"

"Don't call me Kev," he snapped. "I'm convinced you brought this shit in on us and you know damn well who's behind it."

"Damn, you're as immature as the day I left. I told Dad a long time ago to let you pursue your dreams as an attorney. You pick an argument when there's not a cause to fight or a person to represent. Some things never change."

Luke looked up all at once. "What's so special about that bunker?"

"I wondered if you knew. Go ahead, Jett. Tell him," Brock encouraged. "Tell him what it is that has your balls in a tight pinch.

No reason for you to carry the weight of the world on your shoulders all by yourself."

"Well thank you very much for making it a damn heavy load," Jett barked. "There are some things I'd rather not think about."

"I'll bet," Brock said with a little too much satisfaction.

"There's a lot of stuff in that particular unit," Jett said.

"What kind of stuff?" Luke asked.

"Ah," Brock said, finding the topic more interesting than before. "You don't know what Riley and Jett planted there, huh?"

Kevin only glanced at Jett. "I can guess without any problem."

"What about you, pretty boy," Brock teased Luke and then asked, "Can you?"

"Since I've lived with Riley for the better part of his life and all of mine, yeah I can. I imagine you're the one in the dark, if anyone is."

"Oh no, little brother, that's where you're wrong. When I came back here, I went through all of the underground compounds to make sure they were in perfect condition. I know everything about those units. Ask away. Anything you want to know.

"I can tell you how many bottles of water are in each, what meds are in the cabinets and where they're located. I know the brand of sheets on each bed. In the case of where Riley and Sydney are...I can tell you all about the toys there. See, that's the main underground compound. It's the one where we all were supposed to go in the event of major catastrophes or natural disasters. It's state of the art and equipped with everything the family needs in order to stay underground long term."

Luke looked away from Brock. "We agreed to share her anyway, didn't we? As long as Riley is with her, we shouldn't sweat the small stuff."

"I never agreed to anything," Jett said. "And the small stuff is exactly what I'm worried about. The best toys on the property are in that bunker."

Laughing, Brock pushed aside the communal Sydney issue and directed another question Luke's way. "More information than you can stand, huh?"

"Riley's going to have a good time," Kevin said. "End of story."

"That depends on Sydney," Brock advised.

Jett found immediate humor in the whole situation and started laughing. "Knowing Riley, they'll spend the first forty-eight hours fighting."

Brock liked what he heard. He settled against the wall, pulled his collar around his throat and decided to revisit the idea of sleep. He shut his eyes. "Then I'll have her out in twenty-four."

"I doubt it," Kevin said thoughtfully. "Besides, if you're in a rush to save her from Riley, you've underestimated him and his feelings for Sydney. They're probably fucking right now. Sydney is going to want details and Riley will make her fuck for answers."

Brock's eyes popped right open again. Kevin was right and sleeping today was out of the question.

* * * *

Riley propped up on the sofa in the control room. "Pouting, for the record, doesn't sit with me."

"Me either," she remarked.

"Good. We're on the right footing at the start of our little adventure."

"What do you want, Riley?"

"A good blow job would work for me. How about you?"

"In exchange for?"

He tucked his arms behind his head and stretched his long legs out in front of him. "What do you want to know most?"

She studied the bulge in between his thighs. "You're serious about this?"

"I don't tease about getting a blow job especially since I know how good you can give one."

"What if I agree to give you anything you want?"

"You don't have to agree to anything, Sydney. I can bide my time and wait for you to beg for it." He advised, offering her a cocksure wink followed by a wicked smile. "I can make you beg, Sydney. I know how it's done."

She swallowed tightly. Did he have time to talk to Brock about their intimate lives together? Did he know she'd begged for cock, for Brock to make love to her, before?

Sydney slid Riley's shirt over her shoulders and stood in front of him. She lowered her eyes and waited. Spreading her feet apart, almost as second nature, she placed her hands behind her back.

"Shit, Sydney." He growled, shifting his weight on the couch. "Come here."

She took a few steps forward and he reached for her. He pulled her to his lap and hooked his arms around her waist. With one hand, he pressed her head to his shoulder and the second he did, she cried.

He released a tortured sigh and held her close. "I wondered when you were going to stop this act and let it out." He rocked her back and forth.

She sobbed and sobbed. Unable to control it, she unleashed all of her fears in a steady stream of tears, and she never bothered to tell him, it wasn't an act. As a submissive, it was her duty to remain ready for her Master. Right now, while she missed Brock, only one man had her in his arms. In many ways, he was her lifeline, the only way to find sanity and comfort when she needed it most.

"That's it, baby. Cry. Let it all out. I know," he spoke the words against her ear. "You're safe. I've got you, Sydney and I swear it, no one will hurt you as long as I draw air."

Chapter Fifteen

When the sun came up, the Donovans cautiously left their post. They went through the rooms one by one and looked under beds, in closets, and pretty much everywhere. After they secured the Kane home, they shoveled a path to the barn and Kevin and Luke fed the animals.

Once they returned, they made their demands known. They were looking for answers and knew who to approach for them.

"Jett, there's no escaping it. You have to tell us what happened in Caracas." Kevin never could let anything rest. He missed his calling in life. He should've been a corporate attorney.

Luke pressed for information, too. "We found so many scattered tracks out there, it's hard to say how many men were in here last night. There were at least ten snowmobiles. No one around here has snowmobilies except us. This kind of operation took money and manpower. The tracks prove whoever is behind this had both."

"These guys mean business. They'll be back and they'll bring friends. We need to get ready for them and we can't do that if you don't start talking," Kevin said.

Brock only glanced away from the computer monitor. He gave Jett a quick head to toe evaluation and then returned to his work.

Earlier, they moved Sydney's home computer upstairs so they had a bird's eye view of the property surrounding the Kane home. The family room had a loft area and that's where they set up their makeshift command center. They could strategize and easily see anyone approaching from any angle.

Jett sat on the edge of a large walnut table and studied his brothers. A look of disgust only lingered a minute before the true signs of an agonizing experience washed over him. His skin lost its vibrant color and his pain claimed its place in his expression.

Brock felt his chest tighten. He had a good idea of what happened. He'd tortured a few folks in his lifetime, saw the way many of them ran from their own shadows later in life. While Riley wasn't running yet, he definitely had some inner demons working him over pretty good.

Looking at Jett then, he saw Riley wasn't the only one. Jett had a few of them, too.

"Riley was captured by an underground sex ring and most likely tortured beyond what I can even begin to comprehend, much less explain."

Brock narrowed his gaze on Jett then. "Tortured, how?"

He shook his head and kept a stiff upper lip. "I don't know. He never discussed it and I didn't press. I saw where he was held and I can only imagine. It wasn't pretty."

Luke tried to process it. "You mean you think he was—

"That's ridiculous," Kevin interrupted. "I know Riley better than any of you. They might torture him but I doubt they used any kind of sexual coercion to get their answers. It would've changed him."

"It did," Jett reported sadly. "Why do you think he came back here and immediately started the Casanova-act? Huh? Before Sydney, he had two, maybe three girls with him at all times. I walked in on him once and he had four of them in the bed with him and the bodies were so tangled, it was hard to decipher which limb belonged where."

Luke grunted. "You should've joined them."

They all stared at him in disbelief. Brock even looked up in disbelief. "Oh so you protected your prick for years and now all of a sudden, you're the man to see for pussy."

"I'm just saying," he said in a low voice. "And Brock, just so you know, you haven't been here. You don't get to come back home and act like an ass to us just because you think you're the one with the detailed pussy plan for Sydney. It didn't go unnoticed how you guarded all of us last night."

Brock shrugged. "Feel better?"

"Much," he replied.

"Glad I could help," Brock said in his smart-ass tone.

"Riley has always loved women. So he likes to fuck. A lot. Big deal," Kevin said, between his stop and starts toward the window.

Brock scooted his chair back and glared outside. He could tell them. Right then and there, he could probably settle all suspicions. He studied the Oak tree and thought about his little brother.

He and Riley were real close before he left, before the business pulled him in and swallowed his life and his dreams. If Riley never told Jett what happened, he wasn't going to volunteer anything for the rest of them.

Brock realized what went on in those sex ring interrogations. In fact, he refused to think about it because there wasn't any real purpose in it. Nothing good would come of it.

"Yeah, well Kevin, it was a big deal," Jett began. "He never took more than one woman to his bed before that ordeal. He respected women, cherished them. He came home and all he wanted to do was fuck. Show them what a big cock he had."

"I've seen bigger," Brock said, peering down at his bulge.

"Shut up," Kevin said disgusted.

"I don't remember Riley cherishing women," Luke remarked.

"Me either," Brock added.

"So what are you implying?" Kevin demanded.

"I'm not listening to this. Jett, think about what you're doing here before you spout off about something you know nothing about." Luke said, rushing out of the loft and slamming the door below them.

Brock felt his upper jaw twitch and he patted Kevin on the back. He shrugged his hand away and waited for Jett to spill his guts.

"Kevin," Brock said sincerely. "You gotta let this go, man. It's the nature of our business and there are some things even brothers don't want to talk about. This is one of them."

"Shut up, Brock. You don't know anything about family or brothers so stay out of it."

Brock felt the sting but only for a minute. It was another flaw found in the business, the lifestyle. Those in the field knew all about those psychological jabs, the kind of dull aches that jab quick and then twisted away before pity sets in and on occasion it did. *What ifs* and *how comes* irked the hell out of him. He realized a long time ago what he left behind and the brothers he missed stood before him not as he left them, but as men.

Kevin grabbed Jett's arm. "You know. I know you do and I want answers now. Right now!"

"He was tortured, okay. How much? I don't know. What means were used? I can't think about it. How often? For over fourteen days. Now, if he wants you to know more, then ask him. See if he tells you."

Kevin glared at Jett. "And where the fuck were you when all this went down?"

"Believe me, Kevin, I've asked myself that very question time and time again."

Kevin waited for more of an explanation than the one Jett provided. When he didn't get one, he stormed out.

Brock locked eyes with Jett's after Kevin left them alone. "Caracas is full of beautiful women," he said after he thoughtfully considered how to approach him for more insight.

"What are you trying to say?" Jett snapped.

"Nothing. I'm just making a statement," he said. "The women there will suck or fuck a man right past his worries or obligations. Damn if there aren't some great looking babes there."

Jett started downstairs and then turned around to face Brock. "If you think I left Riley to fend for himself so I could chase a piece of pussy, you're wrong."

"I'm right. See, I don't *think* anything, Jett. I know."

* * * *

They probably slept a couple of hours. He wouldn't know how long until he logged onto the computer, but he wasn't in a hurry to get to the control panels with a beautiful woman asleep in his arms.

Once they slipped into hiding, he sent the messages out so everyone on the outside—assuming his brothers were safe—knew they made it. For years the Donovans had realized this day would one day come.

It wasn't until Sam Kane pissed off the wrong cartel that they ran into a scary bunch of lunatics in Caracas. After that, they counted down the hours.

They realized a constant threat loomed and enemies closed in around them. Every day and every night they counted their blessings when their home escaped an invasion. They also realized that with each passing day, the bad guys moved closer, gathered more troops and spent more dirty money gathering the weapons needed to bring them down.

Damn Sam and damn his own father's better judgment. Caracas was a deal gone wrong from the very beginning. They were there for one purpose, to cover up their father's mistakes. Those he made with Sam Kane. It should've been an easy task to complete. Instead, it was chaotic and disastrous.

He folded an arm over his head and watched the blinking lights on one of the security systems. Filtered and coded messages sent upon their arrival gave him a little confidence.

Someone out there already knew which bunker they were in, assuming no one saw them disappear underground. Then again, the way Brock watched her like a scorned hawk, he imagined at least one Donovan knew with absolute certainty which bunker he chose.

It was deliberate and a dumb move, all things considered. He took a deep breath when he mentally retraced his steps. Why did he risk it?

She stirred closer to his body and he didn't question his motives any longer. Her shapely curves provided a little body heat and he held her tighter.

One thing about it, if Brock saw him head for the main unit when he was much closer to the smaller caves, he'd guess the reason behind it. No, on second thought, he probably knew without a doubt because Brock was thorough if nothing else, or at least he imagined he was. He didn't know for sure. He based some of his assumptions on what he remembered from years past.

He was a clone of their father and their dad never left stones unturned. Once Brock came back, he probably demanded to see the bunkers and knowing the agent behind the dark and hardened man, he searched the entire place.

He smiled to himself. Oh yeah, Brock would've found everything he had there. The handcuffs, the crops, the toys, even the harness. He was probably digging them out by hand about right now.

"What are you thinking about?" she asked, opening her eyes and peering up at him.

He jerked at the sound of her voice and tucked her under his arm. "You have to ask?" he teased.

"Yes," she hummed, snuggling against his chest.

He nuzzled the top of her head. "You sleep in your birthday suit and your hard nipples are pressed tight against my skin. You still want to know what I'm thinking?"

He brushed a fallen strand away from her brow. "You sure you want to know?"

"Uh-huh," she muttered. "I do."

"How about I show you? Would you like that?" he asked, shifting his weight. In a smooth move, her arms were confined above her head and his mouth slanted right above hers. "I want you to show me the world. Let me take a trip around Sydney. How about it?"

"You're cornier than your brother."

He loosened his grip but his body went rigid. "Which one?"

She stretched her neck and stole the kiss he refused to give her. It was only a quick smack but a kiss all the same.

"Brock," she said.

The little vixen wanted a reaction. He could tell she was well satisfied with her chosen words.

"Sydney, I'm nothing like Brock," he said rolling off of her. The moment ruined, definitely postponed.

He slid out of bed and right into his pants. He'd tossed those at some point during his short-lived sleep.

"Luke, God love his heart, shopped for you about two months ago. You should find a few things in the closet that will fit you."

"I'd love to find some undergarments there, too," she said making her way to the bedroom.

She pretended not to notice the cancelled romp.

"You gotta be kidding," Riley remarked, glancing away from the computer system. "You stayed with Brock and you expect me to believe he allowed bras and panties?" He rolled the chair under the long counter he apparently planned to use as a desk. "Right."

"I guess not," she said, disappearing into the bedroom.

When she reappeared a few minutes later, Riley checked her out. After a quick visual, he made his inquiry. "How about it? Did you find a thong or something?"

"As a matter of fact, I did." She smoothed her hands over a dark burgundy turtleneck. He stared at the leggings, which made her look taller and clung to her in a way that enticed his erection forward.

"Damn that Luke. I'll have a talk with him about it later." He stared at her breasts. "One thing you didn't find was a bra, huh?"

Her nipples pressed into the material and made it impossible to deny. "No bra but for what you have in mind, I imagine it doesn't matter anyway. I have the important part well covered."

She started by him and he snatched her around the waist.

"Do you now?"

"Yes, Riley, I do. In case you haven't noticed. I have on pants."

If she meant it to draw him into a challenge, it worked and he won.

The second she twisted away from him, he grabbed at her, flipped his wrist, mashed her body against his and held her to the countertop, right next to the computer. With one hand, he yanked her pants and thong down at one time and with the other, he tanned her soft rounded globe with four smacks straight across her ass.

"Riley!"

He slapped her bottom a few more times. "What were you saying about having pants on, baby?"

"Riley, stop this! Why are you punishing me?"

"Truth? I don't want you in panties or a thong and I prefer you in short skirts or something for easy access."

"Uh-huh," she said, sliding her hand across her hip. "You and every Dom around."

"I'm serious, Syd," he said in a low voice.

"Stop," she said with a smile that told him otherwise. He had the green light and her proud nipples pressing against her sweater made for a delightful invitation.

Stepping over the center of the material now bunched around her ankles, he raised his knee in between her legs and forced her to straddle it. He yanked a handful of hair and held it in a closed grip.

"You took me too far, baby. This doesn't stop now until I'm stroking in between these thighs and hearing you cry out my name as hard and as wild as you called out Brock's last night. That's when it stops and baby, by that time, I'll be warmed up and ready to go again."

Chapter Sixteen

She was crazy and not in a certifiable way. She lost all ability to reason or the desire to think on her own. Right now, this experience was about *him*. She thought she might give her life for experiences like this and men like Riley Donovan.

Riley had a way with women. If she had to guess, he earned his place in a lot of beds because of it. He knew what to say and how to say it. Better still, he delivered on promises. There wasn't any bull shit with him. If he said he wanted something, he put his mind to it and his tongue, lips, and teeth worked for a solid reaction.

God help her when he decided to sweeten the deal and add another body part. He promised great activities followed and he made a believer out of her at swipe one. Once he locked his lips over her clit, holy shamolee, life was good.

He lapped at her like a hungry mountain lion and her body kept a pool of hot cream for the taking. Why she climaxed over and over again wasn't something she dared question, but thoroughly enjoyed.

Heaven on earth came to mind, life after death too because if they died there, if by chance, they never escaped, they'd leave this earth together, no question about it. As intimate as they were, as far reaching as his tongue plunged, there wasn't a point of separation. There wasn't a 'him' and a 'her' but rather a quickly developed union…an *us*.

He held her legs apart and worked his tongue like magic, a magnetic force pulling it higher, driving him forward. Lick for lap and suck for sip, he ate her with an aggressive man's hunger.

Pressing down on his head, she arched her back and then pushed her body higher. Her legs instinctively closed against his head and with his elbows, he nudged them open again, determined to stay in control and refusing to leave her pussy in the process.

"Riley," softly spoken, it didn't sound like her voice who said his name. "Higher."

He shifted his body and thrust into her walls and she didn't have a chance to tell him she wasn't talking about his tongue. Oh no, she may have uttered the word but she knew he was pushing her there and all she could do was brace herself for the inevitable fall.

* * * *

"You're spying on them?" Kevin asked.

He couldn't believe Brock's audacity. But he couldn't turn away either so that made him an accomplice to his brother's perversion.

"If you don't want to watch, if you can't stand it, then walk away." Brock leaned back in an executive chair he had discovered in Sam's office. The second he spotted it, he hoisted it up the steps and then dared any of them to sit there. Some things never changed between brothers.

Kevin swallowed hard. "Holy...that's..."

"Beautiful. Sexy." Brock looked down at his tented pants before he checked out Kevin's.

Kevin knocked him over the head with a stack of papers. "It's hard, okay. Turn the damn thing off."

"I prefer to watch," Brock said, crossing his ankles and kicking his feet up on the table. He crooked his head and studied his shoes. No wonder, they needed a spit-shine or better yet, a polish.

"Of course you do," Jett said joining them. "You're a sick prick and always have been."

"Yeah Jett, it takes one cut from the same womb to know it."

Jett walked by them and only glanced at the monitor. "See what I mean?"

He placed the laptop on a nearby end table and then headed straight back for a better look. "Holy shit."

He dropped his head, inched closer, twisted it for a better angle and then licked his lips. "Is he trying to eat her alive or what?"

"I'm the pervert," Brock reminded. *"Right."*

"Got volume on that thing?" Luke asked from behind them.

Brock pointed at the action they were missing. "Pretty boy, you couldn't handle it if I turned up the sound now."

Kevin's own mouth watered. "He has a point, Luke."

Her head pressed against the cushions under her. Riley pushed her knees up all at one time. His body towered over hers and he licked around her opening with perseverance. He stopped abruptly and she spread her legs wider. He looked up and grinned for the camera.

"Fuck him!" Jett exclaimed. "He must know we're spying."

"God help us all if we have to stay here in this snow and watch him put on a show," Kevin said, full of frustration.

"Make no mistake about it," Luke said. "He knows Brock has him on camera. That is most definitely staged."

Brock raised his eyebrows. "No, baby boy. That's not an act. That's the real thing. The best a woman can give. I guarantee it."

* * * *

Sydney reached a decision. Maybe loving all of them wasn't out of the question. She didn't see any reason to fight it. She realized all along it was possible. Her daydreams and little girl fantasies shaped her, maybe even prepared her for this.

Dreams coming true, that's what this was, dreams coming true.

Riley kissed a trail up her leg and snaked his arm around her waist. Forcing her to sit up, he fingered her nice and slow, careful to caress her folds, one at a time while watching her for a reaction.

That's what he wanted. He wanted to see the impact. He'd already tasted it.

"Did you like it?"

She gulped. What a question. "Hated it, actually. Never really had a thing for tongues, you know."

"Is that right?" he asked, yanking her close. He held his mouth over hers. "You may wish you'd given me a different answer."

He rubbed her clit and then inserted two fingers. He added another one.

"Riley," she moaned, trying to lean back. His grip around her neck held and she couldn't move. "Watch. Look down and watch me."

He withdrew his fingers and she saw the transparent web of her juices cling to his middle and forefinger. She felt like her breathing shattered, it caught in her chest and prevented full breaths, constant breathing without interruption. She was in a trance. A Riley-moment.

"Now what, Syd?" He teased her a little more. He withdrew his fingers three quarters of the way, enough to let her believe he might take them away from her altogether or maybe twirl them enough to make her think about a deeper invasion.

"I want to do whatever you want me to do. I...will *do* whatever you want me to."

She lowered her eyes and the submissive gesture made his balls tight. Between the pinching sensation in his scrotum and the obvious fact he was erect and horny as all hell, he wanted her now. He didn't give a shit if he needed to exercise more control.

She became an urgent need. He had a commitment now, an obligation to bury his cock so far inside her walls that she asked for rent. Maybe she'd even charged a deposit because they both understood without a doubt, borrowed time together was unacceptable. Riley suddenly wanted promises of tomorrow and lots of time to spend stroking out their desires.

He watched her body move against his hand. Every time she started to grind into his palm, he pulled back. Soon, she was up on all fours.

"Ah now, Syd, do you know what I want to do to your pretty little ass right now."

"I hope so after all the foreplay."

"My tongue in your cunt is not foreplay."

"Call it anything you want but it felt like a preamble to something." Suddenly, she went pale. "I mean, if you decide to fuck me that is."

His dick twitched. "Is that an offer?"

"Do you need one?" she asked on a whisper. Her mood changed and she was clammy all of a sudden. "No, I don't guess you do," she stated flatly.

Alarmed, he dropped his grip from her nape and took her hand in his. "Syd, is something the matter?"

"No," she shook her head so rapidly, he didn't believe her.

He narrowed his gaze on her and watched the lust fade from her eyes. "What is it, Sydney? Talk to me."

* * * *

Brock turned up the volume after everyone left for a little afternoon nap. They were in for a long night ahead and needed to get some rest. Later, when their anticipated company tried to arrive unnoticed, they'd show their guests a little southern hospitality.

He folded his arms over his chest and studied his shoes. For a man with money, he sure didn't dress the part. He twisted his foot and looked at the soles. Sure enough, he spotted a little breezeway forming in the arch. He thought he felt a hole there earlier. He shrugged and decided after this mission, he might go on a long vacation somewhere near a shopping mall. He bet Sydney would love that. She liked to shop.

With the mention of foreplay coming from the computer speakers, his head snapped to attention. He rolled the chair closer to the monitor and studied her expressions. He turned up the volume so he didn't miss anything the two of them exchanged.

"You did a number on her, I'll give you that much. She can't even enjoy herself with Riley because of you."

Brock turned down the volume and swiveled around to face his accuser. "What if they can't enjoy *each other*? What if Riley is so warped because of what happened in Venezuela that he doesn't know what to do with a woman?"

"You saw him with her. He knows what to do with her."

"Maybe he can lick her pussy but I haven't seen him fuck her since they've been down there."

"You're something else," Jett said. "You really are a piece of work, you know?"

"Yeah," Brock admitted, shooting him a sarcastic wink. "Thanks for noticing. It means a lot to me to have the admiration of my brothers."

"Damn it, Brock. Anyone can take a look at her and see she had a number ran on her by someone. You fucked her up. She has a problem with trust because of you."

"She trusts me," he informed.

"Maybe she did at one time. I don't think so now."

"Oh, you can count on it. In fact, pay attention to them. She's had very little alone time with Riley. She has no reason to believe whatsoever that she will make it out of there. Except one."

"Uh-huh, and what's that?"

"She knows I'll never let her stay down there long with another man."

"And you know this how?" Jett asked.

"I didn't let her stay with you, did I?"

Jett's eyes were wide and with a sudden thought, his face gained a maroon tint. "Explain that."

Brock stretched his arms over his head and planted both palms on the back of his head. "You're a *smart boy*, figure it out. While you're at it, you need to remember something. I always loved the Fourth of July festivities. How about you?"

Jett glared at Brock. "You were there," he said with a solid accusation. It lacked punch but what he lacked in a powerful statement, he made up for in his expression. His face was a shade redder than before. Brock thought about the way he used to act when they were kids. Jett always took things so personally.

Now, he probably had a good reason. There was a big difference between sharing things, like a new bike, and sharing a piece of great looking ass.

"Surely you didn't think I'd let Sydney wonder around late at night without a shadow."

Jett paced. "No one knew you were guarding her," he reminded. "Were you there or not, damn it!"

"I was. I'm the reason she left home the next day. The threat that arrived was one I created, masterfully I might add."

"You sorry—"

"Watch it, we have the same parents. Bastard and SOB don't work here."

"You created some kind of bogus threat to get Sydney away from me?"

He winked. "You're damn straight I did. It worked, too. Her daddy couldn't get her back in my arms quick enough."

"Why?" Jett asked, shaking his head. "I mean why go to that much trouble?"

A few moments more and it sunk in. "You did it to keep her away from me and I wanna know why!"

"You know why."

"Because you love her?"

"I didn't want her to start her life without me," he said before adding, "And I do love her. You're right about that but it's no big surprise. I've already told you how I feel about her. Back then, I didn't want her to commit to someone else. I still don't. Not yet."

"You're self serving. You always have been."

"She waited for me anyway," he said.

"Oh really?" Jett stood taller and pointed at Luke when he walked in to see what the commotion was about. "She waited for you, did she?"

"Yes," he said.

"How do you figure that, Brock, huh? She gave Luke what every man wants."

Brock stood. He kept an intense focus, a set jaw, gritted teeth. "But I was there for every stroke and sigh, Jett. I was there!"

"Is that right?" He probed through the fury. He wanted to see him enraged. "Then pardon me, big brother for the oversight. I could've sworn the one with bragging rights was Luke. What am I thinking?"

"You're not," Brock snapped. "You never have. What Sydney and I have goes way beyond who stroked her sealed snatch first, and Jett, there's where you have the biggest problem, isn't it?"

Chapter Seventeen

They waited up half the night. Brock called his father a few times and each time he assured him he was fine. It didn't matter. Uneasiness surged through his veins and he needed to crash the adrenaline somehow. He needed Sydney with him worse now than ever before.

"Maybe I should go stay with Dad," he finally said.

Kevin's head snapped up immediately. "That's suicide in this weather and you know it. Even though the storm let up some, we don't know what, or who is waiting out there in the darkness. Dad's fine."

"I'm not so sure," Brock stated, pacing the floor. "Besides, he's not a pretty young thing anymore."

"I'd love to tell him you said so," Luke said in amusement.

"Yeah?" Brock asked. He didn't care if Luke looked tougher than the average man, he was still the Donovan baby, his kid brother. "Think the old man is still tough as nails?"

"I know he is. You'd know it too if you'd stuck around."

"Speaking of which, when do the three of you think we can move beyond the past?" Brock braced for their reply.

"When you stop acting like it's no big deal that you vanished from our lives without a phone call or letter goodbye," Jett said without missing a beat.

"Shit, I knew I forgot the Dear John letters to my brothers."

"See!" Kevin said through gritted teeth. "You're a sarcastic ass."

"And you were glad to see me until Riley slid out of sight with Sydney and then your whole demeanor changed. You're in love with her and can't even see it."

"I saw it," Kevin said, shaking his head.

"Yeah, me too," Jett added. "I've seen him with other women. Jeez, Sydney even looked surprised when they were fucking."

Brock grunted and the others enjoyed a hearty laugh.

Kevin moistened his bottom lip and ran his thumb over it. "She sure is sweet, isn't she?"

Brock started to answer but watched Luke instead.

He quickly agreed and said, "Sweetest thing I've ever known."

"Would you die for her?" Brock asked him.

"In a minute."

"Yeah?" he asked, only slightly amused.

"I took a bullet for her, what do you think?"

"Let me remind you," Jett said, pointing to his shoulder. "I didn't dig out the proof of that but between me and you, to make it sound good to Sydney, I'll support your story."

"It won't matter," Brock said. "She already loves him."

They all sat up and paid attention. Jett's gaze held with Brock's before he spoke his mind. "I imagine if anyone knows, you do. Right, Brock?"

"You're catching on, Jett. It's about time, but I'll take it."

* * * *

Jett and Luke took the first post. Brock didn't sleep. He pretended to trust them and agreed to let them have the look out but his eye movement under the lids told a different story.

Around six o'clock, a loud knock crashed against the door. Someone had gotten inside the house. Immediately Brock was on his feet with a gun in hand and ready to fire.

"Open up, it's Sam Kane!"

Brock rolled his neck over to the left signaling his brothers to move to the side. "Get to the loft," he whispered to Kevin. "He shouldn't be here. Something is up."

"Brock, it's Dad. Open this blasted door."

"What the hell?" Luke asked, peering out the window at the snow-covered lawn. "There's no way."

The door crashed in seconds later and Sam said, "I hated to do that but Brock is so damned stubborn, this could've taken all day. He's your son, Mark. No doubt about it."

Sam walked into the center of the room and grinned up Kevin. Mark looked like a proud soldier as he met the gazes of each son.

"Lower your gun boys," Mark ordered, slapping Sam on the back. "The threat is over."

* * * *

Brock's anger wasn't concealed. "You mean to tell me the two of you set this up?"

Mark motioned for him to sit down. "Son, if you'll listen to Sam, you'll understand."

"Hell no! You've gone too far with your tests and training now. Those yahoos you sent in here shot Luke!" he exclaimed, pointing toward his brother.

"What if he'd been killed?" Kevin asked, biting back true rage.

"He wasn't," Mark pointed out.

"Someone shot him!" Brock yelled.

"The bullet grazed the skin," Mark reminded. "You said so yourself in your report."

"I don't understand this," Kevin said, shaking his head. "What kind of men place their families in a direct line of fire?"

"Sam will explain it, if you'll cool your hot heads long enough to listen," Mark said, sounding agitated.

"Hell no!" Brock exclaimed. "You sit down. Dad, you stepped over the line here. You placed Sydney in danger and all of us. Never mind the money you spent to run this little test. The two of you are acting like old men, geezers with nothing else better to do except orchestrate dangerous field tests. They're nothing more than childish pranks!"

Mark and Sam shared a laugh and then the room fell silent. "Are you done?" Mark asked.

"I'm getting warmed up, brace for it," Brock growled.

"I am your father and your superior in the unit. Take a fucking seat!" he yelled, pointing toward an empty chair.

Brock narrowed his gaze on his dad and reluctantly took it. He ran his hand over his long face, still mad as all hell.

Sam, visibly amused, thoughtfully asked, "Brock, tell me something. How is this any different than what you did when you discovered Sydney and Jett had an open fling at the fair?"

Brock fired right back. "Sir, if you don't mind my saying so, every situation is different. For starters, I may have moved Sydney to a safe location but I didn't spend nearly two hundred thousand dollars to do it."

"Oh no?" Sam asked.

"No," he stated flatly.

"Let me refresh your memory," Sam began. "An apartment in New York City ran us three grand a month plus deposit and utilities. How long were you there?"

"Six months."

"Five men on my payroll," he continued. "Each earning ten grand every four weeks. How much is that?"

Brock swallowed tightly. "Sir, I didn't think about the money."

"You're not thinking about it now," his dad remarked. "All you're thinking about is Riley and Sydney, isn't it?"

"So this was a farce?" Kevin asked, steering the conversation to the here and now.

"Not entirely," Sam replied. "We orchestrated the whole thing but we used a middle man to set up the crew. We had intelligence suggesting that some of our men were unhappy with the team. We used this opportunity to allow them to show face, and they did."

"Who?" Jett asked.

"Zaxby," Mark informed regrettably. "And his partner Paul Rines."

"What?" Brock asked, frowning "I've worked with these guys.

"Brock, Zaxby signed first. He didn't even negotiate price," Sam said sourly.

"I don't believe it," Jett said, glancing at Brock. "Riley and I worked with him in Caracas."

Mark looked disappointed. "That's where the problems started, Jett. You left him in Caracas."

"No sir, we didn't," he said, insulted. "We received a message at the hotel the morning we headed home. They caught an earlier flight."

"You mean Zaxby and Rines?" Sam asked for clarification.

"Yes, ask Riley," Jett stated. "He'll confirm it."

Mark shook his head. "It doesn't matter. They believed you and Riley left them. Zaxby pledged his life mission was to bring us down. His expressed hatred for our family was chilling."

"Where is he? I want to talk to him. He needs to know Riley and I wouldn't have left him behind."

Brock narrowed his gaze on Sam. "You took care of the situation?"

"Yes, it's too late to correct the problem," he replied.

Jett placed his head in his hands. "Shit!"

"Son, I asked you to tell me about Caracas. Your feedback was necessary when I asked for it. I wanted to try and understand why Zaxby and Rines signed on to bring our family down. Even though his betrayal was already in progress, I still wanted to find a way to save his life."

"In the end, he made it impossible. Zaxby was corrupt and he had a few ideas in mind for Sydney," Sam said, barely audible.

"So he's dead?" Luke asked, sounding relieved.

"He's resting awhile," Sam said.

"What the hell!" Jett exclaimed. "Your test run cost a man his life?"

"No, son. As I said, we needed to find out where their loyalties were and this provided the opportunity. One mission interlocked with the other."

Brock scrubbed his chin with the ball of his hand. "Why did you test us?"

"Do you really think I tested you, Brock?" Sam asked.

"You did."

Mark looked at his other sons. "No, Sam drew his conclusions about you a long time ago, Brock."

Jett was enraged. "Sure Brock, you proved yourself on those missions with Sydney. She trusts you, remember. Her daddy believes in you, don't you see? They planned this little adventure for the rest of us."

"You're right," Sam said, sounding pissed. "And I won't apologize for it. My daughter's life is precious. I've known for years what extreme measures Brock took to protect her. I had to make sure the rest of you would fight through hell to keep her safe."

"So we passed the test?" Luke asked, grinning.

"Yes," Mark said proudly.

"Well," Sam added. "With one exception."

Brock laughed. "Riley."

"I can't figure out why he didn't take Sydney to the closest bunker," Sam explained. "The smaller bunkers are comfortable enough for two and I can't figure out why he put her at risk in order to make it to that main unit."

"Beats me," Brock grated out.

Jett shrugged. "Doesn't make sense, does it?"

Sam eyed the Donovans. "No, it doesn't. But I'm going to let it go. There are some things a father doesn't need to know about."

"So we've earned your trust and have your blessing?" Kevin asked.

"I might as well give it," he said, peering over at Brock and then Jett.

"Good," Jett said, forcefully. "To clarify, that means Sydney belongs to us now. No more games or training that involves her. Do we all understand one another?"

Sam laughed. "Ah Jett, you're more like Brock than you know." He studied the Donovans and then replied, "We have a deal."

"Perfect," Kevin said. "We have a few bodies to retrieve from down under."

"You also have a garage to clean up," Sam said bitterly.

"Look the other way, Sam," Mark suggested. "Remember, there are some things a father doesn't need to know."

"There are some things a father shouldn't have to see," he reminded, turning to Jett. "I don't have to ask which one of you put that shit together. Now, break it down and let me know when it's out of my house."

"Yes, sir," Jett said sourly.

"I'll stay at your place tonight, Mark. I have a feeling my daughter would prefer it if I didn't know about her shenanigans with your sons."

Brock shook Sam's hand on the way out. "We only wanted her for her feisty personality."

Sam was almost out the door when he stopped. He turned around and pointed his finger up in the air like he thought of something in the nick of time. "You know Brock, as a father, there are a lot of things I have to let slide."

"Yes, sir."

"I trusted Sydney in your care but I want you to know I wasn't in the dark as much as you think."

"I'm sure that's true," he said, biting back a smile.

He shook his head, patted Mark Donovan on the back and started downstairs.

"And Sam?"

He stopped. "Yes?"

Brock winked. "We'll take care of our girl."

Chapter Eighteen

Three days later

"Are you awake?" Riley asked, running his hand up and down her spine before kissing the same path his fingertips trailed over first. She was in heaven and just as wet as she was the night before.

"No," she mumbled into the pillow. "Go away."

"I can't go far," he reminded.

"Then go fix breakfast."

"Breakfast is served," he said rubbing his cock over her hip.

She flipped over and rubbed the sleep from her eyes. "After last night? You're all talk, Riley Donovan. There isn't a man alive who would want more."

"If I'm all talk," he said as he nipped at her lips, "Then you better listen because I'm full of kinky ideas this morning."

"Oh really?" She stretched her arms above her head. "Like what?"

He eased into her mouth with a lazy kiss.

"Good tongue," she said dreamily.

"Hard cock," he responded and when he did, his tip slipped between her folds.

"Riley!" she cried out, his first thrust stroking her breath away. "God help me, you...you could've...waited a second."

"I couldn't," he nuzzled her breast and kissed her nipple as he pressed into her. "I've waited all night long."

How that was remotely possible, she wasn't sure. They'd fucked straight past the night and only slept a few hours.

"Riley," she muttered.

His dark eyes focused on her breasts. He pushed into her with a man's intentions. His intimate punches came harder and his cock twitched with each and every one. Grabbing her hands, he laced his fingers with hers and held them parallel to her head continuing with repetitive strokes.

She swallowed, resisted the first urge to explode around him and held tight to his hands. "I want you to love me."

His expression softened and before she felt the impact of her request, she heard his promise, "I already do, baby. I already do."

* * * *

Riley jumped about three feet the second the door to the compound crashed against the wall. He had a pistol in hand by the time she grabbed the sheet and held it against her chest. When she looked up, she wasn't exactly shocked to find Brock standing in the doorway.

"Well I'll be damned," Riley said shaking his head and tossing the gun aside. "You don't waste any time, do you?"

Luke, Kevin, and Jett were right behind him. All of them looked hungry enough to partake in Riley's leftovers.

"You should've knocked or," he said, grinning at Sydney, "Shown up a little earlier to join the party." He snatched his pants from a nearby chair.

"Put your little Peter Pan back in your pants and let's get her out of here," Brock suggested before he gathered her in his arms.

Luke looked around the room with a devastating thirst in his eyes. "It looks like Tinkerbell had one hell of a party."

"I did," she said. "Riley kept things interesting down here. I never missed the light of day."

"Uh-huh," Brock said as he handed her off to Jett. "Just for that, I'm spanking you the second I get you cleaned up."

"I'm not dirty," she said with a smile.

"No, but you have Riley all over you," he said turning up his nose. "Don't you believe in fucking once?"

Riley pointed to the cameras. "You should know. Did you plant these?"

Sydney blinked. "You mean we were taped?"

"Yes," Luke informed.

"Great," she responded. "Who saw us?"

"We did," Jett told her. "Is that a problem?"

"I don't have secrets from you, any of you," she added quickly.

"Good damn thing," Brock said. "We were around for every stroke and cry. It was more than enough to make a man horny."

"I hope so," she said.

"Count on it, doll." He promised, pinching her on the ass and then focusing on Riley. "What about it? Everything okay down here?"

"Sure. Good company, great sex, what more does a man want in his times of trouble?"

"Good wine," she said.

He shrugged. "So maybe we forgot a few luxury items. Wine, certain kind of nipple clamps, chocolate candles, you know ….necessities."

Luke lazily rubbed the back of his arm. "You know, since we're all here…"

"No way," she said quickly. "I can't wait to get out of here. The company was fabulous but I'd like a breath of fresh air before I get anything lodged in my throat, thank you very much."

"Are you offering, sugar?" Jett asked.

"Yes," she said, lowering her eyes.

"Then I'm all for providing transportation." He knelt down and grabbed her clothes. "Go put something on and then we'll get you back up to the house."

She started for the bathroom and Riley reached out and grabbed her around the waist. When his lips snapped over hers, it was the most natural thing in the world to kiss him then, even with the others watching.

Once she stepped into the bathroom, she dropped the sheets and started to clean up a little before stepping into her black leggings.

"God blessed mercy," Kevin said, unable to tear his eyes away from her.

Brock studied her too and appreciated what he saw because she saw him try to look away twice and both times, he immediately returned his focus to her.

"Let me guess," Jett said. "You don't want her shutting the doors when you're around?"

"You got it," he replied.

Brock acted pleased. "Good man," he said, slapping his back.

"So how's the weather up there?"

"You had internet service. You should know," Brock told him.

"I had my hands full down here," he said with a wide smile before meeting her gaze.

Brock walked over to the bathroom and pulled her into his arms. The sweater she started to put on fell to the floor and he hugged her tight against his chest stroking her head. "I know one thing, I need a vacation."

Riley squinted. "I got the email from Dad this morning. I guess you're pretty pissed, huh?"

"Nay, just tired of playing underground and ready for a little R&R. I'm going to plant my ass on the beach somewhere and stay there long enough to grow roots."

"Brock?" she knew better than to ask questions. Her father told her a long time ago to never ask questions because he'd never answer them. Brock typically lived by those same orders.

"Someday, I'll tell you everything, sugar. I promise."

She believed him.

* * * *

Her eyes closed. She knew which one was there. The calculated way he moved toward her allowed her to search her heart and get in touch with her feelings.

"Kevin?"

"How did you know?"

"It's the way you approached."

"It's off?" he asked as he loosened the buttons on his shirt.

"No, it's on." She grinned before she rose from the bubbles and reached for him.

"Heaven have mercy," he said.

"And you?"

"Me?"

"Will you have mercy on me once you get inside me?"

"You're asking questions you shouldn't ask me right now."

"Why?" she hummed.

"Because I don't know the answer right now, Sydney."

In three or four seconds, his shirt was gone. Five or six more, his pants and underwear. Less than twenty in totality and he slipped in beside her. Five or ten more, he was inside her stroking her like they had no tomorrow to wish for, nothing more to live for except one another.

"Kevin," she released his name as he withdrew slowly before tapping into her center with really sweet beats.

"Submit to me, Sydney?"

"What do you want me to do?"

"I want you to love me and God help me, I want you to do what we tell you to do, what we expect you to do so we always know where you are and that you're safe."

He drew back and held her face in his palms. "Can you do that for me? For us?"

"You mean for all of you don't you?"

"Yes," he hesitated and then assured her. "Brock, too."

"Yes," she said. *Brock, too.*

* * * *

She had big plans but after Kevin made love to her, she fell asleep in his arms. She felt the protective bodies draped around her during the night. Luke came and went. Brock came and stayed.

Kevin, Riley, and Jett each took turns blanketing her with their bodies as they slipped in and out of her bed. Riley was the worst. He tried to wake her up and at one point—with his hard dick pressed against her ass—he almost succeeded.

Brock ran interference. "Let her sleep," he whispered to one and then the next. He never left her and when they were all alone, she blinked her eyes and caught him watching her.

"Brock, I missed you," she confessed.

"I know you did," he said, a tear forming in the corner of his eye. "We survived it." He cleared his throat and added, "I almost didn't make it without you, Sydney."

She wrapped her arms around his waist and fell fast asleep again. She woke up to commotion.

Danger, she thought in a sleepy state. "Gunfire," she said but no one heard her. No one was there to listen.

"Brock?" she called for him. "Jett!" she cried out in a panic, scrambling around on a search for her clothes.

"Luke! Riley! Kevin! Somebody!"

She reached for the lamp and tried to turn the light on. It didn't work. She flipped the switch again and again.

Her heart raced like a locomotive. "Shit! Somebody please!"

The electricity was off and someone was there in the house. She heard the exchange of gunfire and no one was there to protect her.

"Help me!" she cried.

Riley rushed into her room with his pistol drawn and a flashlight. "Sydney, honey, what is it? What's wrong?"

"Someone is shooting at the house," she said breathlessly. "And the lights, the electricity is out."

"Come here, baby," he pulled her to him and held her tight. "There was an ice storm last night. With all the snow we've had, the power lines are down."

She pushed him away with her drawn fists. "You don't understand! Someone is here!"

"With several inches of ice on top of the snow we've had? No, darlin, what we've got outside is a good old fashioned pissing contest."

She tried to read between the lines. "Target practice in this weather?"

He nodded. "Jett and Brock are having a contest. They've already compared cock size, now they're trying to see who can shoot best. I told them since everything they're doing is for you, to prove which one of them is a better man, they just needed to let you tell them. That really set them off. Brock must've thought you'd pick Jett and Jett must've thought Brock had tighter claims or something."

She didn't move.

"I told them the whole thing is ridiculous. You've chased us between these farms for as long as I can remember."

"I know what this is about," she confessed.

"Yeah, so do I. Brock told us this morning."

"Oh," she said.

"Have you ever told him how you feel about him?"

"Who, Brock?" she asked.

"Yeah, who else?"

"No, he knows how I feel about him."

"No, he doesn't," Riley said, brushing her hair away from her face. "What Brock knows is what you've told him and that's all. Men go with what they're told, not always with what's directly in front of them."

"I guess I thought after we've spent so much time together and after everything I've given him, he'd just assume."

"Men like to hear it straight from the source," he said. "Just like women, I suppose."

She caught his point.

"I see," she said, dropping to her knees and working to unhook his belt. Before he let her get too far, Riley reached under her arms and brought her back up to him.

"Sydney, I love you. I've looked for love in every submissive that ever went to my bed, but I always knew I loved you. I thought you should know from the source."

She swallowed hard. "You love me?"

He cupped her face and kissed her lightly on the mouth. "Yes, I do but I have to explain my love to you. It isn't conditional, but it's intense and it's expectant, or should I say, hopeful? Do you understand what I'm saying?"

She gulped. What she recognized as opportunity, he must've feared she'd translate as something else. "I will submit to you, Riley. All of you."

"That's fine, but I want you to know something. Brock and I have discussed this and we're already at odds about it. Do you understand the difference in what we expect and what Brock expects?"

She touched his cheek. "You mean do I know the difference between slaves and submissive women?"

"Yes," he replied.

"I know what it all means. I had the best trainer for this lifestyle. I know you think it's a little peculiar that Brock and I never slept together in the traditional sense, but we didn't have to consummate the relationship with penetration. We knew if we did, what would happen."

"And what happened?"

"I think you know."

"I want you to tell me," Riley said.

"I once gave myself over to him, completely but then he refused me because of my father. I understand it now. My father is dying, Riley. I don't know if you know this or not but I've known it for some time.

"I saw his first test results from the local hospital. He has cancer. Brock knew about those tests. Daddy tells him everything. He knew if he gave me an ultimatum, I'd make a choice to stay here and when he gave me a choice, he also realized it would lead me back to you, his brothers. If I had chosen him back then, I wouldn't have found my way home to you."

"He wants you to serve him as his slave, Sydney. And I don't think he cares if your father knows or not."

She paused a few minutes and held his hands in hers. "I know he does. Riley, I want that, too, more than anything in the world. It's not that different than what you, Kevin, Jett, and maybe even Luke, too will eventually want."

Riley pulled her down with him and they sat on the edge of the bed. "I think we need to be honest here. Something is bothering me about all of this. Why would you turn all of your free will over to another human being?"

She kissed his lips and reached for his cock, "Because Riley Donovan, I'm the real damn deal. I'm not playing house here. I want to submit to the men in my bed. I trust you to make all decisions for me. I plan to make a life with you for as long as you want me."

"But why would you prefer—"

"Shh..." she hummed, holding her fingertips to his smooth lips. "I love you. I'm devoted to you long term. There's a fine line between submissive women and those who want to become their Master's slave and I just want to cross it. That's all. I'm yours for as long as you want me. I don't want to think about it. Just take care of me. I trust you to do that and do it well."

His erection pressed against her hand and he grabbed her wrist and brought her fingertips to his lips. "Do you understand how others often perceive this kind of relationship?"

"Riley, I don't care how others see me. I only care how you and your brothers see me. You make me happy. In many ways, I'm your personal property whether you call me your submissive or your slave, I belong to you. It's the last choice I want to make."

"Damn," Brock said from the doorway. "This is a pretty sight."

"Yeah?" Riley responded. "I guess you prefer her above ground, eh?"

"Yes, but if you liked it there, there's always the possibility that Dad will let you turn it into your own little cave down there."

"You wish," he snapped. "Afraid Sydney here is going to love me more?"

"Not a chance," he answered.

Sydney stood up, bowed her head and parted her legs a few inches. Riley looked up and she saw the change in his expression. He liked the idea of a woman slave a little more than his words of opposition originally indicated.

Brock joined them and ran his fingers under her robe. He parted her folds and then stroked her walls before he withdrew his fingers and brought them to his lips.

"Good girl, at ease," he said.

She immediately fell back onto Riley's lap and Brock walked around them petting her on top of her head in passing.

"Jett shoots better than me," he finally said, watching Kevin and Luke battle it out with an early morning snowball fight.

"I know that's not true," Riley said, frowning. "You know it, too. Think about what this has been about from the beginning."

Brock ran his hand over his sweatpants. His hard erection visible and Sydney's mouth ready.

"He may fire better than you but he shoots blanks," Riley said before adding with agonizing heartache. "Brock, Jett can't have children."

"What?" Brock studied him. "When did he find out something like that?"

"When a gal tried to trap him into marriage," Sydney told him. "Dad told me, Riley. I've never said anything, but I already knew it."

"And you didn't tell me?" Brock asked. "Why not?"

"I never thought about it," she said. "When somebody is suffering, exploiting them doesn't make sense and that wasn't something I planned to share with you or anyone."

Brock narrowed his gaze on her chest. "Open your robe, Sydney."

She did it without question. She knew punishment was in order now. She kept something from him that he felt like she didn't have the right to hide.

"Over the knee," he said pointing at Riley's leg.

"But, I only did it to protect Jett."

"It doesn't matter. We had an agreement," he reminded her. "Anything you knew about the Donovans—my brothers, you were supposed to tell me."

"I didn't know they were your brothers."

"Sydney? Sass warrants more punishment."

"Hardly seems fair," Riley said. "You knew things about us but we were kept in the dark."

"I'm the big brother," he said.

"No, Brock, you left," Riley told him. He gently moved her off of his lap and approached him. "I've been their big brother. I've been here. I stayed and when I was sent on an assignment, I came home. I was here."

Brock stared outside. Sydney went to him. If Riley refused to issue her punishment, Brock might want to give it to her instead. She knelt beside of him and caressed his calf.

"Do you have other secrets?" he asked her.

"No," she shook her head. "I tell you everything."

Riley arched a brow. "Remember what we talked about?"

She quickly bowed her head and lowered her eyes.

"What is it?" Brock asked.

"I haven't always been forthcoming in regards to my feelings for you," she said.

"Look at me, Sydney," he said a new tone in his voice. "Tell me. What haven't you told me that you need to tell me? We don't have secrets."

"We've had secrets and I think if I'd told you a long time ago, maybe you wouldn't have left me."

"Sydney," Brock began. "I didn't leave you because I wanted to leave you."

"I don't care why you left, only relieved you came back, because...Brock, I love you and I always thought you knew."

"I do know," he said reaching for her and then cradling her against his shoulder. "I've always known. That's why..."

"That's why you didn't have sex with me before, isn't it?"

Brock looked away as if to turn away allowed him to escape the question.

"Don't," she said. "Please don't avoid this. I need to know, please. I thought something was wrong with me."

Riley's lips formed a thin, tight line and he looked at her with compassion. "You're amazing," he said.

"Truly," Brock added.

"Then why didn't you ever stay?"

"Sydney, our fathers are the exception in this business. They've lived longer than any operatives in the Underground Unit and the truth is if your father dies of natural causes then he's going to be the first in their particular unit."

Riley shook his head. "No, Sam doesn't want her to know that part."

"I don't care. I want her to know it," Brock said. "I wanted your father to have his last days with you here at home. I wanted you to feel like you made the right decision at the right time to stay with him. You would've chosen me if we were sleeping together."

Riley laughed. "Think you have that much talent, do you?"

"He does," she confirmed. "And you do, too," she added with a smile.

Pinching her nipple, Brock warned her. "Keep those remarks for him when you're one on one."

"Jealous, are you?"

"Damn straight. I had to listen to you orgasm to my toys and my brother's name while you were playing house underground. You better believe I'm one jealous man."

"That's something we're going to have to work on," she said with a whisper.

"Yeah, and I can think of several ways we can straighten me out," he replied. "Come on, let's go check out Jett's so-called Catherine Wheel."

"I like the way it looks," she told him.

"Remind me to spank her, Riley."

"I'll hold her down," he said, following them down the hallway.

"Promise?" she asked excitedly.

"Only if you promise not to like it," he said with a husky laugh. "And that's where we'll always have a problem."

Epilogue

Two Years Later

Sydney's friends, what few she had, refused to come to her ceremony. Her feelings weren't hurt. She even understood. They'd have a hard time facing her after gossiping about her. If life taught her anything at all it was that people often condemned those things they feared or didn't understand. Often, they sported loose tongues and were quick to judge. She didn't need them standing by her now. She had all she needed in the men who chose to claim her as their own.

Few people understood why she wanted to submit to five men. As she stood at the window and peered out over her front lawn she laughed aloud. Maybe if those who questioned her motives took a closer look at her men, they'd understand.

She pressed her palm to the glass and right when she did, all of her boys, her well dressed men, turned to wave. They said something between them and then simultaneously fell to one knee and blew her a kiss.

Yes, she had some brains—albeit between her legs—when she decided to take all of them to her bed. Where they were located was apparently the universal question, just not a foreseeable problem. Her friends and neighbors should've been happy for her, regardless of the men behind her happiness.

It didn't seem to bother her father or theirs. When she thought of her father and Mr. Donovan, she immediately searched the small wedding area for them. Beyond the trees, she spotted them, down by the fence, watching Bitch run.

She watched Mark Donovan pat her father's back and she imagined he probably wanted to give him additional assurance. They turned back toward the house and Mr. Donovan pointed toward her bedroom window and threw up his hand. Her father waved too, his arm not as swift as it would've been a few years earlier but it rose and fell all the same.

Sam Kane was dying.

He had lived longer than he was expected to survive and her men, Brock, Riley, Jett, Kevin, and Luke promised her he would only die of natural causes. She believed them.

Twice they'd to come to his rescue, once they moved him quickly when his cartel enemies approached with a new order to kill. She never blinked an eye or lost one night of sleep. They handled things appropriately, thought fast on their feet, and protected her father when he was too sick to help himself.

Thanks to them, he was going to walk her down the aisle and give her away to the men who promised her father to keep her safe and love her until death parted them. As she swallowed back the fear of losing any of them, she wondered if her men would be as fortunate as her father. Would they suffer their fate at the hands of their enemies or would they live long enough to die of natural causes?

The chimes from the old grandfather clock rang out seven times signifying the arrival of a new life beginning. She walked over to the dresser and picked up the metallic-looking collar.

She placed the small matching padlocks on the tray along with the five separate keys and five white gold wedding bands they all reluctantly agreed to wear, but only for special occasions. Their ceremony counted as one of the few times they verbally agreed.

All five Donovans relayed separate messages. They weren't the kind of men who liked jewelry, besides all of them told her independently—as if each thought up the excuse on an individual basis—rings were dangerous on the job. They could get hooked on anything and cost them their finger, or worse, their life. All because they chose to wear a wedding band. She meant to ask them how they felt about collars.

She strolled through the doorway and headed down stairs. She took the first step in the right direction, after the second they all came easier. She resisted the urge to run.

She didn't have wedding ceremony jitters. She was one lucky woman. A woman who relinquished her rights to five strong and handsome men, Sydney knew those who whispered behind her back would never understand. How could they?

Her right to choose was lost a long time ago. Society and her father's choices ensured she rarely had the pleasure of living the life she wanted to lead.

It didn't matter anyway.

This was far better than freedom. Being enslaved to five lovers who wanted and needed to take care of her trumped anything she ever tried to experience one on one. What she wanted and needed, she found in them. It was far better than overrated freedoms.

After all, what was freedom? If freedom was the right to choose, she thought, she easily possessed it now. She was finally free to love and submit to the sexiest men alive.

Who wouldn't do the same in her place? She couldn't think of anyone.

She stepped out on the porch and looked into the wild eyes of her handsome cowboys. So what if they shared a bizarre relationship? Who cared if the mere joining with them alienated her from those who felt their relationship was abnormal? Right now, she knew without a doubt, she made the right decision. She had the best of all men, and their untamed hearts would forever beat with hers as they joined together as husbands and wife.

THE END
www.myspace.com/natalieacres

ABOUT THE AUTHOR

Natalie Acres is the author of the best selling books Sex Party and Wanted by Outlaws. She writes western ménage romances and in her spare time, reads anything she can find on the historical towns of the Old West. She lives in the south with her family. For more information, visit her at www.myspace.com/natalieacres.

Siren Publishing, Inc.
www.SirenPublishing.com